PRAISE FOR LYN LIAO BUTLER

"*The Fourth Daughter* is one of the best novels I've read in a long time. Effortlessly melding family, food, and history into a multigenerational saga that kept me turning the pages well into the night, Lyn Liao Butler swept me away. I'll be thinking about this story for years to come."
—Camille Pagán, bestselling author of *Good for You*

"Lyn Liao Butler has woven a stunning tale of love, loss, and the unbreakable ties of family. *The Fourth Daughter* is a novel that doesn't flinch from the complexities of truth or the pain of what has been lost—but it also celebrates the resilience of love and the hope that binds generations together. With vivid storytelling and deep emotional resonance, Butler takes us from modern-day New York to the Taiwan of the past, exploring identity, sacrifice, and the power of finding our way home. A rich, wise, and unforgettable novel."
—Patti Callahan Henry, *New York Times* bestselling author of *The Secret Book of Flora Lea*

"A beautiful multigenerational story that asks if we can ever truly regain the things we have loved and lost, *The Fourth Daughter* is a wonderfully transportive novel of family, identity, acceptance, and healing—and a sensory delight for foodies and would-be travelers. Lyn Liao Butler has found the perfect recipe for a satisfying read."
—Jessica Strawser, *USA Today* bestselling author of *The Last Caretaker*

CW01497449

"Up-and-coming chef Liv Kuo must overcome a recent trauma to help her Taiwanese grandmother find the daughter she thought she had lost forever. A heartwarming blend of romance and family drama with roots in martial law–era Taiwan, *The Fourth Daughter* will have you turning pages filled with delicious food, tragic secrets, and the healing power of love."

—Julie Wu, author of *The Third Son*

"Taiwan is a small country, but its history and culture stretch across the entire world. Butler beautifully details the hopes of its people, who are sometimes powerless in the face of unrelenting authority and misfortune, but never defeated."

—Ed Lin, author of *Ghost Month*

"Lyn Liao Butler's *The Fourth Daughter* is a richly woven tapestry of heritage, healing, and the unbreakable bonds of family. Steeped in the vibrant culture of Taiwan, from its tantalizing cuisine to its deep-rooted traditions, this poignant and moving novel explores resilience, love, and the courage to uncover buried truths."

—Jean Kwok, *New York Times* bestselling author of
The Leftover Woman

THE
FOURTH
DAUGHTER

ALSO BY LYN LIAO BUTLER

The Tiger Mom's Tale

Red Thread of Fate

Someone Else's Life

Crazy Bao You

What is Mine

THE
FOURTH
DAUGHTER

A NOVEL

LYN LIAO
BUTLER

LAKE UNION
PUBLISHING

Published by Lake Union Publishing, Seattle

www.apub.com

Amazon, the Amazon logo, and Lake Union Publishing are trademarks of Amazon. com, Inc., or its affiliates.

EU product safety contact:
Amazon Media EU S. à r.l.
38, avenue John F. Kennedy, L-1855 Luxembourg
amazonpublishing-gpsr@amazon.com

ISBN-13: 9781662529054 (paperback)
ISBN-13: 9781662529047 (digital)

Cover design by Alison Impey
Cover image: © Jo Panuwat D, © takamaru / Shutterstock

Printed in the United States of America

For Past Me, who thought I'd never sell another book.
You did it.

Yi-ping

1959, Taichung

The year my fourth daughter was born, our home near the Taichung train station, which housed five families in the Wang household, collapsed during dinnertime. Just as I was putting the *dua mee gee* noodle soup I'd made on the table, a neighbor ran into our building shouting for us to get out because our home was about to fall.

My mother-in-law yelled for the wives to take our coal stoves so that the building wouldn't burn down (but did that really matter if our home was about to be destroyed anyway?). Like the dutiful daughter-in-law I was, I grabbed mine with two dish towels so I wouldn't burn myself as my husband scooped up our two youngest daughters in his arms. I ran for the door, our oldest daughter clinging to my leg and our faithful dog by my side. We rushed outside and stood on the street in shock as our three-story building began to crumble. As a thunderous rumble filled the air and thick plumes of dust rose around us, our home with all our belongings collapsed in front of our eyes.

The month my fourth daughter was born, my father-in-law was in an automobile accident that left him blind and unable to work. My mother-in-law's wails would have woken all the ghosts who haunted the island of Taiwan for the entire seventh lunar month.

The week my fourth daughter was born, my husband's oldest brother's son died of pneumonia in his mother's arms. How the entire family mourned, the oldest son of an oldest son, gone too soon and before he could take his rightful place in the family.

The day my fourth daughter was born, our dog stood just inside the front door of my husband's sister's house, where we'd taken refuge after we'd lost the family building, and howled for over an hour. My husband knew then that the son he'd hoped for was merely a dream, and that a hungry girl child had gobbled him up to take his place. Sure enough, our fourth daughter came into the world bellowing at the top of her lungs, as healthy as could be. I saw the bitter disappointment in my husband's eyes as his mouth twisted in disgust, and my stomach twisted in dismay. After having three daughters, he had prayed and prayed for a son to carry on his legacy. His frustration was a palpable storm cloud, threatening to let loose over us. He stalked out of the room, not even sparing us a glance. But my heart filled with joy at the sight of this perfect baby, and I loved her from the moment I laid eyes on her.

In Taiwan, the number four is considered unlucky, because the word for "four" sounds so similar to the word for "death." Taiwanese people are a superstitious lot. They avoid the number four at all costs. Few Taiwanese buildings have a fourth floor, and not many license plates end in the number four. When my mother packed me snacks when I was young, she never packed four of anything, for fear of dooming me to bad luck. My husband refused to have the number four in his office phone number and threw a fit if I brought home four bags of rice, instead of three or five. I should have known that he would not allow a fourth daughter to taint his life.

But I was young: only sixteen when I married him, and only twenty-one when my fourth daughter was born. I'd been taught to obey my husband, that I was nothing without him. I had no idea that on the day of her birth, he was already thinking how he could get rid of her. For he thought of her as a curse, her very existence the reason for all the bad luck in his family that year. I should have been more vigilant and protected her, shielded her from my husband's wrath. But I hadn't, and my fourth daughter became nothing more than a wisp of incense smoke disappearing into the sky.

PART 1

1
Liv

Present day, Manhattan

"I saw my fourth daughter yesterday," my grandmother, Yi-ping Wang, said when I picked up her FaceTime call.

"Ah-Ma?" My body jolted in alarm as I called her by the Taiwanese words for "grandmother." I sat up fast from the cocoon of blankets I'd buried myself in on my couch, dropping my cell phone in the process. As I fumbled on the floor to retrieve it, my mind spun as I mentally went back over every video call I'd had with her recently, wondering when my active eighty-six-year-old grandmother's mind had started to slip. Why hadn't I seen the signs? Had I been too wrapped up in my own trauma to pay attention to anyone else?

"Liv-ah?" I heard my grandmother's voice from my fallen phone just as my fingers closed around it. "You there?"

My hands shook as I brought the phone back up so I could see my grandmother's face. My eyes skimmed over her familiar features, wondering if dementia was something you could see physically, like a wart on the back of a hand. Ah-Ma had only three daughters—my mother, Felicia, being the youngest one—and a son, my uncle Winston; there was no fourth daughter. How far gone was she to have conjured up another daughter? My heart wouldn't be able to take it if my beloved grandmother was declining just when I needed her most.

"Are you okay?" My voice came out in a tremulous whisper. I'd been holed up inside my studio apartment for the past two months like a spirit stuck in this world, unable to move on, ever since Ah-Ma had gone back to Taiwan and my best friend, Amy Phan, had left on a worldwide solo trip. I was afraid to go outside and face all the danger that was New York City. My brain knew I couldn't live like this forever, but my body refused to cooperate. And when you lived in a city like New York, you never had to step foot outside if you didn't want to. Everything could be delivered, and no one had to know that you'd developed a phobia of the city you'd once loved so much. The only fresh air I'd gotten lately was when I went out onto my little balcony, shivering in the mid-April chill as I watched the traffic go by seven floors below.

"I'm fine." Ah-Ma's voice was impatient, and she waved a hand in the air. "I need you come to Taiwan. Help find her. My husband, he stole her years ago."

"What?" I blinked at her in confusion, my mind trying to make sense of what she was saying. "What are you talking about? You don't have a fourth daughter."

Should I call my mother? Or the companion who'd gone every day to help my grandmother ever since she'd moved back to Taiwan? Did anyone else know about Ah-Ma's declining grasp on reality?

She heaved a sigh and stared at me for a few moments in silence. "Felicia never told you about Yili?"

"Yi who?" I sat up fully, shrugging the blankets off me, my entire attention on my grandmother. I searched her face for signs of disorientation, agitation, or anything else that would give me a clue as to whether my grandmother was losing her mind. But the face I'd always known gazed back at me.

"My fourth daughter, Yili," Ah-Ma said.

I shook my head, confusion clouding my brain. My mom had never once told me she had a younger sister. *No one* in our family had ever said that. I wasn't as close to my mother as I was to Ah-Ma, but we had a good relationship. I called my mom every few days, but there was much we didn't talk about. Apparently, her missing younger sister was one of them.

"Aiya." Ah-Ma shook her head. "It like she never exist." She switched to Mandarin then, her words coming faster in her native language, which I understood but could barely speak. "I had a fourth daughter. My husband gave her away when she was only eighteen months old, when Winston was born. I searched for her for years, but it was like she'd disappeared."

"No." My eyes widened as her words sank in. She'd lived with us for all of my childhood, and she'd never once said anything about a fourth daughter. I'd never met my grandfather, but I couldn't imagine he'd been that evil. How could anyone give away their own child?

"Yesterday, she was in line in front of me at a food stall. And then she disappeared. Poof." Ah-Ma flicked open her hands to emphasize her words. "Just gone. Like magic."

"I . . ." The words got stuck in my throat. My grandmother had always been practical, not one to give in to superstitions or fairy tales. She didn't believe in magic. I'd just seen her a few months ago, when I'd landed in the hospital after that horrible incident at the restaurant where I worked, and she and my mother had flown here to New York to be with me. After I was finally released, my grandmother had stayed with me in my tiny studio for months taking care of me after my mother went back to California.

"I'm sorry I never told you about her." Ah-Ma's tone softened. "It hurt too much to speak the words out loud. I saw her yesterday at Yizhong Shopping Street." Ah-Ma paused, a faraway look in her eyes as a tiny smile flitted around her lips. "I was craving good old-fashioned street food. There's a stall there, they sell the best barbecued squid. I was in line when I saw her."

"How do you know it was her? She must be . . ." I trailed off, trying to do the math, but my brain was still trying to comprehend that my grandmother had had a child stolen from her, and I couldn't make sense of the numbers.

"She would be sixty-five now." Ah-Ma's smile was sad. "The woman I saw was the right age. She looked exactly how I imagined my Yili would have grown up to look like."

"But Ah-Ma, you said she was taken from you when she was eighteen months old. How could you possibly . . ." I didn't want to hurt my grandmother's feelings, but there was no way she could know what her lost daughter looked like all these years later.

"I know it was her." Ah-Ma's voice was steely. "She had this birthmark . . ." Ah-Ma gestured to the back of her head. "Right here, behind her left ear. It looked like a heart. The woman in front of me had the same birthmark. She had her hair pulled back in a low ponytail. I wasn't paying attention, but then the person behind pushed me and I fell against her. And I saw it, Liv." My grandmother's eyes burned with intensity. "She has the exact same birthmark in the exact same place. And when she turned around to see if I was okay, I recognized her. It was her."

I stared at my grandmother, trying to absorb everything she was telling me. If she was right and this woman was actually her missing daughter, it would be a miracle.

"I called her by name. Yili." Ah-Ma's chin trembled with emotion. "But she only looked at me in confusion and said I was mistaken. That wasn't her name. She gave me a sympathetic look and then took off down the street." Ah-Ma stared into my eyes. "She didn't even get her snack. I was so shocked I didn't move for a few moments. Then I took off after her, trying to catch her." Ah-Ma shook her head, as if in regret. "There were too many people. It was so crowded. I lost her. I kept searching, pushing past people, trying to find her, but she was gone."

"I'm so sorry." I brought my hands up to my chest, my heart breaking at the look on her face.

"I know it sounds far-fetched, but I believe in my heart, in my soul, that that was her." Ah-Ma's eyes clouded with sorrow, and she stared at a spot somewhere behind me. "I've dreamed of the moment when I'd see her again so many times over the years. I'd wake up thinking I could smell the sweet scent of her hair, feel her arms around my neck. I believed with all my heart that she'd be returned to me." Ah-Ma sighed. "I never imagined that I'd see her again for the first time in line to buy street food. Or that I'd let her slip away when she was so close."

"Oh, Ah-Ma." My heart constricted. "I don't understand. How could your husband have done that? What kind of monster would give away their own child?"

"It was a different time." Ah-Ma's gaze shifted back to me. "Sons were important, and my husband was very superstitious. He believed it was the right thing to do."

My mind swirled with questions. My family seldom talked about my grandfather, and now I wondered if this was why. And then something occurred to me. "You didn't leave him until Uncle Winston started college. How could you have stayed with him for all those years?"

Winston was her youngest child, and I knew Ah-Ma had followed him to California a few months after he left Taiwan to start his freshman year at Stanford. All of Ah-Ma's children had settled in America, and she'd lived with my aunts and uncle until my mother got pregnant with me. It was a difficult pregnancy, and Ah-Ma came to live with my parents to help and stayed with us all through my childhood and beyond, until she went back to Taiwan seven years ago.

"I had no choice." A tear slid down Ah-Ma's papery-thin cheek, and I longed to reach out through the phone and wipe it away. "His family was very traditional. There was no divorce back then. They were powerful, and I would have had nothing if I left him. He would have taken our three daughters and son. I had to stay." Her voice grew stronger. "When Winston left for college, a friend in Taiwan helped me escape and got me a visa to America without my husband knowing."

"That's terrible." I knew my grandmother had left my grandfather but never knew the reason why. Tears gathered in my eyes as I imagined the emotional torture my grandmother must have lived through, trapped in a life with a man immoral enough to give away one of their children. "Tell me what I can do."

"Help me find her."

I shook my head. "If it was her, how could I possibly help? I know nothing about her, or your story. I've never been to Taiwan. Maybe you should ask Mom for help?"

Ah-Ma tsked impatiently and switched to accented English. "Felicia no good with tech. I need you. I need the young ideas of you."

"Okay, you're right, I'm better than Mom at that stuff." I gave her a faint smile. My mom was a mathematical genius, but she could barely operate her cell. Ah-Ma thought I was a whiz at technology, when in reality, I was just a millennial with passable skills.

"Come to Taiwan. I took DNA test weeks ago because I saw commercial on TV. I've heard people find long-lost relatives that way. Maybe my daughter did one too. I be getting results soon." She looked at me for a few seconds in silence. "Please, Liv." Ah-Ma reached out a hand, as if she wanted to touch me through the screen. "I know you not working."

I flinched, shame pouring through me like hot lava. I'd tried to keep that fact from her, that I hadn't returned to work at the restaurant like I'd promised I would before she went back to Taiwan, but my mother must have told her.

"And you need get out of Manhattan." Her voice softened. "You not okay, ah?"

I dropped my gaze to my lap, wondering how my grandmother could always tell what was going on with me without my saying a word. I'd lied every time we FaceTimed, saying I was doing great and getting back out there. Before the incident, I'd been a sous-chef at 852, a bustling Asian fusion restaurant in Hell's Kitchen named for Hong Kong's country code, and was supposed to return to work two months ago. My rival, Benjamin, also a sous-chef, had been covering for me and, I was sure, garnering favors with the chef de cuisine in my absence.

Chef Wu ran his restaurant like a drill sergeant, but he was more than understanding after what had happened to me in his kitchen. He told me I could return whenever I was ready. But when I tried to go back to work, I had a panic attack in the subway. A kind stranger helped me get aboveground and put me in a taxi back to my apartment, where I'd stayed ever since, afraid to leave. I knew Chef Wu was going to have to replace me if I didn't get my butt back to the kitchen. But how could I, when every time I thought about setting foot in the place where I'd been injured and witnessed my coworker Cat's death, it sent my mind into apoplectic shock and my heart beating out of control?

I threw my shoulders back now, determined to show my grandmother that I was trying. But could I really leave my apartment, get on a plane, and fly halfway around the world to a country I'd never been to? I'd missed my grandmother when she moved back, but I'd been too busy and hadn't taken the time to visit Ah-Ma. Cooking and food had been my life. When I wasn't working, I was experimenting in my own tiny kitchen, eating at one of the thousands of restaurants in New York City with my friends, or traveling to new locations with Amy, who also worked at 852 as the dumpling and pastry chef, creating delectable baos and desserts fused with Asian flavors. But now? Now I had all the time in the world.

When I looked up, I found my grandmother studying me intently. "Tell me about her," I said, twisting my hands together in my lap. I wasn't going to acknowledge the wave of panic that overtook me at the thought of leaving my apartment and going so far away. I needed to stay focused, to listen to my grandmother's story and be strong so that I could help her.

"Oh, Liv." The sigh Ah-Ma expelled could have blown thousands of dandelion seeds away in a field. It was powerful and filled with so much sorrow that I knew whatever she was going to share with me would tug at my heart.

But for the first time since the traumatic day when that crazed man had stormed into the restaurant kitchen and shot Cat and me, something stirred within me, as if waking from a long sleep. The months of apathy and fear I'd endured finally had an end date, and I was determined to hold on to this lifeline with all my might. I couldn't slip back into the oblivion of the past five months, a frightened and hollow shell of my former self. If I couldn't save myself, I could at least pull myself together to help Ah-Ma.

My grandmother began to speak, and I latched on to every word as if they were precious pockets of oxygen that I needed to stay alive.

2
YI-PING

March 1961, Taichung

It should have been a happy time in the Wang household after my son was born. We'd finally moved back into the family building near the Taichung train station, after it had taken almost two years to rebuild from when the building had crumbled. We'd found out later that the collapse was due to the construction going on next door, where a company erecting a new building had dug too deep into the foundation, causing ours to become unstable. Instead of stopping, they'd kept going, and our home had collapsed as a result.

"Make them pay," my brothers-in-law had urged their father.

"Make them pay," my husband had agreed.

And pay they did. The Wang family was powerful back then, *waishengren*, Chinese immigrants who had come to Taiwan starting in 1945 and into the 1950s with the Kuomintang (KMT) Party after losing the Chinese Civil War on the mainland. My husband's father was a high-level official of the KMT and had a lot of clout. He forced the company out of business in order to pay the Wangs for the destruction of the building. I didn't understand most of the political undertones, but I had heard the rumors that my father-in-law's automobile accident later that year was retaliation for what he had done to the company. With him blinded from flying debris, his sons, my husband included, had to step up in the family banking business.

Our neighbors feared us, and many of the *tai tais*, the married women in our neighborhood, kowtowed to my mother-in-law and the rest of the wives in the Wang family, me included. It embarrassed me, because I was only a simple country girl when I'd moved to Taichung to marry Po-wei. Besides, I was nothing in the hierarchy of the Wang family. They could have treated me like a servant since I'd given them only daughters, but my mother-in-law had always been kind to me. I was grateful to her, and it made me even more proud when I finally bore a son, my fifth child, for the family.

After the birth, I stayed at home for a month for *zuo yuezi*, or "sitting the month." I'd done this postpartum confinement with each of my babies, but this time, it was different. The Wangs treated me extra well and hired a nanny to live with us for the month. Her sole purpose was to prepare special health-giving foods along with traditional Chinese herbal remedies for me. She scared me, this woman. She was intense and so focused that I couldn't wait for her to go away.

Every time I turned around, she'd be right there behind me. "Yi-ping, it's time for your remedy." When I poked my head out of my bedroom door, she'd be standing there with a tray. "You didn't finish your lunch." When I came out of the bathroom, she'd be there, a mug in hand. "Drink. Now."

I would comply, gagging and holding my breath as I choked it down. My eyes burned, but I spied my mother-in-law over her shoulder. "Thank you for this, um, delicious concoction. I am honored." For I knew it was a privilege that Abu, as we all called my mother-in-law, was showering so much attention on me.

"You need to eat more. You don't eat enough." The woman ushered me back to bed and then set a bowlful of soup on a portable table in front of me. I beamed at her while tears pooled in my eyes from the strong fumes of the herbal chicken soup heavily laced with alcohol.

Abu came to my side and patted my cheek. "I'm glad she's here to take care of you. You're too skinny."

All I had to do for the month was stay inside and sleep and eat, rejuvenating my body. My husband stopped by more often than he had with the other babies, and once even gave me a gruff pat on the shoulder. From him, that was high praise.

I was secure in the insular bubble of the Wang household, unaware of the political rumblings happening all over Taiwan. I knew the men of the neighborhood were always trying to garner our favor, get on the good side of my father-in-law and his brothers and sons, because they dictated who the KMT would target. The political unrest, the random arrests, men who disappeared and never came back, none of the chaos of a country under martial law affected me directly back then.

My own family had been in Taiwan long before Chiang Kai-shek and his troops had fled here after their defeat in China. My father hadn't wanted to marry me into a KMT family, but it was a good match, and my parents had too many children. I'd caught Po-wei's eyes when I'd gone into Taichung with my father to deliver the vegetables we grew on our farm.

Po, as his family called him, was the fourth son, so standards for his marriage were lower than for his older brothers'. I think his birth order also fed into his superstition about the number four because he had to prove he wasn't bad luck and doomed to failure. His parents allowed the match because the matchmaker had said it would be an auspicious union, and that I would give them a son. My father made me promise not to get involved in politics, while my mother sobbed quietly behind him. I promised, even though I was so naive and oblivious.

And now, at barely twenty-three, I'd just had my fifth child and was finally a respected member of the Wang family. I'd given my husband what he most wanted in the world, a son. I'd proven the matchmaker correct, and my in-laws congratulated themselves on our lucky union. My husband should have been happy and allowed me my own happiness with our daughters, who were growing into beautiful and inquisitive girls. Our oldest, Lun-Shan, was already a gifted pianist at only six years old.

"She's a genius." Abu beamed with pride. "A prodigy." She turned to me. "Don't worry, we'll pay for her piano lessons."

Our second daughter, Lun-Wen, at five years old, loved to cook like me.

"Lun-Wen is such a great little chef," Abu would say, showering her with a radiant smile.

Our third daughter, Lun-Fei, who would later change her name to Felicia when she moved to America, showed signs of being a mathematical genius at only three and a half.

"This one," her ah-gong said, pointing with delight. "She loves numbers like me." He spent hours teaching her to recite numbers and sums, which he could do without sight.

And our fourth daughter was eighteen months old and already charming every person who met her. She would be a peacemaker, I knew, able to soothe frazzled nerves and fraught tension with one beam of her dimpled smile.

I tried not to play favorites, but my fourth daughter held a special place in my heart. I was enamored with her. She walked before our three other daughters and said her first word at only eleven months old. She lit up like a firecracker whenever she saw me and filled my heart with pride. I couldn't wait to see all she'd accomplish when she grew up.

How foolish I was. Life could be a cruel joke, taking away just when you thought you had everything. I was too proud, thinking my four daughters were just as valuable as a son. I was lulled into thinking I was a valued member of my husband's family now that I'd given them a son. But my vanity caused me to be lax, and I paid dearly for it.

At my son's one-month-old ceremony, our building was full of family and friends there to help us celebrate his life. Our home was decorated with red banners proclaiming luck and health to our baby boy. I held my son with my husband at my side, my heart bursting with pride as people brought us gifts and blessings.

"Ah, Yi-ping. Po-wei." My mother-in-law stood next to my father-in-law, one arm hooked into his to guide him and tell him who had stopped in front of them. She leaned in and whispered to me, "Look who's just arrived."

Our heads swiveled to the front door, where the mayor of Taichung was walking in with his wife.

"Oh," I said quietly, in awe.

Abu beamed her approval and whispered again, "Good girl," before guiding my father-in-law forward to greet them.

My face flushed with pride at her praise. She'd fussed for days before the ceremony, making sure there were red eggs (for new life and fertility, their shape symbolizing harmony) and red buns (for good luck and perfection), to give to our guests. Those full-month buns with the red dot on top resembled a mother's breast, and they represented the wish that the mother would have ample milk for her baby, which I did.

I couldn't help but wince every time I saw someone biting into those red buns meant to resemble my breasts. What macabre person had thought that would be a good image for a nursing mother to see? There weren't any celebrations for males where sweet buns in the shape of penises were passed around, meant to symbolize good luck and fortune. I wrinkled my nose and turned my focus back to my son, trying to ignore those red buns. I wasn't used to being in the spotlight, and all the attention had me frazzled. I couldn't wait until we were alone again.

I didn't realize my fourth daughter was missing until long after the guests had gone home, satiated from the feast my mother-in-law had provided, including oil rice served with chicken legs because this baby was a boy. I had finally collapsed into a chair in my room after putting the baby down.

"Daughters," I called out. "Come see your mama."

Three of them gathered around me, chattering about the day, the excitement from the celebration bringing the color high on their cheeks. They regaled me with stories about the guests, how several had given them red envelopes full of money, and another had been so drunk on whiskey that he was as red as a tomato, staggering and singing to himself. I smiled at them and listened to their giggles, but something niggled at me.

When there was a break in their excited babble, I finally asked, "Where's Yili?"

The last time I'd seen her, my youngest daughter had been holding the hand of one of my sisters-in-law, dancing from foot to foot. She'd sent me a dimpled grin from across the room, and I'd waved at her before being pulled away to meet someone new.

"Yili?" my oldest asked.

The other two looked at each other and then at me as they shrugged.

I stood, my heart suddenly thundering in my chest. "Yili?" I called out.

My daughters followed me as I ran back into the main room, where my sisters-in-law were still gathered, talking about the day. They all looked up as I zeroed in on the one whom I'd last seen holding my daughter's hand.

"Where is she?" I grasped my sister-in-law's arm. "Where's Yili?"

Her face blanched and she said, "I don't know. Your husband took her from me at the party. He said there was someone who wanted to meet her."

We stared at each other as wild thoughts ran through my head. I fought to beat them down because there was no justification for them. I was glad my husband had taken an interest in Yili, as he'd mostly ignored her since her birth. He was easy and relaxed around our first three daughters, but I'd noticed a distance when it came to our fourth daughter. I should have been happy that he'd paid attention to Yili. But deep down, my gut was ringing alarm bells.

"Where is he?" I shouted, looking around for my husband. I ran through our part of the building, and when I couldn't find him, I yelled his name again. My mother-in-law rushed in at my loud voice.

"Daughter, what is it?" she asked, hurrying to my side.

"Yili." My hands fluttered uselessly at my side. "Have you seen her?"

She pursed her lips and shook her head, which sent me into another spiraling panic. My children were always either with me, one of my three sisters-in-law, or my mother-in-law. But all of them were here in this room with me, and my daughter was not. I prayed my husband had only taken her on an outing finally, maybe to get ice cream down the street, or for egg tarts at the bakery next door. But my gut knew this was not the case. I let out a mournful scream, and my legs gave out as the women surrounded me. They helped me to the couch as I fought them, telling them I needed to go find Yili. I knew she'd been kidnapped.

And that's when my husband appeared in the doorway from outside.

"Po, Yili is missing. We need to find her!" I broke away from the women and ran to him, my fists beating on his chest as I told him to call the police. But he stopped me with a hand to my arm, and I looked up. And what I saw in my husband's eyes told me more than I ever wanted to know.

He shook his head and said, "She's safe and better off now."

"What?" The word ripped from my mouth, burning me with the sharpness of its edges. "Where is she?" My voice grew shrill as I took a step back. "What have you done?" When he didn't answer, I screamed again, "What have you done to her?"

He gave me a look I couldn't read. "She's fine."

I stared at him in shock, and then the words burst free from my lips. "Tell me where she is, right now. I'll go get her. I'll bring her back home, safe and sound. Where is she?"

But he refused to say and turned away, walking down the hallway that led to his eldest brother's part of the building. I stood there, looking after him, my body numb and my breath hitching. He'd done something to our fourth daughter. He'd taken her from me. The agony that ripped through my body at the realization had me crumbling to the ground. I wailed, a sound so heartbreaking and high-pitched that I still remember it to this day. My sisters-in-law and daughters tried to soothe me, hands reaching out to stroke my back, squeeze my hands, murmuring words of sympathy that I didn't hear. It was only the touch of my mother-in-law that finally broke through my pain as she smoothed the hair back from my forehead and clasped me to her.

"I know you're hurting now, Yi-ping, but please trust my son. He's only trying to do the best for the family." Her voice was low and gentle. "He believes this is the right thing, that Yili has been a curse to our family."

Her words penetrated the fog of my brain, and I stared in disbelief at my mother-in-law. "No." That was the only word I could get out.

She nodded. "Yes. You remember all the bad luck the year she was born. And what's happened in the time since." She paused, and I knew she wanted me to remember how one of my sisters-in-law had been badly burned when a boiling pot of water had fallen on her, or how one of my brothers-in-law had been beaten unconscious and had to be hospitalized.

But none of that was Yili's fault. My sister-in-law was clumsy and had pulled that pot of water off her coal stove by accident. My brother-in-law was an obnoxious know-it-all and had offended so many people I was surprised he hadn't been beaten up before. None of that had anything to do with Yili or her birth. She was just an innocent child and shouldn't have been blamed. I stared at my mother-in-law, unable to believe that she would buy into this superstition. I couldn't accept that she would condone her son stealing my child from me.

"How can you say that? You're a mother." The words flew out of my mouth like bullets spraying from a gun. "He took my child. She's gone." I reached my hands out to her. "If you know where she is, tell me now. Please."

But she only shook her head and averted her eyes. "I don't know anything. My son is a good man. He wouldn't have done what he did unless he believed he had to."

I drew in a sharp breath, full of shock that my mother-in-law couldn't see how wrong this was. How could they rip a child from her mother? What kind of family stole a child without warning? But deep down, I knew they could, and for the first time in my life, I spoke up for myself. And Yili.

"How can you believe that?" I'd always respected my mother-in-law, as was her due, never raised my voice to her, but I couldn't stay quiet. Not when my daughter was gone. "You must have helped him. You would have been the one to make the arrangements. Who did you give her to?" I screamed the last words, past caring about the repercussions of yelling at my mother-in-law. I could hear my sisters-in-law gasping behind me as they drew my daughters to them, but I didn't even turn my head to acknowledge them. "You have no idea what it's like to lose a child." I flung my hands out, indicating her four sons, who all lived in this building with their families, as well as her two daughters, who were married and in their own households.

She regarded me in cold silence, her lips pressed together in a hard line. And then she leaned in close to me, her intricately carved green jadeite pendant swinging forward to tap against my cheek as she said in a low voice, "You have no choice, no rights. The sooner you realize that, the better off you are. You think it was easy for me? I was adopted into the Wang family when I was only two, as a little daughter-in-law for their oldest son. I barely remember my own parents." Her voice hardened. "I have lost children, and there was nothing I could do as a woman." She gestured with a hand to our building. "I don't own any of this. My husband controls everything, including our children. I learned early on to be agreeable and act like I don't care, because if I obeyed, he and his family couldn't hurt me."

I whimpered, horrified at what she was telling me. How many children had she lost? But it was the sixties, and things were progressing.

21

We weren't living in the 1930s or '40s. There had to be laws in place that prevented a husband or in-laws from taking your child.

As if to answer my question, my mother-in-law shook her head slowly. "No one will help you. The Wang men have too much power. Trust me and accept things for what they are. Forget about Yili and focus on your son. He's your ticket to a good life."

And with that, she straightened and gave me a gentle pat on my cheek. I flinched, not willing or able to accept her words. She gave me a mild look of disapproval and then turned and walked out of our section of the building. I was rooted to the spot as I watched her go. My heart cracked in two as I wondered if Yili was terrified, scared wherever she was without me. She'd never been apart from me for more than a few hours. My breath came in gasps as I imagined her bewilderment and terror. I couldn't take it, knowing my baby was out there somewhere, scared out of her mind. She was not where she belonged, here in this building with her family, with me. I'd vowed when each of my children was born to always protect them, and I'd failed with Yili.

A sound filled the room, so loud I wanted to put my hands over my ears. But one of my daughters now held my hands in hers, calling "Mama. Mama!" over and over again, and my head hurt from the noise. It was only as my sisters-in-law crowded around us, making shushing noises and patting me, that I realized I was the one making the terrible noise. I couldn't stop it as the screams tore from my throat and my mind splintered. Nothing could soothe me, because my husband had done the worst thing possible. He'd taken my precious daughter from me, and I never knew her fate.

3
Liv

My throat was raw, as if I'd been the one to scream and scream the day my daughter was torn from me. I stared at my grandmother through the phone screen, wondering how someone could live with that kind of pain, never knowing what had happened.

Ah-Ma sniffed and wiped at her eyes with a tissue. "I wasn't well after that. I was hell-bent on getting Yili back. I couldn't stand to look at my husband. I truly despised him for what he did."

"I'm so sorry." I whispered the words, wishing I were with Ah-Ma so I could give her a hug and hold her as tight as possible to absorb some of her pain.

"I've spent sixty-three years mourning the loss of my daughter, trying to find her, but I've never succeeded. I've wondered what happened to her, imagining the worst but hoping for the best. That she'd found a good home and had a happy life. And now, finally, there's a glimmer of hope that I will see her again before I die." Ah-Ma's voice gained strength, and her face turned fierce. "Please come to Taiwan and help me find her."

And with those words, I reached for the lifeline she was throwing me, a reason to leave my apartment and the city that had become my prison. I longed to be in my grandmother's arms, the familiar scent of the Tiger Balm that she rubbed on her aching joints stinging my nose along with the lemony soap she favored. I could almost smell the herbal and umami flavors of Taiwanese food lingering on her body, for she loved to cook and had passed this passion on to me.

"Okay." I nodded, even though I had no idea how I could possibly be of help to her.

Her face lit up with a wide smile, and she clasped her hands in front of her. "Thank you, Liv." Her heartfelt gratitude had me smiling, even as I wondered at her misplaced trust in me.

I nodded again, a spark of hope, perhaps anticipation, pulsing through my veins. I had something to focus on beside my own tragedy and the nightmares that still woke me almost nightly. I would help Ah-Ma, do everything I could to find my aunt, and hope that it would be enough to fight down the anxiety and fear that had overtaken me ever since the incident at 852 five months ago. I was about to tell her I would start looking for plane tickets when something from her story made me pause.

"Did you say . . ." I scrunched up my forehead, one detail of her story jumping out at me. "Our family is KMT?"

I'd been so emotionally wrapped up in what had happened to her that it was only now that I realized she'd said her husband's family was part of the Chinese Nationalist Party, or the pan-Blue coalition in Taiwanese politics. From everything I'd read in textbooks and on the news, I knew the KMT had ruled Taiwan as an authoritarian one-party state from 1949 to 1987. The country had been under martial law in a period known as the White Terror, when the KMT had curtailed civil liberties under the guise of being anticommunist.

"My husband's family is, so I guess we were, by association." Ah-Ma gave me a rueful shrug. "But I'm not any longer. Not since I left him."

I shook my head slowly in wonder. "There's so much I don't know about our family." Never in all my thirty-five years had my mother ever told me her grandparents had been KMT. My parents were firmly in the pan-Green camp when it came to Taiwanese politics, fighting for Taiwan independence and democracy. They never talked about it with me or my brother, but I'd taken a course on politics in China and Taiwan in college and so had an idea of what had transpired in the last century.

"I pay for plane ticket." Ah-Ma changed the subject, and my attention swung back to her. "I send you . . ."

I cut her off. "No. I got it."

I'd been able to afford not to work the last five months because the family of the man who had stormed into the kitchen of 852 that night had paid Cat's family and me off after what he'd done. They hadn't been ordered to pay us; they'd genuinely been heartsick at what their son had done. When questioned about why he'd shot us, the gunman had said only, "The baos weren't as good that night." I didn't want to accept their blood money, but the lawyer my parents had hired for me nudged me to take it, saying I might need it in the future. It'd been sitting there in my bank account ever since it had landed. I hadn't touched it because it wouldn't bring Cat or my former life back.

"Okay." Ah-Ma nodded. She knew about the money. "When can you come?"

"As soon as I can get a visa." Now that I'd made up my mind, there was no reason to wait. Nothing was keeping me here, and I could afford whatever exorbitant fee the airlines would charge for a last-minute ticket. The spark of interest that I'd felt earlier ignited even more. Here was a chance to learn more about my family. I'd finally get to see all the places Ah-Ma had told me about when I was growing up and visit the night markets that always had my mouth watering when she described the stalls and food. I knew I couldn't go back to work at 852 yet, if ever, and if I was going to lose my job, at least I'd have something else to focus on.

"Thank you." Gratitude shone from my grandmother, and I blinked away the tears. I should've been thanking her, for giving me a purpose in life again.

"I have so many questions," I said.

A ghost of a smile graced her lips as her face softened. "I can't wait to answer them all."

With a last nod and a promise to let her know when my plane would land in Taipei, we hung up so I could apply for a visa and search the airlines.

Hours later, I finally collapsed onto my bed. My application was complete, and I'd put a tentative reservation on a flight out in a few days, depending on when my visa got approved. I'd even upgraded to business class; why not travel in comfort with my blood money? And now it was time to make the hard calls, to Chef Wu at 852, and to my parents.

"How long will you be gone?" I could hear the resignation in Chef Wu's voice. I'd called after the dinner rush, knowing he'd be having a drink at the bar, socializing with patrons.

"I don't know." That was the truth, since I had no idea how long it would take to find a woman on an island with a population of more than twenty-three million.

"Liv." Chef Wu paused, but my name was heavy with meaning.

"I know, Chef."

He wouldn't be able to hold my spot for me. He had a busy restaurant to run, and Benjamin couldn't keep covering for me, working double his normal shifts.

He sighed, and I could hear the disappointment in his voice. "I'm so sorry for what happened to you and Cat. It was horrific, and we all mourn her loss. I wish I could make it go away for you." He paused again, and I waited. "You're a talented chef, Liv. I hope you won't lose that."

"I won't," I said, even though I didn't know if it was a lie. I hadn't cooked a single thing since that night.

"Can I offer a word of advice?"

"Okay."

"You're talented. But you're still searching for your path. The essence of what makes you Chef Liv Kuo." He paused, as if waiting for me to interject, but I stayed silent. "You've been imitating, replicating what you think Asian food should be. Don't. Dig deep. Find out what food means to you, either through your culture or your own experiences. Not what some celebrity chef thinks is the latest thing."

His words stunned me. I'd always thought he'd admired my innovation, combining Asian cuisine with American tastes. "But your restaurant is Asian fusion." The words burst out of me in an indignant rush. Then I remembered myself. "Chef."

"It is. But do you know why it's successful?" He didn't wait for my answer. "Because I cook from the heart. The food on my menu is from my culture. My father is from Hong Kong, and my mother is Chinese American. I cook from my soul, from the memories my grandparents and parents passed down to me. You . . ." I imagined he'd be pointing at me if I could see him. "You don't know what you are. You try a bit of Chinese, a bit of Japanese. Some French, a bit of Cuban Chinese. But who is Liv Kuo? At your essence?"

I couldn't speak. He'd never spoken this way to me before. In fact, he was a man of few words and rarely spoke more than a few sentences. We could tell by his expression if we'd pleased him or created something not up to par for his palate. He let Benjamin and me experiment for the specials menu, and whenever he included one of our creations, we gloated to the other. That was why I'd loved to work for him in his kitchen. Chef Wu had given me wings to try new things, and I'd thought he'd been impressed. To hear that he hadn't been was crushing to my soul.

As if sensing my thoughts, he said, "You *are* good, Liv. I'm not negating that. I just think you could be great. Extraordinary, if you allow yourself to be and dig deep."

"I . . ." No other words came out because I was thinking with shame how I'd never incorporated Taiwanese food into my cooking, because I thought it was too "simple" and not impressive enough for the kind of restaurant I wanted to be associated with.

Chef Wu continued to speak. "Don't give up on yourself because of what happened. Use your trip to Taiwan to explore new things. Be open. Use your senses. Find yourself, your culture. I believe in you."

Those last words finally loosened my tongue. "Thank you, Chef. That means a lot, coming from you."

"I mean them."

"Thank you again for saving my life." My voice broke on the last word.

"I wish I could have saved Cat too." There was a long moment of silence before he spoke again. "Take care of yourself. If you ever want to come back, you know where to find me. But I have a feeling you're on to new and better things." Chef Wu's voice was gruff, and I had a moment of indecision, wondering if I was doing the right thing.

Maybe I should just take the antianxiety medication the doctors had prescribed for me and get back into the restaurant. But I couldn't go to work around knives and hot stoves heavily medicated. At the same time, what was I doing, flying halfway across the world to avoid the circumstances of one night? Why wasn't I stronger, or why hadn't I tried to find a therapist, even a virtual one, since I couldn't seem to leave my apartment? Or gotten a job in another restaurant?

The last question was the easiest to answer. Because Chef Wu was the best as far as I was concerned, and I'd been happy there. Before I could tell him that I'd changed my mind, that I would be back at work the next day, he said goodbye and hung up. I stared at my phone for a few moments, thinking about all he had said. What was the essence of a Liv Kuo dish? Did I even know anymore?

I took a deep breath and then braced myself for the second call.

"Mom?" I said as soon as my mother answered.

"How are you?" There was so much concern in my mother's voice that I grimaced.

"I'm fine. I'm going to Taiwan as soon as I get a visa."

"What?" My mom's voice rose an octave.

From the background, I heard my father ask, "Who is it, Felicia?" My mother had used the name Felicia, instead of her Mandarin name of Lun-Fei, ever since she came to America for college. She'd met my father in California and ended up staying there.

"It's Livia," she called. "She's going to Taiwan." She spoke back into the phone. "Why are you going out of the blue?"

"Ah-Ma called me." I paused for a moment, thinking how my mother had named me Livia, not realizing the name was actually Olivia. Having grown up in Taiwan, certain words and names were unfamiliar to her, and she'd always thought the name was Livia. Which I actually liked.

"Is she okay?" My mom's voice brought me back to our call.

"She saw her fourth daughter yesterday." I bit my bottom lip as I said this.

There was dead silence for a few seconds. And then my mom let out an audible breath. "Oh, wow. What . . . how?"

"How come you've never told me about her?"

"She never talked about Yili after she disappeared." My mom must have put her hand over the phone because I heard muffled words, probably to my father, before she came back on the line. "I was only three and a half, so I don't really remember anything about her. But I grew up knowing not to talk about Yili, and my grandmother and aunts acted as if she never existed. Over time, I kind of forgot I'd had a younger sister at one time. My older sisters didn't talk about her either."

"But how could you all forget her?" I tried to put myself in their shoes, but I couldn't, even though I knew they were just children when Yili was taken.

"Because I never had any real memories of her. And no one ever spoke about her." I could hear the defensiveness in my mother's voice. "I did ask about Yili when my mother moved here from Taiwan. She only said that my father had done a terrible thing, taking Yili away from her, and that she'd never forgiven him."

"I can't even imagine something like that happening." My heart broke again for all my grandmother had been through.

"Taiwanese women didn't have many rights, even back in the 1960s," my mother said. She sighed, and her voice grew wistful. "If someone asked about my childhood, I remember growing up surrounded by family. My grandparents, aunts, uncles, cousins, all lived in the same building. We were in and out of each other's homes all day long. My mother tried so hard not to make my sisters and me feel inferior to our younger brother. We knew he was our father's favorite, but my mother made it clear we were all her favorites. It wasn't a bad childhood."

"But you were KMT then." I still couldn't believe that my mother had lived in a KMT household for years and never told me.

My mother let out another breath. "It was just the way life was back then. The KMT ruled the island, and you either went along with them, or you lived in fear that they were going to throw you in jail for some slight infraction, because they could. My grandfather was a high-level official, but he was just my *ye ye* to me. I didn't really understand the implication until I was a teenager, and then I left for the States for college when I was seventeen."

"What were they like? Your father and grandfather?" I couldn't help asking, because from everything I'd read, the KMT and everyone associated with them had done heinous things.

"At home, they were just Baba and Ye Ye." My mother sighed. "But I heard things. Things they'd done, especially my father. My mother tried to shield us, but we couldn't help hearing rumors. How the intellectual elite—like doctors, professors, bankers—in our neighborhood would disappear, often because of my father."

"What . . . ?" I sputtered, remembering learning about the 228 Massacre of 1947, the antigovernment uprising that was violently suppressed by the KMT, leading to thousands of Taiwanese being killed on February 28, 1947, and in the days after. All the people who'd fought and been jailed and killed for fighting for a democratic Taiwan. And my grandfather had been part of the people responsible? How could my mother not have told me? I was indignant, but then I had to remind myself it was easy to cast blame when I myself hadn't lived through the time and had only read about it in textbooks or watched reports on the news.

"Liv. Your grandmother wanted us to be as unpolitical as possible. People knew who we were and treated us accordingly, but she went out of her way to remain neutral when she could get away with it." The phone rustled, and I imagined my mother must have shifted the phone to her other ear. "Perhaps the rest of the Wangs let her be because of what happened to Yili. I don't know. There are a lot of things that weren't spoken about in the household, and we learned not to ask too many questions."

"I'm just, I guess, shocked by it all." I didn't know how else to express my feelings. "Because you and Dad are so pan-Green."

"We are, and so is your grandmother now."

"But the rest of the family is Blue?" I was confused, thinking it was so black and white, that your family was either Green for Taiwan independence, or Blue, which originally had advocated for reunification with China but now had a more conservative position of maintaining the status quo.

"It's complicated." My mother paused, as if searching for words. "Taiwan is so divided. Within the same extended family, some are Green, and some are Blue. Terrible fights have broken out in families when it comes to election time. Winston's wife and her family are staunchly in the pan-Blue camp, having originally been from China. Winston's daughter sides with him, and his son sides with their mom, dividing their family. We wanted you and Jay to decide for yourselves, so we never pushed our beliefs on you."

"Aunt Lori is Blue?" My mouth dropped open in shock. I'd never known that. After a beat of silence, I said, "There's so much I don't know about our family."

"I'm sure Ah-Ma will tell you when you get to Taiwan. What did she say about Yili?" My mother's voice shook with emotion.

I told her what my grandmother had told me and then said, "I need to go help her. I'd do anything for Ah-Ma, but I also need to get out of New York."

"You do." My mom's voice was resigned. "Maybe you'll meet a nice Taiwanese boy."

"Mom." There was a note of warning in my voice.

"You never know." She paused, as if waiting for me to come to my senses and marry the next man who'd look at me twice.

"No." I left it at that, and to my relief, she let it go.

"This trip will be good for you." Her tone was conciliatory.

"I hope so." I clamped my lips together, trying to keep them from trembling.

The truth was, I was sick of feeling afraid, of being immobile. I'd always lived life to the fullest, doing what made me happy, instead of what I should be doing. I was still single at thirty-five, because I hadn't met anyone I wanted to spend my life with; I'd embraced it instead of obsessing about finding a mate, like some of my friends. Amy felt the same way, and we'd both loved the restaurant lifestyle. We used to go out late after the restaurant closed, knowing we could sleep in the next morning. We'd taken vacations to tropical and far-flung places together. We'd been the envy of our married friends, who were tied down with young children and obligations. We were living our best lives. Until that man burst into the kitchen of 852 that night and wreaked havoc on the place I loved and on my life.

My mom talked a bit more, but my mind drifted, swirling with everything I'd learned today. When we finally said goodbye, with me promising to keep her posted from Taiwan, I was more resolved than ever. I was going to get my life back on track once I returned from Taiwan. I had to. No more wallowing, no more hiding out, ignoring all my friends' calls, texts, and pleas to talk to them. Amy was the only one I'd allowed to visit me during my exile, and now she texted often from wherever she was in the world. My thumbs flew over my phone as I messaged her to tell her I was going to Taiwan. I knew she'd be thrilled, glad I was living again, wherever she was.

But first, I had to get myself out of this apartment and halfway around the world without having a panic attack.

4
LIV

A few days later, I stood in the crowded baggage claim area of Taiwan Taoyuan International Airport in Taipei, triumphant. I'd done it. I couldn't believe I'd not only left my apartment but also traveled over 7,700 miles without a meltdown. I'd taken an antianxiety pill before the Lyft had picked me up from my apartment for the airport, and then a stronger dose right before boarding. I had a moment of panic when the plane was taking off, but the drug did its job and lulled me into a false sense of security. I'd slept most of the fifteen-hour direct flight in business class, and now I was refreshed and invigorated, even at five thirty in the morning. It made me wonder why I hadn't done this earlier, taken the medication my doctor had prescribed, if it would have helped ease my post-traumatic anxiety.

A text dinged, and I looked down at my cell.

Heard you're leaving us. I'll miss you. You pushed me to be better. Stay in touch.

It was from Benjamin. Chef had given him a few days off because he'd been working overtime covering for me. He would be at the restaurant now, getting ready for the dinner service.

I replied, I will. I'll miss you too.

Then I pulled up Amy's number. I made it!

She'd quit her job at 852 after the shooting to go travel the world, feeling guilty that Cat had been killed. Even though I told her it wasn't her fault, I knew Amy blamed herself in part, wondering if she'd been working that night and the baos were what the man was used to, would he have snapped and stormed into the kitchen? Neither of us had voiced out loud that he might have snapped anyway, and Amy would be dead now instead of Cat.

I got a response right away. Yay! So proud of you. Come join me when you find your aunt.

Where are you?

Marrakesh. But only for a few more days. Then off to Portugal. Or maybe Spain.

I shook my head, part of me envying her adventures. Once upon a time, I would have been with her, traveling with no agenda, going wherever the wind took us. But now the thought of traipsing from one unknown place to another terrified me. Especially as this trip had exhausted me.

Announcements crackled in Mandarin, and I looked up from my phone and around at the bustling airport. For once, I was in the majority, just another Asian in the crowd. I'd never learned to read or write Mandarin, but I could understand it well enough to get by. My grandmother had always spoken it to my brother and me, and my parents had used a mixture of English and Mandarin.

"Excuse me," someone said to my left, and I jumped out of the way as a luggage cart full of suitcases rumbled by, pushed by a boy of about thirteen, his parents trailing behind.

Someone else bumped me on the other side, and I drew back, avoiding a heavy backpack that almost clipped me on the side of the head. A prickle of dread began at the back of my neck, and I couldn't wait to find my suitcase and then the driver Ah-Ma had sent for me, who would take me to Taichung. I'd survived the flight, but there were too many people here for my comfort. I needed to get out of the airport as soon as possible. My hands fisted and I dug my nails into the palm of my hands, willing myself to stay calm. I'd gotten this far; I could hold it together until I was in the safety of the car. When the carousel for my flight started up after a loud beep, I breathed a sigh of relief and moved toward it.

But before I could get close, I saw that a little girl ahead of me had dropped her stuffed dog from the top of her suitcase and hadn't noticed. I rushed forward, intending to pick it up, but a man got to it before I could. He called after the little girl, who turned, at first uncertain, and then ran back when she caught sight of her dog in the man's hands. Her father chased after her, and I smiled when she squealed as she accepted the toy.

"I can't believe I dropped Perry!" She hugged the brown dog to her chest. "Thank you."

The man smiled down at her. "He would have been sad to be separated from you."

The father thanked him, and they walked away. I didn't realize I was still staring at the man until he turned and caught my eyes. He raised an eyebrow, and I realized I'd seen him before. He'd been on my flight, across the aisle from me, but since I was medicated and had slept most of the way, I hadn't really paid attention. Something about his brief interaction with the little girl and the way he was currently gazing at me made my cheeks heat.

He was Asian, maybe Taiwanese like me if he'd flown from New York to Taiwan direct. He was somewhere just shy of six feet, and there was an easy confidence in the way he had his backpack slung over a shoulder, his weight shifted onto one hip as his eyes took me in. He had a strong chin, something my grandmother had always said meant the person was steady and dependable, and his dark eyes sparkled with anticipation. His skin was darker than mine, and he smiled at me when I didn't look away. My lips curved up on their own without input from my brain. I couldn't help it, because there was something about him that spoke of ease in his own skin. He didn't pretend he hadn't caught me staring, and his smile said he didn't mind. I wondered if he'd approach, talk to me, and I was just about to walk toward him when his eyes widened in alarm.

Before I could puzzle out why his expression had changed, I heard a shout behind me and then something rammed into my legs hard, causing them to buckle. Suitcases and luggage rained around me, forcing my arms to fly up over my head to shield myself. I hit the ground hard on my left side, my hip stinging as a heavy suitcase landed on me. Voices shouted, something crashed with a bang, and without warning, I was transported back to that night in the kitchen at 852, when that man had burst in from the outside door during the dinner rush.

I was brushing miso paste on a beautiful piece of black cod and looked up to see a large man looming in the doorway. His eyes were cold, his face hard. My heart stopped when he directed his gaze at me. My station was closest to the back door. The fish dropped out of my hands and onto the counter. I came out from behind my station, my senses on alert.

"Can I help you?" I asked. "You shouldn't be here."

Without a word, he closed the distance between us and then pushed me hard. I flew back, right into a busboy just coming in from the dining room with a tray of dirty dishes. The plates rained down around me as I fell to the ground, breaking glass shattering all around me like tiny bombs exploding.

"He's got a gun!" I heard Chef Wu shout, and I saw him sprint out from behind the stove.

No, no, stay back, Chef.

The man fired a shot and I screamed, sure that Chef Wu had been hit. More screams erupted around me as people ducked for cover. I struggled to get off the floor, to see what was happening.

"Are you okay?" the busboy whispered.

I nodded, but my attention was fixed on the man. Someone had to stop him. Who was he, and why was he in the kitchen? I made it back on my feet in time to see him advancing on the pastry station, where Cat, the new hire who was covering for Amy that night because Amy had gotten a migraine earlier, stood frozen, staring at him in fear. Chef Wu was nowhere in sight.

The man raised his arm and aimed his gun at Cat.

"No!" I screamed, intending to run to them, but I slipped and fell to the ground.

Crash.

The suitcase that had landed on top of me fell off as my entire body jerked. I shook like a leaf in the wind, whimpers escaping from my mouth. My heart was galloping as fast as a stallion, and I was barely holding on. I was in full-panic mode, and I was sure I was about to die.

Breathe, Liv, breathe, I chanted to myself, trying to slow my gasps.

A child sobbed, people shouted, but everything around me faded as I relived that night at 852 all over again. I'd been too cocky, thinking I'd made it here to Taiwan without a panic attack, and now I was being rewarded with the mother of all attacks. I stuffed a fist against my mouth, one arm still over my head as terror gripped me, holding me hostage. Someone was speaking to me, but I couldn't hear them over the roar of gunfire and the chaos from the 852 kitchen that was echoing in my mind.

Cat, Cat! *I shouted over and over in my mind.* Get out of the kitchen. He's got a gun!

It went off, once, twice, three times. I saw Cat's body jerk, saw blood spattering over the baos and dumplings on the counter in front of her, and then she disappeared. I sobbed, got to my feet once again, and rushed toward her. And that's when the man turned and, without hesitating, shot me. Pain, searing pain, exploded near my shoulder, and the force of the shot knocked me back. I fell once again, except this time, I couldn't get back up. I couldn't breathe from the pain, smothering me, pulling me under. Darkness beckoned, but I fought it. I had to get up. I struggled to breathe, to leap to my feet, but something pressed down on me, and I was going under. A silent scream stuck in my throat.

The screams from that night echoed in my head, and my entire body shuddered, imaginary pain radiating from my shoulder. Someone was still talking to me, but I couldn't hear the words. It wasn't until a warm hand landed gently on my bad shoulder that the panic that had taken over my whole body receded slightly, and I slowly became aware of my surroundings again.

A child was babbling, people were calling out, and I realized someone was picking up the luggage that had fallen on and around me. But I focused solely on the low voice that was speaking directly into my ear. It was gentle, and when I could finally understand the words, I realized it was saying in English, "You're fine. Nothing's going to hurt you. It was just a luggage cart. A child was pushing it, playing around, and lost control. It crashed into you. You're okay."

Slowly, my arm loosened from around my head, and I looked up, into the eyes of the man I'd exchanged a smile with before the cart hit me. His gaze was steady, and I found myself drawn to his quiet strength as the terror that had clawed at me started retreating slightly. Only then did my mind finally realize the gunman couldn't hurt me anymore. He was in jail, and Chef Wu had saved me by tackling him before he could shoot me again.

I gulped in a breath of air, embarrassment replacing the panic. People gawked at us, the parents of the child who'd crashed the cart into me alternating between scolding him and looking at me in concern. When the mother caught my gaze, she rushed over.

"Are you okay?" she asked in Mandarin. "I'm so sorry. He didn't mean to hurt you. Should we call an ambulance?"

I shook my head, not quite trusting my voice. My hip stung, but I was otherwise intact.

The man who'd talked me out of my panic still had a hand on my shoulder. "Can you stand?"

I nodded and pushed to my feet with his guidance. My legs were weak, and I swayed a bit, grateful he hadn't let go. Everything swam in front of me, and my heart was still going a million beats per minute, the rush of adrenaline wreaking havoc within my body. The child's mother continued to apologize to me, as did her husband, who now had a firm hand on the cart.

The child, a boy of about seven or eight, said with his head hung low, "I'm sorry I hit you."

I nodded and tried to smile, but my mouth had stopped working. I nodded again, hoping that would convey that his apology was accepted. The mother said more words that I didn't catch, and then with one last round of apologies, they were gone.

The man let go of my arm and looked at me. "Okay now?"

I dipped my head even though I was still shaky, embarrassment warring with relief that I no longer felt like my heart was going to give out. My eyes darted to the baggage carousel, noting that most people had retrieved their suitcases and the crowd was starting to thin.

"I'm sorry." My words were shaky, and I gulped in air, trying to slow my breathing. The terror from that night still had me in its grips, even as my brain understood I was in Taiwan, and not at 852 that night.

"You have nothing to be sorry for." His tone was kind.

I couldn't meet his eyes and gestured with my chin to our carousel. "You probably missed your suitcase." I tried for casual, but the tremor in my voice gave me away.

"It's okay." I could tell he was studying me. "What color is yours? I'll get it for you."

"Black. With a red belt around it." I chanced a look in his direction. His mouth quirked into a smirk. "Don't you know not to use red when coming to an Asian country? Everyone uses red for good luck."

His casual teasing calmed me even more, and I tried to match his jocular tone. "What color should I have used then?"

"Blue, or orange, or pink. Anything but red." We walked over to the carousel together, just as my suitcase came around the bend.

I reached out to retrieve it, but he plucked it off the belt before I could. Then he pulled off a black suitcase with a royal blue ribbon wrapped around the handle and turned, catching my eyes with a lift of his eyebrows.

A smile bloomed from my lips. I'd humiliated myself in front of this man who, seconds before the crash, I'd wanted to come over to talk to me. I'd never been shy when it came to dating. If I was interested in someone, I talked to him to see if there was something there. But that was before, and he'd also seen me at my worst, huddled on the floor of the airport in terror. I looked away, unable to meet his eyes. All I wanted to do was get out of this airport and hide out in Ah-Ma's apartment for a few days.

"Thank you again for helping me. You were . . . great," I said, for lack of a better word. I turned, intending to hightail it out of there. But my heart picked up pace again as I surveyed the busy airport, panic settling in at the thought of navigating this crowd and trying to find the driver out there somewhere.

"Hey." He leaned in close to me. "Is the panic attack coming back?" He tilted his head to study me, and I suddenly had the feeling that he understood all I'd been through.

"How did you know?"

He gave me a small smile. "I'm a psychotherapist. I specialize in trauma."

"Oh." No wonder he'd been so good at talking me out of the throes of my panic. Heat rose in my cheeks because I couldn't help noticing the way he smelled like soap even after over fifteen hours of travel, or the way his long eyelashes brushed his face when he blinked.

We looked at each other in silence, and I realized I wanted him to help me find the driver. The thought of being alone after that harrowing experience had my knees trembling.

"I can get you to wherever you need to go." His eyes bored into mine, and I saw the sincerity in them. I latched on to that, refusing to think about how much I was inconveniencing him, when he was probably eager to get to wherever he was going too.

"I'd like that," I whispered. "Thank you."

"No problem." He gestured with his head toward customs and immigration, and I trailed after him, so thankful I'd run into this kind man.

Half an hour later, we sailed through the last obstacle and were released into the arrivals area. He stopped and I halted next to him.

"Where are you going?" he asked.

"Taichung."

"Me too." His eyebrows rose. "Do you have a ride?"

I nodded. "My grandmother sent a driver for me."

"That's good. Let me get you to the car, and then I'll leave you to it."

"Do you have a car too?" I asked, trying to make conversation.

"No." He threw a smile over his shoulder. "I'll take the train."

I stopped walking. This man had been so good to me, and it didn't feel right that he'd have to catch a train when I had a personal driver coming for me. He was a stranger, but somehow, I felt as if I knew him. "My driver can take you to wherever you're going." I blurted this out before I could stop to think about the implications of offering a stranger a ride.

He turned to look at me. "It's okay. I don't mind taking the train."

I shook my head. "You helped me so much. The least I can do is offer you a ride."

He studied my face, and I tried to convey my gratitude with my expression.

"You sure?" His words came out slowly. "I don't want to stress you out."

"You're not." As I said these words, I realized it was the truth. Something about him calmed my nerves, and my instincts told me he was harmless, even if I'd only met him minutes ago. "Besides, the driver will be there and can defend me if you try something funny."

His lips twitched at that. "You don't have to worry about anything funny from me."

I gave him a nod of assertion. "Then it's decided. I'm giving you a ride."

He watched my face for another moment and then nodded too. I let out a breath, not sure why I felt so elated, when moments before, I'd been curled up on the floor in panic.

"My name is Simon. Simon Huang." He held out a hand, and I took it in mine. His hand was warm, and the heat traveled all the way up my arm.

"I'm Liv Kuo."

"Nice to meet you, Liv," he said, and the grin he aimed at me finally chased away the last vestige of the panic attack.

I stared out the window of the car, taking in my first glimpses of Taiwan. It was mostly highways with signs written in both Mandarin and English, but I saw tall buildings in the distance and more greenery than I expected.

"Why are you here?" Simon asked, and I turned to him.

"My grandmother needs my help." I hesitated, wondering if I should tell him about her lost daughter. "It's kind of a long story."

"We've got at least an hour and a half before we get to Taichung."

He was right. I realized I was at ease with him, as if he were an old friend I'd run into. I told him about the aunt I didn't know I had, and when I finished, he shook his head.

"How are you supposed to find her? Do you know how many people are in Taichung? It's like finding a needle in the huge haystack of the city." Simon voiced the same concern I'd had when my grandmother asked me to come.

"I have no idea." My shoulders lifted and then fell. "But my grandmother is so desperate to find her and so hopeful. I had to come and try."

He nodded as if he understood, and I could tell he was turning over the story in his head.

"What about you?" I asked. "What are you doing here?"

"My—" He broke off and looked away. "My best friend's grandfather passed away." His mouth turned down in sadness. "I'm here for the funeral."

"I'm so sorry." I wanted to reach out and touch him, but I held back. "Were you . . . close to him?"

"Yes," he said simply. A pause before he said, "He was like a grandfather to me. My own both passed away when I was a child, so I never got to know them."

"Oh." My heart went out to him. "He lived in New York?" I asked when he didn't elaborate.

"No. He lived in Georgia for years before moving back to Taiwan a few years ago. I'm originally from Georgia."

"I'm so sorry," I said again, not sure how to help him.

"Thank you." He nodded.

I touched him on the forearm then, unable to resist making contact with him. We were both here for our grandparents, or grandfather figure in his case, although our reasons were so different.

He smiled at me as I took my hand back, and we spent the rest of the ride making small talk. I told him I was a chef, but not what had happened at 852. He told me about his work, both at a hospital and a private practice based in Astoria. He was easy to talk to, and he made me laugh a few times, a far cry from the panic I'd experienced in the airport. He'd been to Taiwan many times, even living here for a year for work, and told me about the night markets and all the food I needed to try. I made note of them in my phone as my mouth watered, listening to him wax poetic about stinky tofu. Before we realized it, the car pulled up in front of the building at the address he'd given the driver.

I wanted to ask for his contact information, not willing to let him just disappear. But before I could, he spoke first.

"Can we stay in touch?"

Did I imagine it, or was he looking at me with hope?

I nodded, trying to remain calm. "I'd like that."

We exchanged phone numbers and then got out of the car, the heat of the day already high. He took his suitcase from the driver and handed him a tip. I stood there, awkwardly shifting from foot to foot, wondering why I was so bereft at the thought of driving away without him.

"It was great to meet you, Liv." His voice was gravelly. "Good luck with the search. If I can help in any way, you have my number."

"Thank you again. For everything." I gave him a tremulous smile. "I'd probably still be on the floor in the airport if it hadn't been for you."

His mouth twitched, and then we both moved in for a brief hug. I had the impression of strong arms wrapping around me, the warmth from his skin and the scent of soap tickling my nose. It ended too soon, and then with a wave, he rolled his suitcase toward the building.

I got back into the car, looking after him until he disappeared. I couldn't stop the hopeful feeling that bloomed in my chest whenever I encountered a situation with potential. Whether it be a fresh idea for a recipe or a new person I was excited to get to know, the beginning of something had always invigorated me, because at that point, anything was possible. I didn't know Simon; I had no idea if he was single or married or somewhere in between. But I had a feeling, as I pulled out my phone to text Ah-Ma that I was almost there, that this was the beginning of something intriguing.

5
Liv

Less than five minutes later, the driver pulled up to Ah-Ma's apartment building in a narrow side street. There were no sidewalks, and bicycles and scooters lined the street on both sides, with cars randomly pulled up close to the buildings. My grandmother was waiting in front of a wide burgundy metal gate. I jumped out as soon as the car stopped, and she pulled me to her. My entire body went limp in her embrace as I buried my face in her neck, breathing in the familiar lemon scent of her soap. I'd made it in one piece, barely.

"Liv-ah. You're here," my grandmother said against my ear.

"I am." I pulled back with a rueful laugh. "I almost didn't survive the airport, but here I am." I'd tell her about Simon later, but right now, I wanted to focus on her.

She greeted the driver, and I thanked him when he set my suitcase next to me. My uncle Winston had insisted on paying for a driver and a companion for Ah-Ma when she'd been adamant about moving back to Taiwan despite her children's protests. Ah-Ma had given the companion time off while I was here, but the driver would be taking us around the city.

"Come, let's get you inside." My grandmother put an arm around me, and we stepped through the gate into a small courtyard. "You must be hungry. I made *mue* for you." She spoke to me in a mixture of Taiwanese and English.

"Oh." I sighed out the word. I associated congee with my grandmother, since she used to make the Taiwanese breakfast for us on the weekends.

She gave my shoulder a squeeze and ushered me to her second-floor apartment. It was modern and bright, filled with colorful furniture. Ah-Ma had always loved color, and the vivid blue couch with the two canary-yellow upholstered easy chairs on either side made me smile.

After a visit to the bathroom, I came out to find Ah-Ma had laid out little side dishes on the table. There were pickled cucumbers, wheat gluten, fermented bean curd, pork floss, and salted duck eggs. There was also a dish of Chinese morning glory, a green vegetable with a hollow stem that she'd sautéed with garlic. It was a simple meal, but it filled me with yearning for a past I hadn't thought about in years.

"Sit." She gestured when she noticed me hovering. I complied, and she placed a steaming bowl of congee in front of me before studying my face intently. "How are you, really?"

I let out a breath, not quite ready to tell her about my panic attack in the airport, and that any loud noise could transport me back to that night at 852. I turned the questioning back on Ah-Ma instead.

"I'm okay. I want to know more about Yili. What did you do after she disappeared?" I picked up my chopsticks and used them to bring a small smear of the creamy bean curd into my mouth. I sighed as the briny saltiness mixed with a bit of sweet exploded on my tongue.

She frowned and shook a finger at me. "I know you're deflecting." She reached out to touch my forearm. "I'll tell you about Yili, but then we need to talk about you."

"We will. I promise." I flashed her a smile and then focused on the feast in front of me. I began to eat as my grandmother started to tell me more of her story, my nerves soothed by the familiar flavors of my childhood that I'd ignored for far too long.

YI-PING

March 1961, Taichung

In the days following Yili's disappearance, I was filled with a manic frenzy. I barely slept. I ate just enough to quiet the rumbles of my stomach. I cared about only one thing: finding Yili and bringing her home. I hounded my husband, begging him to tell me where Yili was, who he'd given her to. He refused, and I resorted to shouting at him, beating him with my fists until my sisters-in-law pulled me off him. He started avoiding me and moved out of our bedroom, which was just as well. I couldn't stand to look at him, let alone be near him. I wanted to spit in his eye, kick him where it would hurt, rake my fingers down his cheeks until they bled. A red haze of fury and sorrow wrapped itself around me, and everyone in the household took to tiptoeing away from me, eyeing me as if I were a wild animal.

I didn't care. The Wangs had always treated me well because I'd been a dutiful daughter-in-law and wife. I respected my elders and my husband and knew my place in the family. I helped around the building, not just in my own home, but in those of all my in-laws. I was good with the children, all of them, and the family knew they could depend on me. But no longer. The Wangs had done the worst thing they could have possibly done to me. Let them kick me and my children out into the street. I could find work or go back to my parents' home. I was filled with a sudden longing for the farm where I'd been a carefree child, running with the animals and picking fruit right off the trees, juices running down my chin when I bit into them. My heart yearned to be in the fields with my father, tending the vegetables and fruit trees, harvesting them to be sold.

47

I wanted to go home, my real home, and not the Wang household. The loss of my daughter forced me to remember all those I'd left behind when I was sixteen: my parents, my sisters and brothers, my best friend from down the street, our childhood dog who used to follow me everywhere, and the bunnies my mother raised, who'd nuzzle me with their noses. I felt Yili's absence to the depth of my soul, to the point where there were days I wondered if I would go out of my mind with grief. I could barely contain my emotions, and it was as if everything that made me human had been stripped away.

At the weekly Wang family meal, I didn't wait for my father-in-law and the other men to pick the best pieces of meat first, the way I'd always done. I grabbed at it before they or my mother-in-law could, while my sisters-in-law gaped at me. I didn't go to the market with the other women like I used to, didn't have meals prepared when my husband came home from work, didn't help around the building as I'd always done. I neglected my other children, forcing my sisters-in-law to take over. I was like a feral animal who'd been let loose in the midst of the very civilized Wangs, eavesdropping at doors, sneaking up on my husband, hoping someone would drop a hint as to where Yili had gone, all decorum forgotten. On the fourth day after Yili disappeared, my favorite sister-in-law pulled me aside after lunch.

"You need to stop," she whispered into my ear, after dragging me into my bedroom. "They let you get away with your behavior at first, but you're pushing them too far."

I stared at the sister-in-law we called Mei Mei, or Little Sister, because she was the youngest one of us, a year and a half my junior. "What do I care?" I cried, flinging my arms out. "They took my daughter. They took my heart."

"You still have four other children. Think of them." Mei Mei tugged me to sit by her at the foot of my bed. "You can't act like this." She leaned in close and whispered again: "I heard Abu say this morning that if you didn't get a hold of yourself, she would take care of you." Mei Mei peered around fearfully, as if expecting our mother-in-law to be hiding under the bed. "I don't know what she meant, but you know it can't be good."

We stared at each other, both thinking about what our mother-in-law had done to one of her daughters. Her youngest hadn't wanted to marry the man her parents had arranged for her through a matchmaker. She was in love with another man, a doctor who came from a good family. But that hadn't mattered to her parents. Tradition in the Wang family dictated that they would find her a husband, and when she rebelled, Abu kicked her out of the house, cutting her off from the rest of the family. The daughter had lasted a month before she'd come back, begging for forgiveness on her knees in front of Abu. Her story was now a Wang family story of caution. She'd defied her parents for love, and the love of her life had left her when he found out her family had disowned her. He'd been as in love with the Wang money and power as he'd been with her.

"I don't care." I crossed my arms over my chest. "She can kick me and my children out. I can work." *Or go home,* I didn't say out loud.

"But she'll take your children from you." Mei Mei's gaze was intense. "You have a son. She'll never let him go. And she's very fond of your three older daughters. I don't think she'd let you take them. Or your dog."

I sucked in a breath and stared at Mei Mei. It'd never occurred to me that Abu would keep my children and my dog. I'd thought they would go wherever I went. Now I realized Mei Mei was right. If they could take Yili, what was to stop them from keeping my other children if they disowned me? Abu had invested so much in Lun-Shan's piano lessons. Lun-Wen often helped Abu with the big family meals. And Lun-Fei was the apple of her grandfather's eye. My in-laws would never allow me to keep my children, especially not my son. And they'd keep my dog, just out of spite.

"*Aiya,* what have I done?" I stood, my hands tugging at the ends of my hair. I walked at a frenetic pace, wondering why I'd been so naive.

"Now do you understand?" Mei Mei said, reaching out to grasp one of my hands, halting me in place. "You must stop this. We all miss Yili, but you can't jeopardize your position in the family. You'll lose everything."

My chin quivered as I fought down that thought. I'd been stupid, not thinking clearly. "What am I going to do?"

Mei Mei pursed her lips. "You can fix this. You have to. For your other children."

I flinched at her words because I hadn't thought of them at all. "I'm sorry."

We both froze when we heard our mother-in-law's voice in my main living area.

"Where's Yi-ping?" she called to my daughters, who were gathered in there, watching their baby brother.

"In her room," I heard my oldest daughter say.

Mei Mei and I looked at each other. My eyes widened as I imagined that my mother-in-law was on her way to tell me to leave. Mei Mei must have seen the fear in my eyes because she leaned in and said in a low voice, "I'll tell her you're sleeping and head her off. You leave, go get her favorite *rou geng* soup from that stand—you know the one I mean."

I nodded. My mother-in-law loved the thick soup made with tender pieces of pork wrapped in fish paste and stewed with shiitake mushrooms, bamboo shoots, carrot, and cabbage. There was a particular street stand she'd stumbled upon one day that she hadn't been able to stop talking about. But it was in a bad area of the city, and she didn't like to venture there. If I brought some back for her, it would go a long way in asking for her forgiveness.

"Thank you, Mei Mei." I squeezed her hand in gratitude.

She squeezed back and then let go, standing. "None of us want to see you banished from our home." With a quick smile aimed at me, she slipped out of the room.

I watched her go, my feelings at war. Mei Mei was the clumsy one, the one who had burned herself so badly with boiling water. When Abu mentioned that the day Yili disappeared, I was filled with resentment that Mei Mei's clumsiness had contributed to Yili's disappearance. The other sisters-in-law and I were usually the ones to cover for her, but now she was taking care of me. Mei Mei's husband also adored her and she him; perhaps I was filled with jealousy that my own marriage wasn't as happy as Mei Mei's. I gave a quick prayer of thanks that she'd warned me and was helping me get back into Abu's good graces.

I waited until I heard Mei Mei's and Abu's voices fading down the hallway leading away from our home. Then I grabbed my bag and walked out into the main room, giving each of my children a quick kiss and telling the girls to take their brother to their second aunt's home on the third floor. They obeyed without question. I slipped out the door and headed on foot for the soup stall. I knew what street it was on but not its exact location, and I prayed that I'd be able to find it.

My eyes looked for Yili as I walked, dodging scooters, bicycles, and reckless drivers who drove up onto the sidewalk with no warning. I searched each small face I passed, wondering if it was my daughter. I walked around children darting away from their parents, and high school girls who walked arm in arm in their uniforms, their hair cut in the identical short style dictated by the government. Once, I'd dreamed of going to high school and university like them, but my father had needed my help in the fields, and then I'd been married off. I looked away at the sound of the girls' laughter, envy slicing through me like a blade as I wondered how different my life would have been if my family could have afforded to send me to school. But then, I wouldn't have had my children, and I couldn't imagine a life without them.

I finally reached the street that had become legendary in our home, because my mother-in-law had happened upon it one day when their car had broken down. As she waited for someone to come get her, she saw the *rou geng* stall on the side of the street, and hunger made her take a seat at an uneven table. She ordered one bowl, then another. She'd told the entire family more than a few times how incredible it was, and how it was the best *rou geng* soup she'd ever had in her life. Too bad it was in an area of Taichung she'd never willingly go to again.

I walked up and down the street, looking for the stand. I asked someone in Taiwanese if they knew where it was, and they directed me in the opposite direction. When I finally spotted it, I let out a cry of triumph, glad I wouldn't go back empty-handed. I sat and ordered a bowl for myself, for I hadn't eaten lunch, and my stomach was rumbling from the delicious smells wafting out of the big pot the vendor was stirring.

When she set a bowl in front of me, I leaned forward and inhaled the rich aroma of the thick soup before taking a spoonful. As the delicious soup slid down my throat, I tried to decipher the flavors bursting in my mouth. What was it that made this version so much better than any I'd tried before? *Rou geng*, or *bah gee* in Taiwanese, was one of those dishes that every Taiwanese family had their own version of. I'd learned to make the one I made for my family from my grandmother, but there was something special about this one.

Was it roasted garlic? Or was that shallot I tasted? The type of black vinegar the vendor used to finish off the soup? I ignored the state of the plastic bowl, which was crusted with dried food on the outside, and of the table, which was dirty and held remnants of someone else's meal. I ignored the shouts around me as people argued in Mandarin and traffic squealed by, fumes emitting into the air. I focused only on the flavors in my mouth, wondering if I could re-create it in my own kitchen. Abu was right—this was the best *rou geng* I'd ever had. My children, especially Yili, would love it. Yili loved soups of any kind, and I could already imagine her squeals of delight when I brought some home for her later.

And then I realized anew that Yili was gone. She wasn't waiting for me at home with her sisters and brother. Tears rolled down my cheeks, mingling with the spoonful of soup I was about to put in my mouth. It was salty, seasoned by my tears. The toothless vendor said something to me in Taiwanese, but I didn't answer. I was too busy trying to suppress my sorrow as I continued to eat, rolling the flavors around on my tongue. It suddenly became important for me to re-create this soup for Yili. If I could figure out the special ingredient, I knew Yili would come home.

"What's your secret?" I finally asked the owner of the stall. I waited for her answer as if it would solve all the problems in the world.

She grinned at me, gums showing, and replied in Taiwanese, "Old family recipe. I can't tell. You come back anytime you want." She kept talking and I sat there, lips trembling, wanting to beg her to tell me what it was because I knew it would bring Yili home. Part of my brain realized this was wishful thinking. I was grasping at straws, making bargains with the gods: *Perfect this soup, and Yili could come home. Get Abu to forgive me, and she'll tell me what happened to Yili. Make all of Yili's favorite foods, and she'll be home to eat them.*

When I finished my bowl, I ordered two more to take with me for Abu. Once I had my bags of the thick soup with the black vinegar (that had to be the woman's secret; what type of black vinegar was it? I'd do a taste test when I got home) in its own little pouch tied to the knot of the handle, I pressed a few more coins into the woman's hands and then hurried toward home. I had to walk onto the busy street a few times as there were sections without sidewalks, tempting fate since Taiwanese drivers rarely heeded traffic rules. I held my breath when a scooter zipped by me so close that its occupant literally brushed shoulders with me. I clutched the bags of soup close, not wanting to lose the prized packages I'd slogged all this way to get. I didn't admit to myself that deep down, I'd bought the second one for Yili, hoping she would be at home when I returned.

I finally reached the Wang building and headed upstairs to my mother-in-law's rooms. I found Abu watching a Chinese drama on the television. As soon as she looked up, I dropped to my knees in front of her, bowing my head.

"I'm sorry, Abu," I said, looking at the floor. "My grief made me forget myself and do things I would normally never do. Please forgive me. I went and found the *rou geng* soup you've been dreaming of." *Please forgive me so that my fourth daughter can come home.*

I held up the bags of the still-hot soup and saw her eyes light up. "Yi-ping. Thank you." She took them from me and headed for her kitchen. "Get off your knees," she called over her shoulder. "Help me get this ready."

I followed her to the kitchen and bustled around, pulling down her favorite blue ceramic bowl with peonies on it, untying one bag, and pouring the contents into the bowl. I knew my mother-in-law liked extra cilantro in her soups, so I got some out and washed, then chopped it to sprinkle on top of the soup. Lastly, I added the correct amount of black vinegar and served it to her at her dining table. I tied up the remaining vinegar, intending on taking it home so I could try to figure out what was so special about it.

Then I sat in silence at the table while Abu ate. When at last, not a drop was left, she finally spoke. "I know how you feel. My third daughter was taken from me a month after she was born."

I held my breath, wondering what she was about to tell me.

Abu looked away from me. "But I at least knew where she'd gone, which family had adopted her. I even got to see her a few times as she grew up." She turned to me, and her eyes softened. Was there moisture in them? I'd never seen Abu anything but stern and proud, so this moment of weakness endeared her to me. "This is just how things are done. We have no say."

"But Abu . . ."

She cut me off by holding up a hand, her eyes hardening. "I still believe my son did what he thought was best for the family. But I'm not heartless. You should at least know where your daughter has gone."

I sucked in a breath. "You'll help me find Yili?"

She shook her head. "You won't get her back. But it might put your mind at ease to know she is in a good home. I'll try to find out the name of the family who took her."

My heart leaped with hope. Even if Abu only gave me a surname, it would be more than I had now. I was sure I'd be able to find Yili then and hold her in my arms again. I didn't think about what I would do if I did find my daughter, how I could get her back, but I'd worry about that when I found her. Right now, all I could feel was gratitude that Abu was willing to help me.

"Thank you," I breathed out.

She reached over and tipped a finger under my chin, forcing me to look into her eyes. "I know you're hurting, but I hope we will see the daughter we've known for the past seven years, and not the uncouth animal of the past few days, ah?"

I nodded, afraid to blink for fear she'd change her mind.

She let go of my chin and sighed. "Go. Take care of your children. Tend to your husband."

I stood and ran away, clutching the little bag of black vinegar. But I wouldn't tend to my husband. Not until Yili was back home where she belonged. I realized that night as I huddled on my bed, with only my faithful dog at my side, that I'd have to find her myself. I couldn't trust superstitions or bargaining with the gods or anyone else in this household to help me. They believed she was gone for good, and I refused to accept that. Once Abu got me a name, I'd track Yili down.

When morning came, I'd rise from my bed after a sleepless night and make a big pot of *mue* for my children. The rice porridge was a comfort food during my childhood, and now it would soothe my children and me as we coped with the loss of Yili. I didn't know how much they understood or what I could do to help them. All I knew was that I would never give up looking for my fourth daughter until she was back in my arms where she belonged.

6

LIV

I pushed away from the table, my belly full of *mue* and my nostalgia out in full force. Sitting here with my grandmother had swept me back to my parents' house in Oakland, California, where I'd grown up, and the weekends when my younger brother, Jay, and I would wake up to find Ah-Ma in the kitchen. She'd be dressed in one of her flowery polyester shirts she'd brought from Taiwan, a steaming pot of *mue* on the stove and the side dishes all lined up on the dining room table. I'd stick my face over the pot, the steam giving me a facial, and inhale deeply, even though *mue* has no smell, since it's just white rice cooked down with water.

"You and Jay always loved it so much." Ah-Ma looked at me with affection now, speaking a mixture of Mandarin and English.

"It's the best breakfast." To this day, I preferred a Taiwanese breakfast over eggs with bacon or pancakes or cereal. "We should FaceTime with Jay later." I'd told my brother I was visiting our grandmother, and he'd asked that we call him.

"Yes. We'll call him tonight." Ah-Ma smiled. "Do you need to rest?"

I shook my head, my mind full of everything she'd just told me. "I slept for most of the plane ride. I'm ready to start the search."

Ah-Ma let out a laugh. "I knew I'd asked the right person for help."

"Let's go back to where you saw her." I knew chances were slim that she'd be there, but I couldn't wait to explore Taichung with my grandmother. I also wanted to see the street markets that Taiwan was so famous for.

Ah-Ma looked at the clock hanging over her kitchen sink. "It's almost ten. The shops and vendors will be opening soon, and it won't be so crowded." She had told me Yizhong Shopping Street was both a day and night market.

I jumped off my chair, eager to get out there. My panic attack from that morning was a distant dream, just like my life back in New York. Everything was different here, and I felt as though I'd been given a reprieve, a chance to catch my breath where everything was new, and nothing reminded me of the shooting.

"Let me change out of this." I pointed to the yoga pants and black T-shirt I'd worn on the plane. "And then I'll be ready to go."

"I'll call Mr. Thomas." Ah-Ma had told me the driver liked to go by his English name. "He'll drop us off."

We stood and cleared away our breakfast dishes. Ah-Ma put the leftovers in the fridge and then drew me into a hug.

"I'm glad you're here, Liv-ah."

She felt frail in my arms. I pulled away to study her face, wondering why I hadn't come sooner. She was getting older, our time together becoming limited, yet I'd been too busy living life in New York to visit.

"We'll find her," I said, more confidently than I felt.

She nodded and then let go of me so that I could freshen up.

An hour later, we strolled arm in arm down the middle of Yizhong Shopping Street, which already buzzed with electric energy, even at this early hour. I held tightly to her arm, trying to keep the panic at bay. As if knowing I needed an anchor, she pulled me closer to her when someone opened the metal gate of their shop in a loud rattle. I jumped, unable to stop the way my heart raced, and my body pumped with adrenaline. I felt the blackness start to take over, but then my grandmother squeezed my arm hard, and with a gasp, I swallowed away the panic. Ah-Ma looked at me with concern, but she didn't say anything, for which I was grateful.

Once my heart rate had returned to normal, we headed straight to the barbecued squid stand where Ah-Ma had seen her daughter. Ah-Ma ordered one and then handed me the stick with a whole squid skewered on it.

"This is so good." It was tender and smoky, seasoned with soy and garlic. It had so much flavor and was like nothing I'd ever had in the States. I held it out to my grandmother.

"I missed food like this when I lived in the States," she said, after taking a bite. "You can't find Taiwanese street food there."

We made quick work of the snack as we stood in companionable silence watching people walking by. I could tell by the way my grandmother's eyes darted from one face to another that she was searching for her daughter.

"Have you been cooking?" Ah-Ma asked, once we resumed walking down the middle of the street.

I looked away to avoid her question, taking in how colorful the streets were, with signs of all colors and shapes hanging off the sides of buildings. Some were vertical, some horizontal, sticking away from buildings haphazardly, announcing their goods. There didn't seem to be any sign ordinances here, and the streets were a rainbow of cheerful signage, all trying to attract shoppers' attention.

"There's a lot of young people here," I said instead.

"This area is popular with students. Taichung First Senior High School is over there, and National Taichung University of Science and Technology is there." I looked in the directions that she pointed to. "There's also a lot of *buxibans* in this area too."

I nodded, having heard about these "cram schools" from my mother. She'd told me how the Taiwanese took education seriously; not only did they have school on Saturdays, but also, families who could afford it sent their children to *buxibans* to get extra practice for whatever they were cramming for. High school and university entrance in Taiwan was very competitive, and *buxibans* were supposed to increase their chances of getting in. My mom had told us this when Jay and I complained about all the homework we had when we were in high school.

"How much schooling did you have, Ah-Ma?" I asked, thinking about her comment that she hadn't gone to high school. I'd always assumed my grandmother had gone to the best schools, since my mother and all her siblings had.

"I only went to the local school by our farm until I was ten."

I stared at her in surprise, halting in the middle of the street. "Ten? But you can read and write so well." She stopped too and then tugged me to keep walking when a big group of students brushed by us. Their proximity made me nervous, and I quickly caught up to Ah-Ma.

"I did have some schooling," she chided me, but she smiled to soften it. "A friend helped with my reading and writing. After Yili disappeared."

"Really? How do I not know this?"

"I guess it never came up. I was married to your grandfather when I was only sixteen."

I stopped walking again, almost pulling Ah-Ma's arm out of its socket because she'd kept going. "You were sixteen when you got married?" I stared at her in shock. I'd known she'd gotten married young, but not *that* young. At sixteen, I was mooning over a boy named David Martinez, wishing he'd ask me to his prom, and giggling with my friends whenever he smiled at me when we passed in the halls. Ah-Ma had been married at *sixteen*?

"Liv. You can't keep stopping in the middle of a busy street like this," Ah-Ma scolded me gently. She pulled on my arm to get me walking again.

I did, but I couldn't help notice how many people were all around us. Ah-Ma said it wasn't crowded, but there were too many people for my comfort. I forced my mind back to what she'd just said. "How did I not know that either?"

"Because I rarely speak about your grandfather. There would have been no reason to tell you how old I was when I got married."

But I could have done the math myself, if I'd taken into consideration how old my oldest aunt was in comparison to Ah-Ma's age. Instead, I'd been absorbed in my own life and never thought about what Ah-Ma's life had been like before I came along.

"There's so much I don't know about you," I said.

Ah-Ma shook her head, her eyes scanning the crowd, looking for her daughter. "You don't want to hear an old woman's stories."

"Maybe not when I was young, but I do now." And I really did. Ah-Ma's plea for help had made me realize I'd never known her as anything other than my grandmother. She'd been a girl once, and then a young woman. "Did you have other dreams? Or did you always want to be a wife and mother?"

She shook her head. "Life was different back then. I did what was expected of me. I didn't have choices, like you do. As for dreams?" She glanced at me briefly before resuming her search of the crowd. "I've always loved to cook. Maybe I might have wanted to write a cookbook once or open my own little restaurant."

"That would have been great."

"I also wished to be independent, to be able to make my own decisions."

I squeezed her on the arm that was hooked through mine. "Is this why you've always told me that it's better to be alone than to be with someone not right for me? Because of what happened with your husband?"

She nodded. "I lived for twenty-five years with a man I didn't love, and sometimes despised." She sighed. "I try not to remember him with hatred, though, because he was the father of my children."

"Was he . . . good to the rest of them?" I was curious, because from everything I'd heard so far, my grandfather did not sound like a very nice man.

61

She pursed her lips and then said, "He did make an effort with them. Showed interest in their activities. He was proud of them."

I wrinkled my nose, thinking that that was what a father *should* do, but I bit my tongue. I didn't know what it was like to live during that time, and I was still learning what had happened. It wasn't my position to judge.

"Is that why you've never remarried, and why you live alone now?" I was so curious. It was as if I'd discovered a whole new person I'd never known before. Had she been lonely all these years? She'd always told me she cherished her freedom and had fostered the same independence in me. While my parents lamented that I was still single at thirty-five, Ah-Ma supported my choices.

"Yes. When I came to the States, I had nothing. No money, no assets, because I'd run away from my husband. He refused to give me a divorce." She pulled me into a side street, where it was shaded from a building. The day was already getting hot, and she must have sensed my growing unease at being out in a crowded market.

"That must have been hard."

"It was." She gazed at me, but her eyes were far away. "I hated having to depend on my children, to get an allowance to buy clothes and food, as if I was the child. But what could I do?"

Something occurred to me then. "If that's the case, how did you afford to move back here?" Her apartment might be small, but it was a new building in a great area.

"When your grandfather died, I got the shock of my life." There was a faint smile on her lips. "We were still married because, like I said, he'd refused to consider a divorce. We hadn't had contact since I left him. He kept in touch with our children, and you know Winston and your oldest aunt visited him a few times." She turned so that she could meet my eyes. "He left me money in his will, along with a note. All it said was that he'd done terrible things to people he cared about, and he was sorry. I imagined it was his way of telling me he was sorry about Yili, by making sure I was taken care of after he was gone."

"Wow." I stared at her, conflicting thoughts racing through my head. I was more curious than ever about my grandfather. Was he the monster I'd imagined, or was there a human side to him that must have cared for Ah-Ma in some way?

Someone pushed by us, and I looked toward the main street. The crowd had grown so much that the street, which had been lightly populated when we first arrived, was now wall to wall with people. I'd never seen so many people in one place in my life. Not even in Times Square. My heart raced, and my palms were suddenly sweaty.

"I don't know how we'll ever find her." I tried to distract myself from my panic as I surveyed the crowd and listened to the Mandarin and Taiwanese all around me. Music from clothing stores poured out into the street, and excited voices chattered and called out to each other.

"Not like this." Ah-Ma shook her head. "I didn't mean we'd walk up and down the street looking." Even though that was exactly what we'd been doing. "We need to use the internet. Use those . . ." She gestured with her hand, as if trying to think of the word.

"Social media?" I provided, taking in deep breaths before releasing them.

"Yes." She snapped her fingers. "Someone must know who she is."

"You're right. We could post something, maybe an ad, asking if anyone knows her. Too bad we don't have a picture."

"I should have taken a picture with my phone." Ah-Ma smacked herself on the forehead. "Why didn't I think of it?"

"It's okay." I patted her arm. "We'll figure it out."

We headed back to the main street once I felt strong enough. Ah-Ma stopped in front of a stand selling Taiwanese sausage on a stick and bought one for us to share. It was piping hot and smelled heavenly. Once it cooled enough, we each took a bite and then passed it back and forth.

"I could do this all day," I said, munching on the sausage, which was sweeter and firmer than a sausage from America. "Eat my way through every food stall."

"You should have come visit me earlier." Ah-Ma poked me in the side with an elbow, and I poked her back, trying to shove her into someone. She gave me a stern look, but just when I least expected, her elbow jabbed me again, making me yelp. She gave me a victorious look and I burst into laughter, much like I did when I was young and we'd have these elbow fights while walking around the mall near our house.

My mom used to roll her eyes at us, telling us how childish we were and leaving us to it, making plans to meet us later at the food court. Ah-Ma and I would wander around the mall for hours, and she'd buy me all the things Mom wouldn't let me have: tinted lip gloss, pink underwear from Victoria's Secret, and a skirt so short I couldn't bend over for fear of showing my underwear. My grandmother understood my desire to fit in at my school, to have the things my friends talked about but my mom wouldn't let me have. It was our secret, and now, I looked over at her and knew she was remembering the times we'd shopped at the mall and then eaten at the Japanese takeout at the food court, ordering our chicken teriyaki and vegetables with extra sauce so that the rice was drenched, just how we both liked it.

"I had no idea what I was missing," I said.

I was stupid for not coming earlier. Being here was like being immersed in a culture that I was familiar with but never realized I craved. All the food we passed that I'd never tasted but had heard so much about, all the people and the language that was so familiar, even if I wasn't fluent. The energy was so different from New York. The mix of Mandarin and Taiwanese felt as comforting as a favorite blanket, and I was at home here in a way I'd never been in California. Which was strange, since I was born in California. I wanted to take everything in: the heat of the day, all the people, food stalls for as far as you could see, all the apparel and accessory stores. My eyes landed on a pair of colorful graffiti jogger pants hanging outside one clothing store.

"Mom would hate these." I fingered the lightweight material, thinking it would be cool in the heat.

"Let's buy them." Ah-Ma raised her eyebrows at me.

I looked from the loud pants to my staid grandmother and grinned. "And send Mom pictures." We'd done this when I was younger too, buying matching outfits that scandalized my mother.

Ah-Ma grinned back at me, and we flipped through the rack, looking for our sizes. Ten minutes later, we were the proud owners of graffiti elastic-waist joggers.

"How about *niu rou mien* for lunch?" Ah-Ma asked as we headed back to the car, which was waiting for us in a side street.

"You're still hungry?" My eyes widened in surprise.

"Liv, you'll learn soon that all we do in Taiwan is eat." Ah-Ma's eyes twinkled. "Taiwanese people are passionate about food."

I patted my belly and groaned. "I'm going to gain so much weight here."

My grandmother frowned at me. "You need to gain weight. You look even skinnier than the last time I saw you. Have you been eating?"

I ducked my head and looked away. I'd lost so much weight while I was in the hospital, and after, my usually healthy appetite had deserted me. I no longer found pleasure in food like I once had, even though Amy had brought my favorites to me weekly, hoping to tempt me.

"You don't need to hide things from me, Liv-ah," my grandmother chided. "I knew you weren't doing well, and that you hadn't gone back to work like you told me."

I grimaced. I should have known I couldn't hide anything from my grandmother. I might have been able to fool my mother, but Ah-Ma always intuitively knew when I was lying or stretching the truth.

"I'm sorry." We reached the car, and I opened the door, letting her get in before going around to the other side.

Ah-Ma had been my champion when I wanted to go to culinary school, instead of law school like my father or engineering like my mother. My parents couldn't understand why I wanted to cook, something they didn't see as a good career. It was my grandmother who had convinced them to let me pursue my dream and supported me through all the ups and downs of life as a chef.

Once we were settled in the car and I could breathe easier again, I asked, "Are there any chat groups or Facebook pages for Taichung?" I knew Facebook was still very popular with the older Taiwanese generation.

"Hm, I'm sure. But I'm not on social media." My grandmother looked out the window as the driver drove us to the stewed beef noodle shop that my grandmother said had the best *niu rou mien* in Taichung.

"You know anyone who is?" I too was looking out the window at all the buildings, crowded so close together, the people walking on the sidewalks, and the scooters (I'd never seen so many scooters and motorcycles in my life) that weaved in and out between cars.

"Ziyi."

"Who's that?" I turned to my grandmother.

"The friend I told you about earlier. The one who helped me with my reading and writing. And who helped me get out of Taiwan."

"You've never mentioned her."

"When I got to the States, it was hard to talk about the life I'd left behind." Ah-Ma looked at me. "Ziyi was my closest friend. Like Amy is to you. But we . . ." She broke off a moment, her mouth in a grim line. "We lost touch. For many years."

I thought I knew my grandmother very well. I knew what she liked to eat, do, wear, what she was thinking without having to say so, that she liked warm weather better than cold, and that we were kindred spirits and as close as we could be. But she'd lived a whole life that I was just starting to discover, filled with people I'd never met or heard about.

"What's she like?" I asked.

"Ziyi is eighty-eight," Ah-Ma said. "She's a human rights advocate, especially of women's rights. She was still very involved until about six months ago." Ah-Ma looked down at her hands. "She suddenly slowed down. Doctors couldn't find anything wrong physically, but she no longer has the energy she once had. I hate having to bother her. She's already helped me so much in the past with my search for Yili."

"I'm sorry." I reached out to take her hand. If Ziyi meant as much to her as Amy did to me, I knew it was painful for her to watch her friend's decline.

"I'll take you to meet Ziyi one of these days. If she's having a good day."

"I'd like that." I didn't let go of Ah-Ma's hand. I suddenly wanted to meet this Ziyi very much, to get a glimpse of who Ah-Ma had been as a young woman.

"What really happened that day at the restaurant?" Ah-Ma asked, out of the blue.

My head jerked in her direction. Ah-Ma knew the basic details, that a random man had stormed into the restaurant and shot Cat and me for no reason, but I hadn't been able to talk about it. I was grateful my mother and grandmother didn't push when they came to New York to take care of me after the shooting. But now, looking at Ah-Ma, I knew I would tell her about my debilitating fear. Soon.

"I'll tell you everything. But I want to hear about Ziyi first. How did you meet her? Why did you lose touch?" My curiosity overrode everything. Or maybe I was stalling.

"We tried to stay in touch. But she was . . ." Ah-Ma broke off and turned away from me, staring out the car window. There was a beat of silence, and then Ah-Ma looked back at me, her eyes brimming with unshed tears. "She found me one day when I'd collapsed in the street after another fruitless day of searching for Yili. Ziyi saved me. I wish I could have done the same for her."

7
Yi-ping

April 1961, Taichung

I took to roaming the streets, looking for Yili. The day I'd gone to the *rou geng* stand, I realized I should be out looking for my daughter. If my husband wouldn't tell me where she'd gone, I'd find her myself. Abu had found out the surname of the family who had taken Yili. Ong. I'd rolled the name over and over on my tongue. It wasn't that common of a name, and I thought it would be easy to figure out who they were.

I asked everyone I encountered if they knew a family named Ong. And despaired when I realized there were Ongs everywhere. Abu wasn't sure if they lived in Taichung, so that widened the circle even more. I spent so much time out of our building that my sisters-in-law took over minding my children. When I wasn't searching, I was in my kitchen trying to perfect the *rou geng* soup. I usually cooked without following a recipe, but this time, I wrote everything down as I experimented with batch after batch, adding a little bit of this and a little bit of that. It had to be perfect for when Yili came home. I was finally able to replicate the soup from the stand, and Abu beamed at me in approval as my daughters devoured it. But it was like a knife to the heart watching their happy faces because Yili wasn't with them.

When the pain got to be too much, I'd flee the building, trying to outrun my thoughts. The more I walked, the more I let go of the Yi-ping I'd been before Yili disappeared. I looked nothing like my former self, my usually styled shoulder-length hair unkempt and sticking up around my head, my skin pale, and as the days, and then weeks went by, my clothes hung off my body. I walked the streets like a hungry ghost during Ghost Month, looking for food and entertainment from the living. I carried a picture of Yili always and approached strangers, asking if they'd seen her. I started in our neighborhood before venturing farther and farther away into unfamiliar streets.

One day, I got turned around and couldn't find my way back. I'd been walking since dawn and hadn't had any food. My feet burned, my heart ached, and the pervasive loss of Yili followed me everywhere. I walked until I couldn't any longer and collapsed to the sidewalk in front of a food stand selling fried turnip cakes. I had no idea if I was near our home or had wandered so far away that I would need a boat to get back to the Wang building. Did I even want to go back? How could I survive this heartbreak and loss? How could the Wangs believe I'd be able to keep going, to live my life, when my child was out there somewhere without me? At the same time, I knew I had to keep going, for my other children's sake, even though I was neglecting them. But they were safe with my in-laws, while Yili was out there, scared and missing me.

I succumbed to tears in my defeat and slumped against a rickety stool, too weak to get up.

"Aiya!" a voice said, somewhere near my head. "Xia nua?"

I didn't move, even though I knew the woman was asking what was the matter in Taiwanese. Her voice rose, her Taiwanese coming fast as she asked what I needed and then shouted to another vendor to come help. Hands pulled at me, the cacophony of women's voices sounding like crows warning of danger to come. I let them haul me up to sit on a stool, ignoring their questions as tears rained down my face, and I wondered if it was possible to die of a broken heart. Someone handed me a cup of lukewarm water, and I gulped at it gratefully.

Suddenly, a familiar voice broke through my grief.

"Wang Tai Tai? What are you doing here? Are you all right?" The cultured voice calling me by the formal address of women in Taiwan belonged to a neighbor, a woman I knew slightly who was married to a KMT official. She was only a year or two older than me, but so beautiful I'd never been able to look at her directly.

Relief flooded me, and I saw sympathy in her dark eyes when I raised my head, rather than condemnation or scorn for finding me like this.

"I got lost." Tears continued to stream down my cheeks.

"Come, come." She gestured with a hand. "I'll get you home. You're not that far away."

I let her help me up, even though she was smaller than me, as the food vendors fluttered around us. I used to speak Taiwanese at home with my family, so I understood that they were asking each other what was wrong with me, if I was sick, or pregnant, or running away from a bad husband. I almost laughed at that last one, because it was close to the truth. The Wangs didn't speak Taiwanese, and because the government dictated that only Mandarin should be spoken and taught in schools, my Taiwanese was rusty. But the women's chatter made me long for home, my *real* home with my parents and siblings, where my grandparents had cherished me and spoken to me only in Taiwanese.

My savior thanked the vendors and then tugged at my arm, leading me down the street.

"Thank you, uh . . ." I couldn't remember her name. Whenever I'd gone out with Abu or my sisters-in-law, I always kept my eyes downcast and followed along, not really looking at the people they stopped to converse with.

"My name is Lim Ziyi." She seemed to guess my dilemma. "Or Lim Tai Tai, as your sisters call me." Her eyes sparkled when I glanced in her direction.

I nodded and whispered, "I'm Yi-ping."

"I know," she said, linking her arm through mine. "What are you doing here by yourself?"

"Looking for . . ." I trailed off, not sure what to say. Did anyone outside the family know what had happened to Yili? Should I keep my mouth shut? But what if Ziyi knew something? Her husband traveled in the same circle as mine. Maybe she knew where my daughter had gone.

Before I could decide what to say, Ziyi spoke in a quiet voice: "Looking for your daughter?"

I stopped walking, forcing her to jerk back slightly. I searched her face, wondering what she knew. "Yes. Do you know where she went?"

She shook her head, regret drawing her mouth down. "I don't. I just heard from the neighborhood *tai tais* that one of your daughters was given away."

"My Yili." Tears started down my cheeks again. Ziyi dug in her bag and took out a handkerchief to dab at my cheeks before giving it to me.

"You need to eat something," she said. "You look like you're about to pass out."

She looked around and then led me into a quiet alley, away from the busy street. She headed for a *ba-wan* shop, one that I now recognized and was known around these parts for having the best traditional Taiwanese dumplings made from rice and potato starch dough, filled with pork, bamboo, and mushrooms. I'd wandered almost half an hour away from the Wang building.

Ziyi found us a table in the back and told me to sit, while she went and ordered the *ba-wans*. When she was finally seated across from me, each of us with a steaming bowl of the gelatinous sticky-dough dumpling with a thick, sweet, and spicy pink-and-brown sauce on top, she regarded me over the table as we ate. I was starving, and the savory food was just what my empty stomach needed. The dough was chewy, the filling delicious, and tears pooled in my eyes again as I remembered how much Yili loved them. I'd never made them before, but now I was determined to try. Maybe she'd come home if I cooked them for her.

"What happened to your daughter?" I looked up from my half-eaten *ba-wan* at Ziyi's question.

"My husband. He gave her away. I don't know where she is." I poked at the remains of my dumpling with my chopsticks.

"I'm so sorry." Ziyi's voice was kind, and more tears threatened to break loose. Instead, I stabbed my dumpling again and forced back the torrent. "You know about your husband, right?" Her next words made my eyes snap to hers. I searched her face, wondering what she was talking about. She cocked her head and then leaned toward me and said in a whisper, "The arrests in our neighborhood."

I pulled back. "What are you talking about?"

She grimaced, biting her lips, as if unsure whether to tell me.

"What is it, Ziyi?" I was starting to realize I knew very little about the man I was married to. He was gone all day, and I had no idea what he did in the bank office with his father, uncles, and brothers. When he was home, after our nightly meal, he and his brothers and father would gather in the small courtyard, smoking and talking about more business, or so I assumed. We spent very little time together, and I'd never thought about what he did with his days.

"I overheard my husband recently, when he didn't know I was in the next room." Ziyi looked around, as if expecting someone to be eavesdropping on us. "You know Dr. Li?"

I nodded. Dr. Li was a kindly family doctor who lived on our street. I hadn't seen him in a while and thought he'd retired, even though he was only in his late fifties.

"Your husband had him arrested. Claimed he's a dissident, resisting KMT rule and siding with the Communists." Ziyi's voice was quiet, and she watched me carefully.

I dropped the chopsticks in my hand. "What?" It took me a few moments to form more words. "He didn't retire?"

Ziyi shook her head. "No. He was sent to prison." She lowered her voice again. "I've heard terrible things. His wife was able to visit him. They tortured him, Yi-ping."

My mouth dropped in horror, and the *ba-wan* I'd eaten threatened to come back up. Dr. Li had always been so nice to me and my children. He wasn't our doctor but always made a point to talk to the girls and often had a treat for them, a bag of dried fruit or a package of crackers. To think he was in jail, tortured . . .

Ziyi reached out and squeezed my forearm. "You didn't know." It wasn't a question, since she could see how shocked I was.

"No." I met her eyes, realizing how foolish I'd been. No one ever told me Dr. Li had retired. I'd just assumed it, because suddenly he was gone. I'd been oblivious, wrapped up in our daily lives, not paying attention to what was happening in our country. Whenever the men talked about politics, I excused myself. When my oldest sister-in-law listened to the news on the radio and then clucked in disgust at something she'd heard, I tuned her out. I'd kept my eyes down and my ears shut, and as a result, I didn't even know my own husband was responsible for sending men we knew to prison.

"Yi-ping." Ziyi's gaze was intense. "My husband said something the other day at dinner about *tongyangxi.* I wasn't really paying attention, as my youngest wouldn't eat, but now I wonder if he was referring to your daughter."

I nodded, my breath hitching. "My mother-in-law confirmed that Yili was adopted into a family as a future bride for one of their sons. She told me their surname is Ong. But that's all I know about them."

Ziyi pursed her lips. "You don't know where they live?"

I shook my head, sorrow filling my heart that my daughter was going to be brought up in a different household so that her future mother-in-law could rear her to assimilate into the family more easily. I whispered, *"Shim-pua."* That was a Taiwanese phrase that literally meant "little daughter-in-law."

Ziyi nodded. "Yes, *shim-pua.* I wish I'd paid more attention, but I hadn't known your daughter was gone at the time."

My eyebrows lifted. Ziyi could speak Taiwanese? I'd assumed she was *waishengren* like the Wangs.

She tilted her head at my look. "My family is *benshengren,*" she explained.

"Oh." My eyebrows rose. "Mine too." I wondered how long her family had been in Taiwan before the KMT took over.

We looked at each other in a moment of solidarity. Kindness shone from her eyes, and I suddenly longed to have a friend again. I got along with my sisters-in-law, especially Mei Mei, but there was always an edge of competition, as if we were trying to win the "best daughter-in-law of the Wang family" award.

"I'm sorry." Ziyi reached out and took my hand. "I don't know what I'd do if my husband—" She broke off and looked away.

"I . . ." There was so much I wanted to say to her. But I didn't know anything about her, except who she was married to and, now, that she was *benshengren.* Could I trust her? Where did her loyalties lie? Where did mine? I'd thought my loyalties had been with my husband, but after what he'd done, I no longer knew.

Ziyi turned back to me. "You don't know anything about your husband, do you?"

I shook my head, embarrassment heating my cheeks.

Ziyi sighed and looked away. She muttered something to herself before addressing me. "Your husband and his family are powerful. They make people disappear."

My heart thudded in my chest. Who else had vanished?

Ziyi shook her head at my expression. "You are so sweet and naive."

I bristled at that, but really, she wasn't wrong. If I'd been more aware of the world we lived in, could I have prevented my husband from taking Yili? Was it my fault for never questioning?

Ziyi sighed again. "I might be foolish to offer this, but I like you. It's not fair what they've done to you. Do you want my help?"

"Help with what?" I clasped my hands together in front of my chest.

"I don't know that I can do anything. I have no idea what happened to your daughter." She reached out and grasped one of my hands in hers. "But if my husband ever took one of our children, I'd hope someone

75

would be there for me." She squeezed my hand so hard I should have grimaced, but instead, the pressure was reassuring, grounding me.

"Help me how?" I asked again. "Find Yili?"

"I'll try. But at least you should know the truth about your husband." She gazed into my eyes, as if to see if I could be trusted.

I nodded because I had no other choice. Maybe learning more about what Po was up to would help me find Yili.

"Keep your ears open. Listen to his phone conversations. Search his home office if he has one." Ziyi's stare was intense. "I'll see what my husband knows too."

I nodded, the idea of the two of us spying on our husbands oddly appealing. Before Yili disappeared, I'd never even dared to think about doing that. But now, desperation made me a willing accomplice. If Po wouldn't tell me what he'd done to my daughter, I'd have to find out myself.

We gathered our garbage, and when we went to throw it away, I accidentally bumped into Ziyi's side. She winced and gasped. I froze, not sure what had happened.

"Are you okay?" I asked, scanning her face. Was there a faint shadow around her eyes, under her face powder?

She had a hand on her hip, her face twisted in a grimace. "I'm fine. I ran into a table the other day. Left a big bruise. Come, my driver is just down the road. I'll give you a ride home."

I studied her, sure she was lying but not knowing how I knew. My eyes traveled over her form, and I saw more bruises on her upper-left arm, peeking out of the short sleeves of the shirt she was wearing. They looked like fingerprints to me. But before I could open my mouth to ask what had happened, Ziyi turned and sailed out the door and back onto the street.

"Wait . . ." I followed, determined to ask about the bruises, but Ziyi cut me off.

"You sure you're ready to find out the truth about your husband?"

I paused, and then my need to find Yili won out over my curiosity about her injuries. "Yes," I said.

Ziyi stared at me for a moment, her delicate face screwed up in concentration. Whatever she saw must have satisfied her, for with a firm lift of her chin, she turned away and started walking back to the main street. I hurried behind her, my steps lighter now that I had someone on my side. I would ask her about the bruises later.

8

Liv

After lunch of the most delicious *niu rou mien*, Ah-Ma and I explored her neighborhood so she could show me around. As we walked, I thought about what she'd told me about her friend Ziyi. I wanted to ask questions, but we kept running into people who knew Ah-Ma, including her sister-in-law Mei Mei, who'd stopped by to meet me.

"Liv," Mei Mei had cried as she took me in her arms. We'd run into them as we were heading back to the apartment. "You look just like your grandmother at that age." Mei Mei had an ample bosom, and she gathered me against her, rocking me back and forth as my grandmother looked on in amusement. Mei Mei pushed a red envelope, which I knew would be filled with money, into my hands. "For you. It's so good to finally meet you."

Mei Mei's husband had accompanied her, and he too greeted me. "We can't stay long because we have to pick up our granddaughter. But Mei Mei wanted to meet you." They held hands as they talked to us, and I could see the affection between them. They left, after making Ah-Ma promise to bring me to their place soon.

We met more neighbors as we returned to the building, and I listened as my grandmother conversed in Taiwanese and sometimes Mandarin. I wished I could speak both. I knew a few words in

Taiwanese, but not enough to hold a conversation. Maybe Ah-Ma could teach me while I was here.

That night, she took me to a side street near her apartment, and we had dinner at a tiny, simple restaurant with seating both indoors and out on the sidewalk. Ah-Ma chose a small table inside away from the hustle and bustle of the road, and I shot her a grateful look. I let her order for us.

Once the waitress had left to put in our order, I finally spoke up, needing to voice what I suspected had happened to Ah-Ma's old friend. "Was Ziyi . . ." I trailed off as I watched Ah-Ma wiping our teacups with a napkin. "Was someone hurting her?"

My grandmother's hands stilled, and her eyes darted to meet mine. "Yes. Her husband. I sensed something was wrong that day, but I was too naive to understand. Whenever I asked, she brushed it off. It wasn't until much later that she finally told me the truth."

"That's terrible." I sucked in a breath.

"It *was* terrible. For Ziyi." Ah-Ma put the cup down and laid a hand over one of mine. There was a faraway look in her eyes before she focused back on me. "She almost died once."

We stared at each other for a moment, and then I wasn't thinking of Ziyi anymore. I was thinking about myself, and the words I hadn't been able to utter when she was in New York came pouring out.

"I should be dead right now." My free hand played with my glass of ice water.

"What?" Ah-Ma was about to ask more when the waitress approached and placed steaming dishes of stir-fried rice cakes with vegetables, chicken-and-leek dumplings, and wonton noodle soup, along with dried tofu cakes cut into slices, a cold cucumber salad, and a dish of beef stomach stewed with soy sauce and herbs. My mouth salivated, and I gave Ah-Ma a slight nod, indicating I would answer her as soon as I'd had a taste of the food in front of us. We were silent as we dug into the hearty feast. My eyes fluttered as I sampled a bit of everything, my taste buds exploding with the rich flavors and textures of a culture I'd always felt on the edge of because I wasn't born here. But it was delicious, and I didn't know how I'd lived so long without it.

I could feel Ah-Ma's eyes on me, her unspoken questions hanging in the air. I put my chopsticks down because there was suddenly a lump in my throat so big that I knew I wouldn't be able to swallow another bite. I looked at Ah-Ma, tears filling my eyes. "That man, the one who burst into the kitchen. He would have killed me too, if Chef Wu hadn't jumped him."

Ah-Ma's eyes widened in surprise, and she reached out and grabbed one of my hands. I'd never told her or my mother that I should have been dead. That, if not for Chef Wu's quick thinking, the man would have shot me again and again, until I was dead like Cat. They knew what the news had reported, that Chef Wu had subdued the gunman and was lauded as a hero, but not that he was aiming at me when Chef Wu tackled him.

"Liv." Ah-Ma's chin wobbled, and I saw that she was about to cry too.

"It's okay. I'm here." I took in a deep breath to control my emotions. "I'm still here. He didn't kill me."

She stood and came to my side, gathering me against her. "You're here. My strong, strong, Liv. I've got you."

I turned and buried my face into her side, and the tears finally escaped, coursing down my cheeks and dampening Ah-Ma's shirt as her arms held me safe against her.

Two days later I woke refreshed. I'd slept fitfully my first night, after the cathartic cry at the restaurant. The waitress didn't say anything but did bring us more tea and a box of tissues, which made me smile. We called my brother when we got home, and he made us both laugh so hard with stories about his work in hospitality and the demanding customers he encountered that I was spent. But I woke in the middle of night, since the twelve-hour time difference was wreaking havoc with my body, and I wasn't able to go back to sleep. The jet lag was hitting me hard, and I slogged through my first two full days here, barely aware of my surroundings. Now here it was the third day, and I finally felt a little bit more human.

I sat up and looked around the room. Ah-Ma had been using it as an office, and she gave me a box of Yili's things that she'd kept from the past, as well as pictures and information she'd gathered over the years. I'd looked through it, but my foggy brain hadn't really registered anything. I couldn't wait to go through everything again now that my head was clear. After getting out of bed, I walked to the door and stuck my head outside.

"Ah-Ma?" I called when I saw that her bedroom door was open.

Silence greeted me. I knew she got up early most days, and she'd said last night that she'd run to the market to pick up breakfast for us.

I walked to where the big box was sitting on the desk. Before I could open it, my cell buzzed on the night table. I picked it up, thinking it was Ah-Ma, but then smiled when I saw the text was from Amy.

Morning. How're you feeling? Is the jet lag better?

Much better, I texted back. Like a new person. Where are you?

Mykonos. Eating kopanisti with tomatoes, bread and louza. And of course, wine.

My stomach rumbled at the mention of food. Wow. What's kopanisti and louza?

Instead of getting an answer by text, I heard my cell ring.

"Liv!" Amy shouted. "It's this really good cheese, and louza is a spiced pork. I miss you. Why aren't you here with me? I think we're too old for Mykonos. I can't keep up with the nightlife and energy."

My mouth curved, and for a moment, I almost wished I were with her in Greece. But the thought of a crowded nightclub filled with young people all grinding close to each other sent a shudder through my body.

"You know I would have a panic attack there," I said quietly.

Amy immediately sobered. "I know."

We were both quiet for a moment, and I wondered if she was remembering the day she'd come to my apartment and told me she'd quit her job and was going to travel the world. She'd asked me to go with her, saying it would be healing for us, but I hadn't been able to leave my apartment.

"How're you doing?" I asked. Because as enthusiastic as she sounded, I knew she had her own demons to slay.

"I'm good." Her voice was soft. "I know I did the right thing, leaving 852, but I still have nightmares about Cat. If I hadn't called out sick . . ."

"Amy—" I started, but she cut me off.

"I know. It's not my fault." She blew out a breath. "We were both given a second chance. I'm glad you finally left your apartment."

"Me too." I couldn't deny that tiny burst of pride in my chest that I'd not only left my apartment, but I'd gotten on a plane and flown all the way here to Taiwan.

"Have you heard from Simon?" she asked. I'd told her all about Simon via text, and how excited I was that he'd asked for my number. She'd texted back the clapping hands emoji, along with a thumbs-up and confetti. I'd told her to simmer down. I didn't even know if he was single, and besides, I was too much of a wreck for anyone to take an interest in.

"He texted me yesterday to see how I was." I couldn't help the smile that crept across my face.

"Call him!" Amy yelled, her mood suddenly light again.

I rolled my eyes at her bossiness, but I really didn't mind. It felt good to banter with Amy again, instead of her looking at me with concern and pity in her eyes the times she'd come to visit me after the shooting.

"We'll see. What have you been up to?"

She started telling me everything she was seeing and doing, and I laughed at her stories. While I was glad for her, I was sad for myself. I was like that before. We were impulsive, living for the moment, the now, instead of getting bogged down by what we should've been doing. But now, she was even more of the free spirit, while I'd been reduced to a scared mouse. But then I straightened my spine. I'd gotten myself here, hadn't I? Maybe I was stronger than I thought.

In the middle of Amy's stories, another text came through. When I saw it was from Simon, my heart gave a hopeful thump.

"Who's that?" Amy asked, obviously having heard the text ding. "Simon?"

"Um, yeah."

Amy's peal of laughter made me smile while I read Simon's text.

How're you feeling? I was thinking about your search for your aunt. Maybe try social media? All my Taiwanese relatives love Facebook.

"Is he asking you out?"

"No." I rolled my eyes, even though Amy couldn't see. "He's helping me and Ah-Ma with the search."

"Okay, well, I'll let you go. But don't forget to live a little. Enjoy Simon, if he's unattached." She cackled, a signature Amy sound that always made me crack up, and it made me miss her that much more.

"Keep me posted on where you are," I said. "And be safe."

"I always am."

We hung up, and I turned my attention to Simon's message, a smile on my face from my conversation with Amy. How rare to have a friend who understood me the same way I understood her. I was thankful again that her life had been spared, but then a twinge of guilt at Cat's death made me squirm. I shook it off and texted Simon back.

Ah-Ma and I had the same idea. I sat and played with the cover of the box as I waited for Simon to respond.

My friend Ken's mom and aunt are very active in Taichung Facebook groups. I'm staying with his aunt Clare. I can ask them for help?

Ken's grandfather is the one who passed away? I typed out.

Yes.

I bit my lip. I don't want to bother them in their time of grief.

It's fine. They could use the distraction.

Are you sure? I really wanted to see Simon again, regardless of whether his friend's family could help. I was just wondering how to respond when his next text stirred the butterflies in my stomach.

I'll ask them. Have you gone to a night market yet?

Not yet. I smiled, remembering our conversation in the ride from the airport to Taichung.

We should go one night. I can show you around. Might help you to be exposed to crowds.

I grabbed my bottom lip with my teeth again, anticipation blooming in my chest. Was he just being friendly, speaking as a doctor, or was there more behind the invitation?

That would be nice, I texted back, and then I winced. "Nice"? I could do better than nice.

Okay, text more later. We'll make a plan.

I hearted that message and then put my phone down. I didn't know what was happening between us, but I liked it. I wouldn't analyze it, wouldn't make more of it than what it probably was. After a moment, I turned back to the box holding Yili's belongings.

Rifling through it, I pulled out the photo album I'd already flipped through. When I'd first opened it, a much younger Ah-Ma stared back at me, a baby in her arms, her face radiant. How pretty my grandmother was, so young and fresh faced, her short hair styled and so black, even in the faded photo. I knew that was Yili she held in her arms.

I'd flipped the pages, my face softening at the joy on young Ah-Ma's face as she gazed at her baby. In one photo, a stern-looking man was standing behind her, one hand on her shoulder. This was my grandfather. I'd seen pictures of him once, a long time ago, from a pack of photos my mother had from her childhood. He wasn't smiling, and I stared into his eyes, as if I could decipher his past.

I kept turning pages, and the baby grew. By the end of the album, Yili was a toddler, standing up while holding on to someone's hands, her face lit in happiness and a tiny tongue peeking out of her mouth. She was adorable, a deep dimple in one cheek and big round eyes gazing into the camera with no fear.

I put the album aside. There was another one, but I dug through the box, taking out a red hair ribbon, a stuffed monkey with an O for a mouth and a thumb that you could put into the mouth, and a tiny pink hat. I found more articles of clothing, mementos of Yili, the only things Ah-Ma had left of her daughter. They were in great condition, considering they were over sixty years old, because Ah-Ma had preserved them well. I was about to pick up the second photo album when a black-and-white notebook at the bottom of the box that I hadn't yet seen caught my eyes.

I took it out and opened it. It was all in Mandarin, so I couldn't read it. But as I flipped through the pages, I recognized the format of a cookbook, with hand-drawn illustrations of the dishes. I recognized *tsai bo neng*, the preserved-radish omelet that Ah-Ma used to make for us to go with our congee in the morning. There was *niu rou mien*, just like the beef noodle soup we'd had the other day at the noodle stand. I kept turning pages, and dish after dish from my childhood fanned out in front of me. I was suddenly ravenous.

"You found my old cookbook?"

Ah-Ma's voice in the doorway made me look up. I held the book aloft to show her.

"This is amazing. All the food I remember from when I was growing up." I turned back to it and flipped another page.

Ah-Ma smiled, but it didn't reach her eyes. "I started that cookbook when Yili was taken. At first, I was convinced if I could perfect a dish that she loved, she'd come home." Ah-Ma walked to my side and reached out to turn back to the first page. "This"—she pointed to the picture of *rou geng* soup she'd drawn—"this was the first recipe I wrote down. When Yili disappeared, I became obsessed with re-creating dishes for when she came home."

I closed my eyes, remembering the year in high school when I'd gotten a horrible case of the flu. I was miserable, so sick I couldn't move, couldn't do anything but lie in bed, missing the winter ball and the Christmas exchange with my friends. I woke up one day to find that Ah-Ma had brought me *rou geng* soup. She propped me up with pillows and placed a portable table over my lap before putting the steaming bowl of soup in front of me. I picked up the spoon, and that first taste of her homemade soup made me feel better than any medication could have.

My eyes opened now, and I pointed to the book. "This is my childhood. Everything that reminds me of you."

Ah-Ma gave me a small smile and then stared off into space. "At first, I only wrote down the foods that I knew Yili loved. But as time went on and the years passed, I started to add dishes that she hadn't tried yet but that I thought she would like." She looked down and flipped a few pages. "I was sure she would come back one day, and I wanted to be able to make her everything she'd missed."

I reached out and put an arm around my grandmother, drawing her close. We stood like that for a moment, both staring at the handwritten cookbook. Then Ah-Ma shook her head. "You look much better." She pointed to the bags she'd put on the desk when she came in. "I got you *shaobing youtiao*, and soy milk to go along with it."

My mouth watered as I looked at the crisp sesame pancake wrapped around a long strip of fried dough that she took out of a paper bag.

"That smells so good." I took the bag from her but then looked down at the cookbook. "I also just had a craving for *tsai bo neng*."

Ah-Ma laughed. "I can make a pot of *mue*, and it won't take long for me to whip up the eggs, if you really want it."

"Yes." I nodded my head for emphasis. "Maybe you can teach me how to make it. Translate your cookbook for me."

"Liv, *tsai bo neng* is easy. I don't need the cookbook for that."

"But still," I said, my brain working. I'd never made Taiwanese dishes before. Maybe it was time I learned. "It'd be nice for me to have it." I picked up the notebook and took it with me as we walked out of my room and to the kitchen.

"Eat the *youtiao* while it's hot," my grandmother said.

I stood in the kitchen and took a bite of the crisp flavorful pancake, and then dunked the *youtiao* into the cup of soy milk she handed me. The *youtiao* was so light and airy, still warm and soft in the middle. My eyes fluttered closed. I took another bite before my eyes opened to find my grandmother smiling at me.

"I'm glad you like it." She went to the fridge and took out a small bag of preserved radishes. After taking down a small bowl, she poured some of the radishes in and then filled it with water before setting the bowl aside. "This needs to soak for at least ten minutes. Otherwise, the radish will be too salty."

"Oh." I hadn't known that you had to soak the radish. I put my *youtiao* down and opened to the page with the egg omelet. "Is that what this says?" My fingers traced over the recipe book. "Wait. I just had a great idea."

I pulled out my phone and clicked on the camera icon as my grandmother paused her actions, looking at me with curiosity.

"What're you doing?"

"I'm going to film you making this and post it to my social media." I had a really popular YouTube channel, where I used to post videos with recipes and short clips of my life as a chef in New York City. I hadn't posted anything since the shooting. I couldn't. All my creativity had dried up. But now, I couldn't pass up the opportunity to make a video with my grandmother.

She let out a laugh. "No one wants to see an old woman on that TikkyTok thing."

I grinned at her. "You're mistaken. I follow this eighty-year-old woman, and her videos are the funniest. Besides, I want to capture this for me. Do you mind if I mention I'm here to help you look for your lost daughter?"

"Sure." She shrugged and then ignored me as I aimed the camera at her.

"While the radish soaks, dice up the garlic and scallions." She got the ingredients out as she spoke. "I also like to add these." She held up a package of tiny salted dry shrimp. "This original version didn't use milk or cream, since so many Asians are lactose intolerant, but when I lived in the States, I always added a dash of milk to the eggs, along with salt and pepper, before whisking it together."

I watched Ah-Ma's hands as I filmed, noting how agile they still were, despite the age spots and wrinkles. Those hands had taken care of her children, and then her grandchildren after that, and made so many wonderful meals for us. I wondered why I'd never thought to ask her for her recipes. Then my face flamed in embarrassment. Because I'd thought the Taiwanese food that she'd made wasn't elevated enough for a restaurant. It was home cooking; comforting though it was, it wasn't high-end cooking, like Benjamin and I had strived to create. That was why I'd always unconsciously ignored my Taiwanese roots when experimenting in the kitchen. I flushed with shame, remembering Chef Wu's words.

The camera on my phone followed Ah-Ma's hands as she stir-fried the garlic in a bit of butter, then added the drained radishes and scallions, along with the dried shrimp. Then she poured the egg mixture over the herbs and allowed it to settle into the circle of the pan. A few minutes later, she flipped it expertly, showing the perfectly browned side. The smell was nostalgic and comforting all at the same time.

While the other side cooked, Ah-Ma took leftover rice out of the fridge and added water to the pot, setting it over a low flame to make *mue*. She took the egg omelet off the stove and slid it easily onto a plate. She indulged me as I filmed it all.

"I'll edit the video and film an intro before posting it to YouTube and my social media later," I said as I sat down. "Maybe we can make everything that's in the book while I'm here."

Ah-Ma nodded, but there was a distant look in her eyes. "I'd love to."

"Oh, and my friend Simon said his friend's mom, Genevieve, and his aunt Clare might be able to help with the search."

"Simon?" Ah-Ma asked with her eyebrows raised.

I blushed and looked away. I then told her how Simon had helped me at the airport.

"He sounds like a wonderful man." Ah-Ma gave me a questioning look.

I dropped my gaze, my cheeks heating. "He wants to take me to a night market." The mere thought of being immersed in a crowd at night sent a shiver down my back.

"I was going to suggest that. My old bones can't take all the noise and people that late at night." Her eyes twinkled with mirth.

"You're not old, Ah-Ma," I protested, wondering if *I* could handle the noise and people.

"I'm still hanging on, but the night markets are better off left to the young." Ah-Ma sat down across from me. "Would you . . . be okay in a crowd like that, though?" Once again, my grandmother knew me too well.

"I don't know." My chin wobbled for a moment before I pressed my lips together.

"Tell him to pick you up here when you go so I can meet him," Ah-Ma commanded.

I rolled my eyes at her, but I didn't really mean it. I wanted Ah-Ma to meet Simon. "About the search." I took a deep breath and forced my mind away from Simon or crowded street fairs. "I need all the info you have. You said your mother-in-law told you the last name of the family who took Yili?" I cut off a piece of the egg omelet with my chopsticks and popped it in my mouth.

My grandmother nodded. "Yes. And about four months after Yili disappeared, Ziyi finally overheard a conversation that told us where the family lived. They were in Taichung, about fifteen minutes by car to the north. Fifteen minutes, Liv. Only fifteen minutes away from me." Her eyes clouded. "But by the time we tracked them down . . ." She broke off and shook her head.

My heart sank, and the egg I'd just swallowed sat like a lump in my throat. I reached out to take Ah-Ma's hand and waited until she'd gotten her emotions under control. I gave her hand a squeeze, and the years between us fell away until we were just two souls sharing a loss that reached across generations.

9
YI-PING

August 1961, Taichung

"Yi-ping!" Ziyi burst into my home without knocking. Her hair stuck to her forehead, and sweat streamed down her face from the oppressive summer heat.

We'd taken to visiting each other often in the past few months, and her presence made my life bearable. She held me up on the days when I thought I couldn't go on, and she made me laugh when all I wanted to do was cry. She helped me with my other children and slowly made me realize I'd been neglecting them. She read books with me when she found out I didn't have a lot of formal schooling and challenged me to write more in-depth letters home to my family. With her by my side, I learned to live without Yili, even though the hole in my heart continued to ache with every day that passed without my fourth daughter.

I looked up now at the urgency in Ziyi's voice.

"What is it?" I asked as I plated the *tsai bo neng* I'd cooked for my children's breakfast. I placed it on the table where they waited. My oldest, Lun-Shan, immediately started dividing up the egg omelet with her chopstick, sliding the pieces into her younger sisters' bowls. I ran a hand over the top of her head, and she flashed me a smile.

"Come." Ziyi gestured toward my bedroom, and I followed her.

I closed the door and turned to my friend. "You found something." I could tell by the way she was literally vibrating with excitement that she had news to share. My spirits were low, for after months of spying on my husband, looking through his paperwork, keeping my ears open around my in-laws, and just being more aware, I'd learned nothing except that my husband had definitely given Yili away to a family named Ong as a *shim-pua*, as Abu had suspected.

One day, I'd been about to open our front gate after another fruitless search when I'd overheard my husband in the courtyard with his father as they shared a smoke. I froze by the gate when I heard their voices.

"I need to get rid of her . . ."

My brows scrunched in confusion. Was he talking about Yili? But he'd already gotten rid of her.

". . . won't stop bothering me . . ." My husband's voice started to fade, and I knew they were walking toward the inside door. I leaned even closer to catch whatever words I could. ". . . political prisoner . . . thought . . . gave her my daughter for their blind son."

And then his voice died off, and I was left hovering at our gate, my entire body trembling. Here was finally proof that my husband had indeed given Yili away. But what kind of family was it? And who was "her"?

"Yi-ping, are you listening to me?" Ziyi reached out and shook my arm slightly.

"What?" I started, focusing back on her as my husband's words faded in my mind.

"I think I've found the Ongs who took Yili." Ziyi's eyes were wide.

"What?" I repeated, not sure I'd heard correctly. It had been five months since Yili disappeared. Was it possible we finally had a clue?

"You said you think Yili was given to a family with a blind son, right?"

I nodded. I'd told Ziyi what I'd overheard months ago.

"My husband is having a meeting at our place right now, and as I was serving them tea, I overheard a man talking about a political prisoner who had just died. He had a blind son." Ziyi's voice bubbled with anticipation, but my heart sank.

"Wait, you left your house while your husband has visitors?" Even though Ziyi didn't talk about her relationship with her husband, I'd seen enough to know that her husband was strict. He would be most displeased if Ziyi wasn't there to take care of their guests. "You need to get back."

She waved a hand in the air. "It's fine. I'm fine. But did you hear what I said?"

"That doesn't mean anything. There must be many men who have blind sons." I turned away, not wanting Ziyi to see the disappointment on my face.

"They referred to the prisoner as Ong." Ziyi tugged at my arm. "This has to be the family who adopted Yili."

I turned to my friend, unable to contain the hitch of hope in my chest. Could this be them? But I still didn't allow myself to believe. Because every lead I'd followed had always led to dead ends.

"Yi-ping, they said this family lives in the Beitun District." And she named a street that meant nothing to me.

I stared at her, yearning blooming within. Could my daughter right now be just fifteen minutes away from me? Was it possible we'd finally found her? I sprinted for the door. "We need to go find her."

"Wait." Ziyi stopped me by stepping in front of me. "I'll go with you. I can have my driver take us." She knew my husband had forbidden our driver from taking me on "useless errands," as he'd referred to my searching for Yili.

"But what about your guests?" I was torn between wanting to protect her and needing a ride to find Yili.

"It's fine," Ziyi said, but a cloud passed over her face for a moment. It was so brief I wondered if I'd imagined it. "My husband can take care of them. This is more important."

I stared at her, gratitude filling my heart. Taiwanese people were reserved in general. We didn't do much touching or hugging, but I needed Ziyi to know how much her support meant to me, so I reached out and pulled her close. She let out a gasp when my arms pressed into her back, and I pulled away sharply.

"Are you okay?"

"Yes, sorry." She gave a short laugh. "You know how clumsy I am. I ran into something the other day."

"Ziyi." I dropped my hands to my side. "You're not clumsy. What's going on?" She'd always brushed me off whenever I asked, but this time I wasn't going to let her push my questions aside.

"Nothing." Ziyi's voice was firm. "Seriously. I'm always walking into furniture or walls and running into things." She stared into my eyes. "I'm fine, I promise."

"Ziyi . . ."

She pushed by me and opened the door. "Meet me downstairs in twenty minutes." And then she was gone, a whirlwind of dark hair and flying skirts.

I stared after her, sure that someone was hurting her but not knowing how to get Ziyi to tell me. Then I shook my head as my mind screamed at me to go find Yili. This was the first clue I'd had of her whereabouts. I had to focus on finding my daughter. Then I'd get Ziyi to tell me what was going on.

But we didn't find Yili that day. We knocked on doors and stopped people on the street, asking about the Ong family who had a blind son. The only clue we had that we were in the right place was when we questioned a woman who owned a traditional Chinese medicine shop on a corner of the street, and I saw the way her eyebrows twitched when I showed her my daughter's picture.

"Where is she?" I demanded, not caring how rude I sounded.

But the woman shook her head, a look of disdain on her face, and she turned away to help a customer. I was about to go after her when Ziyi pulled me back.

"Don't antagonize her." She said this softly so that we couldn't be overheard.

"She knows something." I stared at the woman, willing her to turn around. "She acts like I threw my daughter away like trash. Like I don't love her. I hate my husband for doing this." My voice rose, and Ziyi put a warning hand on my arm.

"Yi-ping. Shh." Ziyi looked around to see if anyone was listening.

"We're so close, and I'd do anything to get back—" Ziyi shushed me again, and I lowered my voice. "Get my Yili back."

"Not like this. You can't get hysterical." Ziyi pulled me out of the store, and I could feel the shop woman's eyes boring holes in my back.

"We need to get her on our side. She doesn't trust us," Ziyi said when we were in the car on the way back to our neighborhood. I was slumped dejectedly, feeling worse than ever. I'd been so filled with hope on the ride there, sure that I'd soon hold Yili in my arms again. The disappointment that I hadn't found her or gotten concrete proof she was in the neighborhood was crushing.

I didn't give up, though. Ziyi took me back a few days later. I was jittery, bouncing up and down in the car, filled with nervous anticipation. I did notice dimly that Ziyi was quiet and had dark circles under her eyes, but I was too hyped up on hope to give her more than a cursory glance. How I regretted my inattention later, when I finally learned the truth about Ziyi's marriage. But that day, my need to search the neighborhood until Yili was found outweighed everything else in my life. Even though we got nowhere, I felt in my bones that we were on the right track. The neighbors were hiding something, and I was determined to find out what.

Ziyi couldn't take me the next couple of weeks, and I didn't ask why. My entire focus was on haunting the neighborhood in the Beitun District until I found the Ong family. I decided if I couldn't get a lift, I would get myself there somehow. I used to ride my bicycle all over the farm and knew I had the stamina and determination to get myself there. It was a long, tiring ride, but I'd do anything for Yili. Not having a bicycle of my own, I'd taken to borrowing the old bikes that were always parked on the sidewalks in our neighborhood. For the next six months, I went to Beitun every chance I could.

February 1962, Taichung

I jumped on a bike leaning against a pillar on the sidewalk and rode away from the Wang building without a backward glance. My legs pedaled furiously, taking me back to the street where the Ongs supposedly lived. By the time I got there, I was dripping with sweat, my hair damp around the hairline. I took a big gulp of the water I'd brought in a bottle and then leaned the bike against a wall. The street wasn't very big, only about three blocks long, but it was filled with residential buildings. Ziyi and I had knocked on every door we could, but there were many more in buildings we couldn't get into. I'd combed the street tirelessly, looking at every person, every child I passed. Today, I was headed for the traditional Chinese medicine shop. Every time I'd shown up over the months, the proprietor watched me with keen eyes. She seemed to be the keeper of the street, and I knew she had answers. I'd tried to talk to her a few times, but she'd always turned away to help the customers who filled her store. Today, though, I wasn't going to let her thwart me. I would wait as long as I had to until she talked to me.

To my surprise, the shop was empty. She sat on a high stool behind a glass counter that housed all sorts of mysterious herbs and animal parts. The earthy and musty smell of the store permeated my senses, causing my head to spin. I steadied myself with a hand on the counter and looked up to see her watching me over her newspaper.

"Wong Tai Tai." I'd heard her customer addressing her as such. "I'm Wang Tai Tai." Perhaps the similarities in our names would soften her to me.

She nodded but didn't speak. We stared at each other for a moment before I spoke again.

"Please, if you know the Ong family, the one with the blind son . . ." I switched to Taiwanese and brought my hands up in front of my chest and clasped them together. "Please tell me how to find them."

Her eyebrows rose. "What do you want with them?" she asked in Taiwanese, after a pause.

"My daughter." I blew out a breath, keeping my gaze on hers. "I have reason to believe they adopted my youngest daughter as a future bride for their son."

If I hadn't been staring at her so intently, I would have missed how her eyes narrowed ever so slightly. But I did see it and my breath caught, sure now that she knew something.

"What do you intend to do?" The woman regarded me with suspicion in her eyes.

"Nothing. I just want to see my daughter again, to know that she's taken care of and happy." I held my breath, praying she'd tell me. I was close, so close to finding Yili.

The woman didn't speak for a moment, instead sweeping her eyes at me from head to foot. Finally, she said, "You're one of them." I knew she was referring to the KMT.

"I . . . I mean . . . I . . . ," I stuttered, not sure what to say.

The woman narrowed her eyes. "Why are you harassing good people like them?"

"I'm not." I held up my hands to show her I wasn't there to harm anyone, while my heart rate picked up because she'd just confirmed the Ongs did in fact live on this street. "Please. You don't understand. My husband took my daughter away from me. He's . . . I mean, I'm not . . . but . . . I'm just . . ." I trailed off, realizing I wasn't making any sense.

She regarded me for another moment in silence. "Your husband, he's the man in the black suit. Always smokes those President cigarettes. Has a mole on his cheek, right here." She touched her right cheekbone.

I nodded, not daring to breathe. She could have described any of thousands of men in Taiwan, but the mole clinched it.

"I overheard what you said that first day you came. You threw your daughter away. Like garbage." Wong Tai Tai glared at me, and I was taken aback by the force of her disapproval.

"I didn't." I reached out to her. "I love her with all my heart. My husband stole her from me."

She continued to stare at me, her face hard and unyielding. Another few minutes ticked by as she scrutinized me in silence. Then she said, "Give me your right palm."

I complied, confusion twisting my thoughts. Why did she want to see it? I held still while she studied my hand. She muttered something to herself and used a finger to trace a line down my palm. It tickled, but I didn't dare move. After a moment, she dropped my hand and met my eyes.

"Ong is a good person. They didn't deserve what your husband did to them."

I gasped, not only because of what she said, but that she was giving me information.

"Your husband, he came here a few times. They'd have a drink over there—" She gestured across the street to a pub. "They struck some kind of bargain. I don't know the details, but one day, he showed up with a little girl."

My hands flew to my mouth, and tears prickled at my eyes. Yili. The little girl had to be Yili. My eyes never left the woman's as I waited for her to tell me more.

"I'm very fond of their little boy, the one who was blinded from a childhood illness. He's a sweet boy. The little girl was a *shim-pua* for him." The woman started pacing behind the counter. "I don't know what happened, but one day, soon after the little girl came to live with them, they took her away."

"Her? The little girl?" I was getting confused.

"No. Ong's wife, Jin." Wong Tai Tai stopped pacing to face me.

I gasped. "They put a woman in prison?" I'd assumed that, when Ziyi heard Ong had been executed, she meant the husband. Did that mean they had killed a woman?

"Yes. They accused Jin of espionage." Wong Tai Tai had a fierce frown on her face. "It was all made up. Jin would never spy for the Communists."

"But her family . . ." My voice came out raw and hoarse. "They still live here?"

She studied me again, and I willed her to tell me, tell me which building, which apartment my Yili was in. I was ready to sprint out of the store, my arms already itching to clasp my daughter to me again.

The woman shook her head. "No. They're not here."

"You mean they went to visit someone, and they'll be back soon?" I looked out her store window, my eyes frantic, not wanting to make eye contact with her, afraid of what I'd find if I did. "Where do they live? I'll wait outside their door for them."

Her next words shattered my hope, shattered my heart and my soul, even as I was anticipating the sweet reunion with my Yili. I could already feel my daughter in my arms again as I buried my face in her sweet-smelling neck. She'd been gone for over a year now, and my body physically ached to hold her fast against me and never let go.

"They left soon after Jin was executed." The regret in the woman's voice made me turn to her. "I have no idea where they went, only that they're no longer in Taiwan. But I know for a fact that they're never coming back."

10
Liv

I opened the door to find Simon leaning against the doorframe, a smile curving his lips. The white linen shirt he wore showed off his deep tan, and I had to tear my gaze away from his forearms, which for some reason were making me hot.

"Hi," I said, swallowing hard. My breath hitched in my chest and my body tensed as the same wave of awareness that had hit me when our eyes connected in the airport swept through me now.

"Hi back at you," he said. "Ready to go to the night market?" He'd texted yesterday after Ah-Ma and I made the cooking video to say he was free tonight. While I looked forward to the culinary experience, my body tingled in dread. Would I be able to handle the crowds at night? Simon had reassured me he'd be with me every step of the way, and that if it became too much, we'd leave.

I nodded and then noticed the bouquet of pink roses he held cradled in one arm.

"Are those for me?" I reached to take them from him, but he pulled them out of my reach.

"These are for your grandmother." He gave me a devilish grin, lifting the ache in my heart that had lodged itself ever since hearing last night that Yili and her adoptive family had left Taiwan forever. After

Ah-Ma told me the story, we'd called my mother. She hadn't known the details about Ah-Ma's search for Yili and had so many questions. Part of me wished I'd be staying in tonight to hear more about what had happened, but now, seeing Simon again, I was really glad I'd get to spend more time with him.

"Smart." I tapped the side of my head. "Butter up the grandmother." I stepped back to let him through, willing my heart to calm down. Ah-Ma appeared behind us.

"*Ni hao.*" She greeted Simon with her hands outstretched.

"Ah-Ma, this is Simon Huang. Simon, my grandmother, Yi-ping Wang."

Simon took one of my grandmother's hands and gave her the flowers in the other. "It's a pleasure to meet you." He spoke to her in Mandarin.

"Likewise." My grandmother took the bouquet and admired them. "These are beautiful." She looked up at him. "Thank you for taking care of my Liv at the airport."

He gave a self-deprecating lift of a shoulder. "I'm just glad I was there. I hope you don't mind she told me about your search for your daughter."

My grandmother shook her head. "We need all the help we can get."

"We'll brainstorm some more at the night market," Simon said.

"Go, go. Enjoy. I'm glad you can show Liv around. It's past my bedtime." Ah-Ma pretended to yawn and made a shooing motion with her hands.

"Thanks for the ride," Simon said. Ah-Ma had sent Mr. Thomas to pick Simon up before coming back for me.

"Of course. Mr. Thomas gets bored, since I don't usually go anywhere, so you're providing him a thrill by driving you up to Feng Chia." Ah-Ma waved her fingers at us and then closed the door in our faces.

Simon caught my eyes, and we burst into laughter at my grandmother's obvious hint.

"Ready?" Simon held out an arm.

I took a deep breath. "Ready." I hoped.

I hooked one arm through his, and we left. I couldn't wait to finally see the Feng Chia night market, purportedly the biggest one in Taiwan. If I stayed close to Simon, like I had with Ah-Ma at the street market, maybe I could keep the panic away. Ten minutes later, Mr. Thomas dropped us off at the gates of Feng Chia University, which served as the unofficial start of the market.

"Text me when you're ready to go home." The kindly driver waved and then took off.

I stood in the darkened night and looked around me. Colorful lanterns hung over our heads, and bright lights illuminated the streets. They came from stores, signs high and low, and the hundreds of stalls and carts that lined both sides of the street ahead of us. Hordes of people created a ruckus, a highly charged environment that buzzed with excitement. More lights spilled out of stores while lit-up signs tried to outdo each other by blinking and flashing. The air was full of tantalizing scents coming from all directions. The energy was as electric as the lighting as people shouted to be heard, calling out to each other and pointing in all directions. It was chaotic, crowded, and loud, the perfect recipe for a panic attack, but when Simon slipped his hand into mine, a sense of calm washed over me. I was exhilarated, not terrified.

"I've never seen anything like it before." Simon's hand was warm and strong, making me feel rooted and not unmoored. I moved closer to him, not only because of the crush of people pushing by us, but because I was drawn to his quiet composure. I knew I was safe with him, and I was suddenly so glad I was here.

"It's great, right?" He gestured with his other hand. "This is what I dream of when I'm back in the States." He gave my hand a quick squeeze. "You good?"

My heart skipped a beat that he was checking in on me. I nodded and then clenched my jaw, determined to enjoy the night and not let my trauma ruin this experience.

"You're about to have some of the best food you'll ever have in your life."

"I can't wait." My mouth was already salivating from the heavenly aromas, and my eyes followed someone who had just walked by with a giant corn on a stick, coated in some sort of brown sauce.

We walked into the market and were soon engulfed by the eager crowd. Friends and couples walked arm in arm, while children darted between people, chasing each other. Vendors called out to the passersby, while shop owners hawked their wares from the entrance of their stores. My breath quickened, and even with Simon's hand clasped firmly in mine, my heart raced and sweat broke out on my forehead. He looked down at me and then drew me to the side, out of the middle of the crowd, where I could breathe.

"Okay?" he asked, leaning toward me. "Is this too much for you?"

I blew out a breath, willing my body not to betray me. I was finally here, at a night market I had heard so much about, and with a man who intrigued me. I wasn't about to let a panic attack spoil the moment. I took a few deep breaths, filling my body with air, before blowing them out through my mouth. Once my heart rate had returned to normal, I nodded at him.

"We'll stick to the outskirts of the crowd," he said, tightening his hand around mine.

I nodded again, and we started walking. Everywhere I looked was more and more food, things I'd never seen before, as well as more familiar sights like scallion pancakes and Taiwanese fried chicken.

"What do you want to start with?" Simon kept a firm grip on my hand, helping to stave off an attack. Occasionally, our sides bumped together, sending a pleasant hum through me.

"I want to try it all. You pick." My stomach grumbled because Simon had instructed me to arrive hungry.

He stopped in front of a stall with a line that was ten people deep. "Why don't we start off easy with the popcorn chicken?"

I peered around people to look at the stall, where a tantalizing mix of spices I couldn't identify wafted toward us. The line went quickly, and when it was our turn, Simon ordered in Mandarin. He handed me the box, and I used one of the toothpicks to pop a piece in my mouth.

"Oh wow," I said after I swallowed. "It's so tender and juicy. And so much flavor." My chef's palate was busy trying to decipher the spices as my foodie side groaned in happiness.

"This is just the beginning." I turned to find Simon watching me, a half smile on his lips. "I forgot that I'm eating with a chef. Glad to see this meets your approval so far."

"Let's get stinky tofu next. I've been dying to try it." I'd never had it before, since it wasn't readily available in the States, but it was one of my grandmother's favorite snacks.

"There's a good vendor over there." Simon guided me to the line for stinky tofu, and we ate more chicken as we waited.

When we got to the front of the line, we dropped hands as Simon ordered in Taiwanese.

"How do you know whether to speak Mandarin or Taiwanese?" I asked as we waited for our order. The food was helping me focus on something beside the crush of people all around us.

"By listening to them speak with other people." He nudged me with his shoulder, a mischievous smile lighting his face.

"Very funny." I narrowed my eyes at him. "I wish I could speak Taiwanese and improve my Mandarin."

"The best way is by being here in Taiwan," Simon said. "Both my Mandarin and Taiwanese get better whenever I'm here."

The vendor called out to him, and Simon accepted a box of the stinky tofu, which came with a side of pickled cabbage. We moved out of the way of the line, and once the tofu was cool enough, I took a bite.

"This is good. Really good." I was surprised at how mild the tofu was because the strong smell of the fermentation would have turned off most people. For me, it was enticing, and I was glad it tasted as good as I was expecting. My mind started concocting sauces to go with the gently fried tofu.

"I'm glad you like it. Cheers." Simon tapped his tofu against mine before taking a bite.

I looked around as we ate, thinking this night market was the kind of vibe I used to revel in before the shooting. It was everything that Amy and I had always craved: food, people, excitement, and new things. It was a scene unlike anything I'd grown up with or experienced in New York City. I could have happily stayed here all night, as long as Simon was at my side.

"I think my lack of language skills is going to be a problem when it comes to looking for my aunt," I said when I was finally satiated enough to talk.

"I can help." Simon speared a piece of cabbage on his toothpick, and I watched, entranced, as he brought it to his lips. I realized I was staring and looked away quickly, a blush staining my cheeks even as I leaned closer to him.

"How are you so fluent?" I asked, trying to distract myself from his full lips.

"We spoke it at home, mostly Taiwanese, and I went to Chinese school and then studied it at college." He gave me a mock scowl. "Don't tell me you never went to Chinese school, the bane of every Chinese and Taiwanese American child?"

"My parents didn't send us." Now I wondered why. I hadn't questioned it back then because it wasn't something I even knew existed.

"But you seem to understand some Mandarin?"

I nodded. "I can understand simple conversations, as long as it doesn't get too technical and you don't speak too fast. My grandmother spoke Mandarin to us growing up."

Simon nodded. "I also lived in Taipei for a year doing research and teaching classes at a university. They've been trying to get me back here again, but I like the work I'm doing at the hospital in New York. And I have a good private practice with a partner." His eyes gleamed as he looked me. "I've been able to see many of my patients via video since being here."

"It's important work you're doing." I flushed and looked away, remembering how he'd helped me at the airport. I spied a bubble tea shop up ahead. "I'm thirsty."

Simon nodded and threw out our empty containers. We joined the end of the line. "Has your grandmother ever done a DNA test to see if she has any matches? Maybe her lost daughter has done one, looking for her birth family."

"Actually, she did one out of the blue weeks ago." I stepped toward him when two kids barreled by us, yelling at each other. "She should be getting the results any day now."

"That's good." Simon put his arm around my shoulders, drawing me closer to him. "I know they can take a while to get the results. Even if she doesn't match to her missing daughter, there might be relatives that could be traced to her."

Once we had our boba teas, we continued navigating through the crowd. Simon kept his arm around my shoulders so that when a big group pushed by us, I didn't panic. Maybe I really was starting to heal.

"Tell me about yourself, Liv Kuo. Why did you decide to become a chef?" Simon played with the ends of my hair with the hand that was around my shoulders.

"Well, I love to eat, as you can tell. And I like to create. My grandmother taught me. We used to spend hours in the kitchen. There's something about mixing flavors together—it's almost like chemistry. My grandmother told me I had a more refined palate at ten than most adults. I could almost always guess exactly what spices and herbs were used in a dish."

"That's amazing."

"What about you? What made you want to be a psychotherapist?" I was curious about his profession. I didn't know many Taiwanese people in that line of work.

Simon gave me a quick glance and then guided me toward a side area that wasn't as crowded. "My best friend, Ken, whose grandfather's funeral I'm here for, took his own life when he was twenty-one. His roommate found him. He'd hung himself."

I gasped. Simon hadn't given any indication that his friend was no longer with us when he'd mentioned him before. I thought he'd come to support Ken. Now my question seemed wrong in such a lively atmosphere, and I wished I could take it back. "I'm so sorry."

"It's okay. I don't mind talking about it. We'd known each other since grade school. He had the same last name as me, Huang, so we were always seated next to each other." His arm dropped from my shoulders, but he stayed close to my side. "Ken was Taiwanese too and came from a family that didn't talk about mental health. Instead, his parents gave him ginseng and other herbs. He covered up his depression well. I didn't know how bad it was because he always put up such a happy front. The super-smart firstborn son who got into an Ivy League school and on the fast track to becoming a doctor. Even his older sister didn't know the depth of his depression. Nor did his girlfriend." Simon had a sad smile tugging at his lips. "Everyone was shocked when he died, including me."

"I'm sorry." I reached out to touch his forearm.

"We were more like brothers than just friends. Ken was really close to his grandfather Ang-Li. We used to go to Ang-Li's house after school a lot. We both loved Taiwanese food, and his grandfather would cook all his favorites for us."

I kept my hand on his arm, not knowing what to say.

"Ang-Li took Ken's death hard, as if he were responsible for not stopping what happened. I stayed in close touch with Ang-Li and Ken's father George after . . ." He trailed off and glanced at me before continuing. "Ang-Li told me once he wished he'd known how to help Ken. If only Ken had gone to someone, talked with someone, maybe he wouldn't have felt so alone, so hopeless."

"And now you do that for other people?"

"Yes. I want more Asian families to know that mental health issues are real, and that there is a way to help." He let out a soft laugh. "My parents had no idea what it was I was doing when I told them what I wanted to study. Even though my father basically grew up in the States and my mom moved there when she was eighteen, they come from that old-school Asian thought where mental illness is seen as the ultimate form of shame."

"I'm sorry." I looked down as I said it because I realized this was true in my family too. I talked to my mom, but I never told her if I was upset about something. I always put up a brave front, not wanting her to know when I was hurting, as if to admit weakness would bring shame to my parents.

Simon reached out to take my hand. "Let's talk about something happier." He must have seen the cloud that had passed over my face. "Have you ever had pork blood rice cake?"

"No, but Ah-Ma said to try it." I took a sip of my tea and chewed the tapioca pearls that gave the drink their name. "It's one of her favorites."

"You're not scared of it?"

I shook my head. "My grandmother made all kinds of stuff for us when we were growing up. Intestines, stomach, you name it."

"It's really good." He pointed ahead. "There's a stand up there."

"I'm glad I came with you," I said, meaning it in more ways than one.

"I'm glad I got to share your first Taiwanese night market with you."

We didn't say anything more until he handed me the rice cake, which came on a stick coated with a sweet soy sauce, spicy sauce, peanut powder, and cilantro.

I took a bite, giving a humming sound as I bit into the soft rice, and the mixture of sweet, spicy, and salty danced over my taste buds. "Perfection."

I handed him the stick, and just like I'd done with my grandmother the first day at the Yizhong Shopping Street, we passed the snack back and forth between us until it was gone. For the next hour, we absorbed the energy of the night. We strolled through the night market, going into stores, watching kids try to win prizes at the arcade, and buying more food to share, including *takoyaki*, octopus balls, from a place with a giant purple squid on top. We also sat to have a bowl of shaved ice heaped with all sorts of toppings.

When a large group of giggling girls shoved between us, breaking my hold on Simon's hand, I looked around for him, panic starting to prickle at the back of my neck. I'd thought I was doing well because he'd stuck close to my side, but now my eyes scanned the crowd in fear as the world around me started to swirl and the lights and sounds overwhelmed me.

Just as I was about to hyperventilate, I spotted him beyond the group of girls. He was scanning the crowd with his eyes, his movements agitated and frantic as he forced his way past the people who separated us. Breathing a giant sigh of relief, I pushed my way through the crowd toward him, forcing myself to slow my breath and not show him that I'd been about to have a panic attack.

"There you are." Simon grabbed my hands and pulled me into him for a brief moment. "I'm sorry I lost you. You okay?" His eyes roamed over my face and I nodded.

Trying to find a distraction, I blew out a breath and looked around. My eyes lighted on a display just behind Simon. I blinked until I could decipher what the vendor was selling. They were cute little stickers with things like dogs, hearts, and flowers on them.

Simon's eyes followed mine and he said, "My sister loves those customized stickers."

"You have a sister?" I focused on that fact as I struggled to steady my breath. I would *not* have another panic attack in front of this man.

"Stephanie is three years younger than me. She's an oncology nurse in Seattle." He turned back to the display. "She asked me to get her some. Which one do you like?"

"This one." I pointed to the one that came with a variety of dogs, one on each sticker. "But what should it say?"

"How about 'Liv Kuo, Chef'?" His eyes twinkled at me. "Or you can make address labels."

I took out my cell and videotaped the display as I debated. Was I still a chef if I hadn't cooked a thing since the shooting? But being in Taiwan was starting to awaken the urge to create again as I experienced flavors and textures I'd never encountered before. Watching Ah-Ma cook, even something as simple as an egg omelet, was making me itch to experiment.

I decided that Simon was right. I would get one that said "Liv Kuo, Chef." I would stick it on things to remind myself that I was a chef. I'd taken a hiatus, but I was on my way back. Ah-Ma and I were going to cook everything in her book together, and I'd discover that passion for cooking again that had been dormant for the past few months.

Simon and I stood side by side and watched the vendor making the stickers we'd ordered. I looked up and caught Simon's eyes. He held my gaze for a moment, and I had the feeling that if we weren't in a crowded street surrounded by so many people, he would have leaned down and kissed me.

"Liv Kuo." He said my name softly, but I heard it. He leaned in closer to me. "Are you seeing anyone? In a relationship?"

"No," I breathed out, my heart beating faster. "Are you?"

He shook his head with a crooked smile on his face. My stomach swirled; I shivered slightly, overwhelmed by my feelings as he drew me close against him. And then my head landed against his shoulder, and I let out a sigh. I wasn't going to worry about anything right now. I was going to enjoy the moment for what it was, an amazing night out with someone I was beginning to like a lot. I'd kept it together more or less in the midst of this crowded night market, and that in itself was a major accomplishment.

Simon's arm around me tightened, and I leaned into him, forgetting all about my panic attacks when I felt his lips whisper lightly against my temple. I closed my eyes, content.

11
Lɪv

"Are we going to Simon's friend's place today?" Ah-Ma put down her mug of coffee.

We were seated at the dining table enjoying a late breakfast because I'd slept in again. I hadn't slept so well since that night at 852 and had taken to lounging in bed and texting with Simon and Amy in the mornings instead of jumping up as soon as my eyes opened, which used to be my norm.

"Yes." I picked up my mug of green tea sweetened with a bit of honey. "He said they'll all be home today."

Simon had gone to Tainan to visit some relatives, since Ang-Li's family had been busy preparing for his funeral. I hadn't seen Simon since the night market three days ago, except for a quick trip to get bubble tea yesterday. "I'm hoping they can help put out the word on Facebook about the woman you saw."

"I hope so too." Ah-Ma dabbed at her mouth with a napkin. I could see the emotions in her eyes. We hadn't gotten anywhere the last few days and were still waiting for her DNA results. I knew my grandmother was starting to lose hope.

"We'll find her. I've only been in Taiwan for a week." I got up and leaned down to hug her around the shoulders.

She pulled away to study me. "You look much better."

I nodded. "I am." But then I thought back to that moment of panic at the night market when I realized Simon wasn't at my side. Could I really navigate the outside world alone? I was proud of myself for even being in Taiwan, but those panic attacks were still appearing with no warning. It was a struggle to keep myself together sometimes, and I had the urge to wrap my arms around my body, holding on as tight as I could lest I fall apart and break into a million pieces.

"What time are we going over?" Ah-Ma's words broke into my thoughts.

"After lunch. I think they're wrapping up with the lawyer this morning." I walked over to where we'd placed the old cookbook in a safe corner of the kitchen counter. "Let's make something else from here, and you can tell me more about the past."

"I was going to make a batch of dumplings from the filling we mixed up last night." Ah-Ma walked to my side and turned a few pages. She pointed at it. "I like to do this occasionally and freeze them, so I always have a ready snack or meal when I need it. There's enough to make some for Simon's family." She paused for a moment. "And for Ziyi."

"How is she?" I asked softly.

"Her companion says she's better. We might be able to visit later." Ah-Ma pushed away from the counter. "I hope your idea of using ground turkey and shrimp works."

When she was preparing the mixture that would become the filling last night, I'd grimaced when she said she was using ground pork. I was craving something lighter. "Maybe we can use ground turkey instead?" I'd thought for a moment. "And mix in pieces of shrimp?"

My grandmother gave me a skeptical look. "I've never done that before. It's always been ground pork and vegetables, or just vegetables."

"I think it could be good." My brain was already turning, my mind buzzing with energy as I tried to imagine the flavors on my tongue. Dumplings and baos always reminded me of Amy. She was half-Vietnamese and half-Chinese and had created so many different kinds, fusing her two heritages. I'd been a willing guinea pig from the first dumpling she'd made.

I picked up my phone now to text her.

Miss you. What's new?

She responded right away. Drinking Arrack in Sri Lanka.

Wow, you're in Sri Lanka now? And what's Arrack?

Yup. I met the nicest couple from South Africa. I'm traveling with them right now. Arrack is coconut whiskey fermented from the sap of the coconut flower. Delish! Wish you were here!

Me too. And for a moment, I did. But then I realized I was content with Ah-Ma, finally learning about her history and the food that was part of our culture.

Love you. And she sent a heart emoji.

Send me a picture of the couple and their names and social security numbers. I was serious. I worried about Amy, out in the big world by herself.

Haha very funny. But a photo of her with a couple in their early thirties arrived a few minutes later, along with their full names and where they lived.

Satisfied, I put my phone down and looked at Ah-Ma. "Let's make those dumplings. What did you add to the turkey and shrimp mixture again last night?" I hadn't written down the ingredients and wanted to do so now.

"Soy sauce, sesame oil, a little bit of sugar, and cooking wine. I like to let it marinate in the fridge overnight. We'll mix in the scallions, Taiwanese cabbage, and chives now."

I took the bowl out and gave it an appreciative sniff. "It smells so good."

"Ziyi has the best dumpling sauce recipe. You should ask her for it if we visit later." Ah-Ma gave the mixture a gentle stir, and I leaned down to inhale the umami flavors again.

"I can't wait to meet her. Tell me more about her." I straightened up from the bowl, thinking about Ah-Ma's friend. She sounded like a force of nature, someone who wasn't afraid to take on the world. But I knew there was more to her story, as I could see the sorrow and guilt in Ah-Ma's eyes whenever she spoke of her friend.

"She can't wait to meet you too." Ah-Ma was laying out everything we needed to fold the dumplings, including a little bowl of water to moisten the edges of the dumpling peels and some flour so they wouldn't stick together. "She was so mad that she got sick right as you arrived." Ah-Ma laughed but then sobered. "Her story is not a happy one. Are you sure you want to hear it?"

I nodded. By now, I was so invested in what my grandmother and her friend had endured as young wives that they felt like new friends. I wanted to know more about this formidable woman who my grandmother said was willing to take on the Taiwanese government to help people who couldn't defend themselves.

YI-PING

June 1963, Taichung

I wiped the sweat off my brow as I hurried to the school where all three of my daughters attended. Three of my four daughters, I corrected myself. My son was now two, which was a constant reminder that it'd been two years since Yili disappeared.

I was going to be late. I'd lost track of time, as I'd been making dumplings for dinner that night, enough for the entire extended family. I'd gotten caught up in the hypnotic rhythm of scooping out the filling and placing it in the middle of the dumpling skin before folding the two edges together and crimping them with my fingers to make a perfect dumpling. My son had been playing by my feet, and I was lost in a fantasy where Yili was next to me, dipping her tiny fingers into a bowl of water and ringing each dumpling skin before I put the filling in, so the skin would stick together and not burst apart when we boiled them in water.

I was picturing how she'd look in my mind. She'd be almost four now, with long hair past her shoulders, either in braids on either side of her head, or possibly with a headband holding it back so that it wouldn't get in the way as she helped me. Her tongue would peek out of her mouth as she concentrated on her task, and she'd be kneeling on the chair so she could reach across the table to hand me the skin.

My daydreams were interrupted when my eldest sister-in-law banged into our home without knocking.

"Aren't you supposed to be picking up your girls?" she said in a loud voice. As befitting her position in our family, she was the bossiest of my sisters-in-law, always telling us what to do and voicing her opinions, even when they weren't welcome. But I'd found that beneath her brashness was a heart of gold, and I knew I could count on her to help me whenever I needed.

"Oh no." I jumped up when I caught sight of the time on the clock in the kitchen. "Can you watch them for me? I'm going to be late." I gestured to the children.

"Them?" She looked at me, curiosity and concern warring in her eyes.

"I mean . . ." I trailed off, flustered. I'd told no one that I often imagined Yili was with me. "I meant my son."

She nodded, although there was still an air of uncertainty about her as she regarded me. I didn't wait for her to say more, just grabbed my keys and ran out the door.

Now, I huffed out a breath as the school building came into sight. I rushed through the front gates and ran to where I usually picked up my children, expecting them to be the last ones waiting. To my surprise, they were standing with Ziyi's two children, a girl, who at nine was one year older than my oldest daughter, and a son two years younger.

"Mama," Lun-Shan called as I ran up to them. She planted her fists on her hips. "You're late." Her little face was scrunched up in indignation. "Where have you been? You were supposed to be here fifteen minutes ago. Teacher was just about to call you."

"I'm so sorry." I knelt, and my two younger daughters ran into my arms. "I was making dumplings and lost track of time."

Lun-Shan wasn't as quick to forgive me as the younger ones. "You need to set a timer. Teacher isn't pleased that you made her stay late."

I looked over at the woman who was waiting with my children and was about to apologize when she said, "Don't worry, it's fine. Have you heard from Lim Tai Tai? I tried her first, and no one is answering at her home."

"That's strange." This wasn't like Ziyi. She was way more organized than me and had never forgotten to pick up her children (unlike me; this wasn't the first time I'd been late, hence the glare Lun-Shan was still directing my way).

The teacher shifted from foot to foot and then glanced behind her, and I knew she needed to leave. I beckoned to Ziyi's children.

"I'll take them with me," I told the teacher.

She sighed in relief and, after saying goodbye to us, took off back to her classroom.

The five children held a lively conversation as we walked home. I trailed behind them, wondering what had happened to Ziyi. A feeling of foreboding filled me. She had never forgotten her children before. I'd tried many times to get her to talk to me about her marriage, but she always brushed me off, saying she was fine. Had I been a selfish friend, too wrapped up in my own grief to make her tell me what was happening at home?

I decided I was indeed a selfish friend and vowed to do better.

"Mama?" Lun-Shan hung back and slipped her hand into mine, her way of telling me she'd forgiven me. "Are you sad?"

I smiled, trying to convey I wasn't sad because of her. "I'm fine."

"Are you thinking of Yili?" She glanced at me quickly before looking straight ahead, where the other four children had linked arms, creating a blockage to anyone trying to get around them. I should say something, tell them to let go, but it was heartwarming to see how Ziyi's children and mine had grown so close over the last two years that I didn't have the heart to.

I turned back to my eldest daughter. "How did you know I was thinking about her?"

"You always get this look in your eyes, like you're looking at something really, really far away." Her voice was as melodic as her piano playing. Abu had been right. Even at eight years old, Lun-Shan played with a passion and skill of someone twice her age. "Was that why you were late? Because you were thinking about her?"

I shook my head quickly. I didn't want my children to ever think I was neglecting them because of my grief over Yili. I'd learned in the past two years how to compartmentalize my feelings, trying to be as present as I could for my other children, and only nursing my grief alone at night in my room or if I managed to get away by myself during the day.

"Why don't you ever talk about her?" Lun-Shan's keen eyes bored into the side of my head, making me flush. "Are you afraid to make us sad?"

"No." I looked away from those sharp eyes. "The others were so young when she was taken. I don't know if they remember her. I don't want to remind them and make them afraid."

"Afraid of what?" We were almost home, and I thought distractedly that I would drop my girls at home and then take Ziyi's children to her place. I'd check up on Ziyi at the same time. But my daughter's next words made me halt in place. "Afraid Baba will get rid of us like he did Yili?"

"Oh, Lun-Shan. No. Baba would never do that." But wouldn't he? He'd done it to their youngest sister. "Are your sisters afraid of that?"

"No. Like you said, they don't seem to remember. But I wonder sometimes." Her voice was nonchalant, but I heard a current of worry threading through her words.

I started walking again, holding on to my daughter's hand tightly. "I promise you I won't let your baba ever take you away."

"He took Yili." I knew Lun-Shan wasn't trying to wound me, but her words were like a dagger to my heart. She was right. I hadn't protected Yili.

"I'm sorry." I didn't know what else to say. We were at our door, and before I could unlock the front door, she said suddenly, "You can talk to me about Yili anytime you want. I miss her."

"Thank you." I stroked her hair and unlocked the door. "Get started on homework. I'm going to Ziyi's."

She nodded, and then I walked Ziyi's children around the corner to their building. Their front door was unlocked, and they ran in, greeted by Ah-Ji, the housekeeper who worked for them. Ah-Ji hustled them into the kitchen for a snack as I headed toward the living quarters.

"Ziyi, are you here?" She wasn't in the living room, or the large playroom where her children did homework. Was she even home?

Just as I was going to head to the kitchen to ask the housekeeper, I heard a noise coming from her bedroom. Was she sick? But what if she was in there with her husband doing husbandly duties? My cheeks flushed pink as I thought about bursting in on them during an intimate moment.

I was about to leave when I heard her voice calling my name, so softly I thought I'd imagined it. I crept to the door and hovered outside of it.

"Ziyi," I said, softly. I gave the door a gentle tap, and then I heard my name again.

I pushed the door open, and at first, I didn't see my friend. Their bed was empty, the blankets folded neatly, and no one was sitting in the two cane-back chairs inlaid with marble dragons that lined one side of the room. Had I imagined her voice?

But then I heard, "Yi-ping. Help me."

I rushed to the other side of the bed and then stopped still at what I saw. Ziyi lay on her back in a heap by the bed, a pool of blood under her head. I didn't recognize her face. It was as if someone had blown it up and rearranged her features, and I could already see it turning different shades of purple and red.

"Ziyi! What happened?" I bent down, but I was afraid to touch her. I couldn't tell if she had any broken bones, and I didn't know how bad her head injury was.

"I . . . I fell. Hit my head." She tried to open her eyes.

"You did not fall." My voice was stern, even as my heart was breaking for my poor friend. "Your husband did this to you, didn't he?"

"No, Yi-ping. I fell." She tried to push herself up, but I motioned for her to stay still.

"What hurts? Can you move your arms? Your legs?" I had absolutely no medical training, but even I knew she needed attention right away.

"I don't know." She tried again to sit up, and this time, she succeeded. I could see that the blood on the side of her head had congealed and stopped, for which I was thankful. How long had she been lying here like this?

"I'm going to get Ah-Ji. She'll call your driver, and I'll go with you to the hospital."

"No. No hospital. He'll kill me," Ziyi whispered.

My heart sank as I realized she had finally confirmed that her husband had been hurting her. "He already almost killed you. I don't care what story you want to tell the hospital, but you need to go." I got up swiftly, the urgent need to take care of my friend making me brave.

I opened the door and yelled out, "Ah-Ji. Come here, now. Keep the children in the kitchen."

The housekeeper came scrambling down the hall, her face concerned at the urgency in my voice. I never yelled. And here I was, shouting in a home not my own. I ushered her into the room and slammed the door behind me. When she rounded the corner and saw Ziyi leaning against the bed, she gasped, and her hands flew to her mouth.

"Lim Tai Tai, what happened?"

"You need to call the driver, tell him to come take us to the hospital. But get the children out first." I didn't recognize the controlling tone of my voice. "Take them to my house. They can't see their mother like this." I didn't wait to hear what Ah-Ji replied before she flew out of the room. I bent down to Ziyi. "Can you stand? Test your limbs first."

Always before, it had been Ziyi who'd taken care of me, but now I was the one to care for her. I made her check each limb, and when none seemed to be broken, I helped her to stand. She held on to the bed and swayed, and I could see that most of the damage was to her face. Her poor delicate face. He'd lashed out at it, and without being told, I knew he'd punched and slapped her, and probably hit her over the head with something sharp, judging by the wound on the side of her head. My blood boiled with anger, and I wanted to claw his eyes out. I was also mad at myself for suspecting that he'd been hurting my friend but never once making her tell me the truth, until it was too late. I vowed then and there that I would do whatever I could for my friend, that I would be as strong for her as she'd always been for me.

12
YI-PING

June 1963, Taichung

I went to visit Ziyi in the hospital the next day. They'd wanted to keep her a couple of days because of the severity of her internal injuries. Her head wound needed stitches, and the doctor gave her something for the pain. She'd been fast asleep when I left her yesterday, returning home to take care of my children. Ah-Ji came over and took Ziyi's children after I'd told her Ziyi would need to stay in the hospital.

I walked in to find her awake, sitting propped up in the bed. I tried to control my facial expression when I caught sight of her, but I couldn't contain a gasp of shock. She was unrecognizable from my dear friend. It was as if her husband had gone after the one thing he couldn't control, her beauty, and pummeled her until she no long resembled herself. Her eyes followed mine as I pulled up a chair to sit at her side. I took her hand in both of mine gingerly, afraid she was going to break.

"How bad do I look?"

"Um . . ." I bit my lip, not wanting to lie to her, but also not wanting her to see I was this close to weeping at the sight of her.

"They wouldn't let me look in the mirror." It sounded like the words leaving her mouth hurt, and I longed to shush her, but I needed to know what had happened.

"It's really bad." Ziyi had never lied to me, and I wouldn't lie to her.

"Oh, Ziyi, what did he do to you?"

Her mouth thinned, and she looked away for a moment. "I thought I had made a good match. The handsome officer from a good family, even if they were KMT. My parents thought the union would help make sure our family stayed safe, as my father is a professor and under constant government watch."

I held my breath because she'd never talked about her marriage. She'd listened to me for hours, helping me search for Yili, even after the Ong family disappeared from their neighborhood. She'd been tireless, never giving up, and she encouraged me to keep asking questions, keep going back to the neighborhood, because maybe someone else knew something. She'd kept me going when all I wanted to do was curl up and die, and yet all this time, she'd been hiding this dark secret.

"At first, he liked when I talked back. He told me he enjoyed a confident woman, someone who knew her own mind. He said it turned him on, and he was rough in bed whenever I—" She broke off as a sob caught in her chest. I had never seen her cry in the over two years we'd been friends.

I stroked her hand. "You don't have to talk about it if you're not ready."

She turned so that she could look directly at me, and my heart split open again at what he'd done to her face. "I can't hold it back anymore. If I don't tell someone, I'm going to explode."

"Then talk. I'm here." I kept stroking her hand because I didn't know what else to do.

"He didn't hit me until after our daughter was born." Ziyi took a breath. "Weili was about eight months old. He had to go to some sort of dinner and wanted me to go with him. But Weili was sick, and I didn't want to leave her. I was distracted because she was crying, and I guess I didn't pay enough attention to him. He took the baby from me, put her in her crib, and then backhanded me across the face." Ziyi sucked in a breath of air. "He left me lying there and went off to his dinner without another word. I didn't move for what felt like hours. I couldn't believe he'd hit me. I just couldn't move, not even when Weili was screaming her head off. It wasn't until Ah-Ji came to see why the baby was still crying that I finally unfroze. I told her I'd dropped something and was looking for it on the floor."

"Oh, Ziyi." I could feel tears gathering in my eyes, but I blinked them away. I'd cried too much to Ziyi; it was my turn to listen and comfort.

"We never spoke about that day, and everything went back to normal. You know me, I always have an opinion, and it didn't occur to me to watch what I said. When months went by without another incident, I thought I'd imagined the whole thing. But one night, we had a friend of his and his wife over for dinner. The man was belittling his wife, saying how she was a slob and didn't keep their home clean. I defended her, because she has six children, saying maybe he should hire someone to help her." Ziyi paused and picked up the glass of water on the portable table in front of her. "The man laughed and elbowed my husband, saying, 'You have a feisty one, don't you?'"

I knew what she was going to say. It physically hurt me, as if I could feel the blows her husband must have rained on her after the couple left.

"Except for that first slap, he was always careful to hit me where I could cover it up. Not so much because he worried what others would think of him, but because he wanted me to always look perfect. He wanted to brag about his beautiful wife, to show me off to his cohorts, and I could never appear in public looking anything less than perfect." Ziyi turned toward me. "He told me he owned me, that I was his to do as he wanted. And he wanted the world to see me as his beautiful and flawless wife."

"Why didn't you tell me, all those times I asked about your injuries?" My words were barely more than a whisper.

"What could you have done? You had worse problems of your own." Ziyi tried to shrug but ended up wincing instead. "And if I didn't think about it, pretended it didn't happen from time to time, I could ignore it."

"Worse problems?" What could be worse than your husband hitting you? "Ziyi, he hurt you." I'd heard stories in the neighborhood about this or that man beating his wife, or jokes about how a man needed to keep his wife in line. The Chinese soap operas that Abu liked to watch were full of spousal abuse, a man slapping a woman across the face, throwing her to the ground. But I'd never met anyone in person who was actually physically harmed.

"Your husband took one of your children from you." Her gaze was direct, even though her eyes were mere slits in her swollen flesh. "To me, that's the worst thing that could happen to me. As long as he doesn't harm my children, as long it's just me he's hitting, I can deal with it." Her expression turned fierce, and her voice deepened. "If he ever takes one of my children or hurts them, I'll kill him."

"Ziyi." I drew back in shock, then looked around to make sure no one had overheard her. To threaten an officer of the KMT, even one's own husband, was to ask to be thrown in jail. "You shouldn't say such things."

"Why not?" She turned her fierce stare back on me. "If I had been you, I would have poisoned your husband by now. I don't care what people say, that we have no choice." Even through her puffy face, I could see the murderous gleam in her eyes. "If anyone ever touches my children, they will regret it."

I let go of her hand, scared by her words, but also in awe of this woman in front of me. She lay here in this hospital bed, beaten beyond recognition, yet she still had a fire of conviction deep within her that her husband could never touch. He might hurt her physically, but I knew in that instance that he could never touch her spiritually.

Then a thought occurred to me. "You said he's never hurt you where you couldn't cover it up. What changed this time?" I was almost afraid of her answer.

She put the glass down before answering. "I have a friend, a schoolmate I've known since we were children. He works at the US embassy, and I was trying to help a friend of a friend get a visa out of Taiwan." She swallowed and looked down at her hands. "This woman's husband is trying to leave because he's been targeted by the KMT. They were desperate, and I tried to help." She looked up at me. "Someone saw me meeting with my schoolmate in the park. They told my husband."

She didn't need to say more. I knew enough about her husband to know that he'd never tolerate having his wife seen in public with another man. And if he'd found out *why* she'd been meeting with him . . . I shuddered, marveling at Ziyi's bravery. Where did she find the fortitude to go up against not only her husband, but our government? I suddenly felt so small and futile next to this formidable woman who stood up for her beliefs and tried to help others.

"What can I do? How can I help you?" I hated feeling so useless. I wasn't brave or smart like Ziyi. But I would do whatever she needed of me.

"Nothing. That's the problem." She met my eyes. "We have no rights. I'll fine once this"—she gestured to her face—"heals. I'm used to it. I can take care of myself."

"This isn't right. Your face . . ." I reached over as if to touch her on the cheek but then thought better of it. I knew she'd never look like her old self again. Even when she healed, she'd have scars, and her nose was now crooked.

"I don't care what I look like." She covered my hand with one of hers. "My husband thinks the worst thing he can do is to mar my beauty, but I care nothing about my looks." She let out a dry laugh. "Joke's on him if he now has a hideous-looking wife. I'd like to see how he explains my appearance."

"Oh, Ziyi . . ."

She closed her eyes, and I stared at her helplessly. Her words made me think, really think, about how little independence we had. We couldn't just walk away and leave an abusive husband, or a husband who'd given away one of our children. What was important to me? She said if her husband ever hurt her children, she would kill him, yet she'd done nothing whenever he hurt her. And here I was, my husband doing what I thought was the worst thing he could do to me by taking away my child, and still I stayed with him. But the thought of him laying a finger on me made anger rise in me in a way that surprised me. Ziyi and I were both helpless to change our fates or the fates of our children, in different ways.

Which one of us had it the worst?

LIV

The dumpling I'd just stuffed in my mouth suddenly felt like lead. I chewed and swallowed, even though I was sick to my stomach about what had happened to Ziyi. To have lived in a time when a woman could do nothing about domestic abuse, knowing it was a common occurrence but that there was nothing she could do about it, was unfathomable to me.

"I don't even know what to say." I stared at my grandmother, disgust and horror warring within me. "What you two lived through."

"It was just the way it was back then." My grandmother put down her chopsticks and sighed. She stood to take another tray of dumplings out of the freezer, where we'd put them so they could set, before putting them in a freezer bag. This ensured they wouldn't stick to each other as they froze.

"I have so much admiration for you and Ziyi." My cell dinged, and I looked down to see a message from Simon. "They're home." He'd told me he'd text us when they were back at Ken's aunt Clare's place. "We can go over anytime."

Ah-Ma zipped up the last bag and put it back in the freezer. I brought our bowls to the sink, and as I was rinsing them, her phone rang.

"It's Ziyi." She shot me a look as she answered the call.

I paused in my dish washing to listen to her side of the conversation.

"No bother at all. You know I'd do anything for you." She paused and then nodded. "I'm sure. I'll be right there." She said goodbye and hung up.

"Everything okay?" I asked.

"Ziyi fell getting out of bed, and Ah-Ji is food shopping and not answering her phone."

"Ah-Ji?" I broke in, recognizing the name. "The housekeeper who'd been with her when you found her beaten?"

Ah-Ma nodded. "She's stayed faithfully with Ziyi all these years and is now her companion." She picked up her purse. "Ziyi says she's okay and just needs help getting up." She headed for the door. "I'll try to get to Clare's as soon as I can."

"I hope Ziyi is okay." Even though I'd never met her and had only found out about her a few days ago, I felt a connection to her from my grandmother's stories.

"Me too. I'll catch a cab so that Mr. Thomas can drive you." She slipped her shoes on and then was gone.

I got myself ready and then went downstairs to meet Mr. Thomas. He greeted me in his usual cheerful way and taught me a few words of Taiwanese on our way.

"*Lí hó bô?*" I muttered to myself as I got out of the car. "*Lí hó bô?*" I said again, determined to greet Simon's friends in Taiwanese.

Ken's aunt Clare lived on the fifteenth floor in a modern high-rise building with all the amenities. Simon opened the apartment door as I got out of the elevator. He came into the hallway and closed the door behind him. My breath caught to see how handsome he looked in a light-blue button-down shirt and jeans, the sleeves rolled up to expose his tanned forearms. I didn't know what it was about his forearms that always made me weak, but I had trouble tearing my eyes away. I hadn't wanted to admit that I'd missed him these past few days, but now, with the way my entire body was yearning toward him, I couldn't deny it.

"You look beautiful." He hovered at the doorway, and when I got close enough, he hugged me close.

I inhaled the brief scent of soap and sunshine before he pulled away and grinned down at me. My lips curved too, and we fell silent, but it wasn't an uncomfortable silence. It was a quiet silence, full of possibilities of what could come.

I finally moved and broke the spell. "My grandmother and I made dumplings for you and your friends." I held up the soft-sided cooler. "We used her recipe but updated it with my ideas."

They'd turned out amazing. My grandmother had admitted that substituting ground turkey and shrimp for the pork made for a tasty and surprisingly light dumpling.

"Where is she?" Simon looked behind me. "I thought she was coming with you?"

I blew out a breath. "Her friend Ziyi fell. She went over to help her."

"She okay?" Simon raised his eyebrows.

"She said she's fine. Ah-Ma is hoping to make it over after she checks on Ziyi."

Simon nodded and gestured to the door. "Ready? Ken's mother and aunt are looking forward to hearing your grandmother's story." He opened the door, and I stepped into the foyer of a very modern space with stark furniture.

A woman about my mom's age came bustling out of the kitchen. "Hi! I'm Genevieve." She held out a hand to me. "You must be Liv. Simon's told us all about you."

I shot him a quick glance and he lifted a shoulder at me.

"So great to meet you." I shook her hand. *"Lí hó bô?"* Genevieve had short hair styled in waves off her face, with an angular jawline and high cheekbones. She was tall for an Asian woman, about five eight, and I wondered if Ken had been tall too. "Thank you for allowing us to intrude on you during your time of grief."

"Oh, you speak Taiwanese." Genevieve launched into a long phrase in Taiwanese.

I sputtered out a laugh and put up my hands in surrender. "No, I don't. My grandmother's driver just taught me that."

Genevieve and Simon smiled. "Well, it sounded pretty good," Genevieve said. "Where's your grandmother? Wasn't she supposed to come with you?"

"She had to go help a friend who fell, but she's planning on coming over after. We made you dumplings." I gave her the bag.

"Oh." Genevieve's face lit up. "Simon said you're a chef. I'm sure these are delicious. Thank you." She set the bag on the counter and opened it. "My husband George is at his father Ang-Li's apartment with his younger sister Sue. They're sorting through their father's things. He's sorry to miss your visit."

We walked to the living room and sat down. In contrast to my grandmother's apartment, Clare's place was all steel and chrome. Very modern, sleek furniture filled the space, giving it a sophisticated but cold look.

"Where's Clare?" Simon asked as Genevieve took the bag of dumplings out of the cooler and put them in the freezer.

"She got a phone call. She'll be right out." Genevieve handed the cooler back to me, and I placed it on the floor by my foot. "But I can't wait. Tell me about your grandmother." She sat in an armchair and crossed her legs. "You know, it's more common than people think, those *shim-pua* adoptions."

"Really?" I leaned toward her. She had a way about her that made me feel immediately at ease, unlike the apartment. Her interest in my grandmother's story warmed her to me even more.

She nodded. "Many of my relatives, aunts, second cousins, were given away as *shim-puas*." She shook her head slightly. "No one ever talks about it. It's just something that was done."

"I can't imagine." How was this a common practice in Taiwan even back in the day? It sounded barbaric to me, ripping a child from their family and sending them to live with strangers.

"It's so unbelievable that your grandmother thinks she saw her lost daughter after all this time. Can you imagine if that really was her?" Genevieve suddenly jumped up, waving her hands in the air as she frowned. "I forgot my manners. Do you want something to drink before I start grilling you like a murder suspect?"

I pressed my lips together to keep back my amusement. "I'm fine, don't worry. And I'm just as eager to see if you can help my grandmother." I looked at Simon. "Simon thought maybe you could help us by posting a description of the woman she saw in any Taichung Facebook groups you're a part of?"

"Of course." Genevieve nodded vigorously. "He only told us that your grandfather gave away your aunt when she was eighteen months old, and she never saw her again." She placed a hand over her heart. "I know what it's like losing a child. The agony and self-blame."

"I'm so sorry for your loss." My heart twisted, sorry too that this was bringing up memories of Genevieve's loss of her son, Ken.

"Thank you." She looked down for a moment and then back at me, her eyes resolute. "What do you know about your missing aunt?"

"The only thing my grandmother knew about the family who took her daughter was their surname." I gave Genevieve a brief overview of what my grandmother had told me. "As far as I know, they disappeared without a trace, and my grandmother has never been able to track them down."

"That's so sad." Genevieve brought her hands together in front of her chest. "I feel for your grandmother so deeply."

I was about to reply when another woman came rushing into the room. "I'm so sorry," she said, coming to our side. "That was work. They know I'm out of office because of my father, and yet, they still call with urgent questions." She rolled her eyes and turned her attention to me.

She was an attractive woman with salt-and-pepper hair who had just turned seventy-one, according to Simon, and was unwilling to retire. She had a sturdy build that gave off waves of authority. I imagined she was an attorney or business consultant by her no-nonsense air, and not an editor as Simon had told me.

"You must be Liv. Simon told us all about you. I'm Clare Shih." She reached over, and I stood to shake her hand. I winced at her grip. I knew instinctively she wasn't someone I ever wanted to cross.

"Thank you for having me over. I'm so sorry about your father." I sat back down after she'd let go of my hand.

She nodded to acknowledge my condolences. Then she turned to Genevieve. "Genny, you didn't put out the refreshments?" she scolded, heading for the kitchen. She opened the fridge and brought out a platter. "I've got fresh fruit and pastries and made iced tea."

She brought the platter to the coffee table before Genevieve could stand up.

"I did ask Liv if she wanted something to drink, and she said no," Genevieve said.

"I did." I was quick to jump in. "You don't need to go to the bother."

"Nonsense." Clare had already turned and returned to the fridge for a pitcher. Simon got up to help her bring in a tray of glasses. "It's not a bother." Clare poured a glass of tea and handed it to me. "We take care of our friends."

Once everyone was served, Clare finally sat down. "Tell me more about your grandmother."

I told her what I'd just told Genevieve.

"What's the surname of the family that your aunt was given to?" Clare asked before biting into the sweet potato ball in her hand.

"Ong," I said. I'd just taken a bite of a pineapple cake, and the buttery crust, mingled with the slight tang of the pineapple filling, had me rolling my eyes heavenward, so I didn't notice that Clare's face had darkened until I looked up at her sharp intake of breath.

"Ong." Clare's voice was low, but something in it made me pause in my chewing. "What's your grandmother's name?"

"Wang Yi-ping," I replied, wondering why Clare suddenly looked so stiff.

"Wang." Clare bit out the name and then put her plate down on the coffee table and stood abruptly, almost knocking over her glass. "Married to Wang Po-wei?"

I nodded. "Yes, that was my grandfather." I looked at her hopefully. "Do you know them?"

Clare stared at me for a few seconds as a range of emotions crossed her face. Fear, anger, disbelief, and something I couldn't decipher. I could feel Simon and Genevieve exchanging glances, probably wondering what was going on. I was about to ask Clare if everything was okay when she whirled away from me.

"We can't help you," she said in a dark voice. "I'm sorry. You need to go." And she left the room, leaving the three of us staring at each other in shock.

13
LIV

"What just happened?" I asked Simon after Genevieve had run out of the room, following Clare.

"I have no idea." His forehead was furrowed in confusion. "Clare is usually so forthcoming. And she said she wanted to help your grandmother."

"Do you think she knows Ah-Ma? Her attitude changed after I told her my grandmother's name." I put my glass of iced tea down, standing because I couldn't sit still. Clare had seemed so friendly and Genevieve so eager. Had I offended Clare somehow?

"How would they have known each other?" Simon stood too and started pacing. "You said your grandmother lived in the States from 1979 until recently, right?"

"Yes. She's been back here for about seven years." I thought for a moment. "How long has Clare been living here?"

"She moved back soon after attending college at Cornell." Simon turned to me. "All her siblings and her father, Ang-Li, stayed in the States, but Clare said she missed Taiwan. I think she moved back in 1976 or 1977?"

"So she could have known my grandmother before Ah-Ma moved to California." I was getting confused, trying to figure out the dates and timeline. But even if they knew each other, why had Clare reacted so strongly? As far as I knew, my grandmother had no enemies. Everyone who knew her loved her.

We stared at each other in silence and then swung our gazes toward the raised voices coming from a room at the back of the apartment.

I turned to Simon, my heart rate picking up. "I'm so sorry. I don't want to cause trouble. Especially since they're all mourning Ang-Li." I hated that it sounded like Clare and Genevieve were arguing because of me.

Simon was about to answer when a door slammed, making me jump, and Genevieve appeared. Her cheeks were flushed, her hands fluttering in the air.

"I'm sorry, Liv. You must think we're so rude." She stopped in front of me. "Clare apologizes also, but—" She looked over at Simon and then back at me. "Our family has had many relatives killed by the KMT, and she recognized your grandfather's name. She knows he was a KMT officer."

"Oh no." I covered my mouth in dismay. "I'm so sorry. I only found out my grandfather's side of the family were KMT a few days ago." I looked up as Simon walked to my side. "Simon told me your family is Green like his."

"Yes." Genevieve nodded. "Clare is a big advocate for a free Taiwan. She . . ." Genevieve glanced back at the doorway she'd come from. "She's so passionate about it, especially because it hits close to home."

"I understand." My voice came out as a whisper even as my body was poised to flee. The situation was uncomfortable, and I wanted nothing more than to leave this apartment. "I'm sorry to cause her more pain, especially in this hard time."

Genevieve had a helpless look on her face. "I really want to help you." Her fingers were knotted together, and she shifted from foot to foot. "But Clare is really against it. She doesn't want me to get involved."

"Okay." I pressed a hand to my chest, willing my heart rate to slow down. "I don't want to cause rifts in your family."

"No, it's not right." I was startled when Simon spoke up so forcibly. "I get that Clare has gone through things and has strong opinions about Taiwanese politics, but Liv's grandmother isn't to blame for what the KMT did."

"Simon . . ." I put a hand on his forearm. "It's okay." I didn't want him to be on the outs with his close family friends.

"No, it's not." His jaw tightened, and I felt even worse.

"I'm . . . I'm just going to go." I looked at the front door, wishing to flee. "I'll let you talk in private."

Simon nodded. "I'll call you later, okay?" He walked with me to the door after I'd bid Genevieve goodbye. He leaned in and gave me a quick hug. "I'm sorry."

"It's okay. It's not your fault." I had only a few seconds to enjoy his strong arms before he released me. I gave him a quick smile and then turned to the elevator with a sigh of relief as I pulled out my cell so I could call Ah-Ma and tell her not to come.

Twenty minutes later, I was in the car with my grandmother as Mr. Thomas drove us to Ziyi's apartment.

"Are you sure she's up to seeing me?" I asked Ah-Ma.

She told me Ziyi was fine (actually great) when she found her, and really just needed help to get off the floor. Ziyi asked about me, and my grandmother told her how I'd gone to see Simon's friends. Ah-Ma was on her way over in a taxi when I'd texted to tell her about Clare's strange reaction, so I'd waited for her to arrive, and now we were heading back to Ziyi's place.

"Yes. I was supposed to bring you to her after meeting Simon's friends, so now we're just going over a little earlier than planned." My grandmother looked over at me. "That's too bad about Clare. We might have to ask Ziyi for help."

"I know." I shook my head, still taken aback at Clare's strong reaction. I knew people got heated about politics, especially if things affected their family personally, but it seemed unfair for her to hold something against my grandmother just because she'd been married to a KMT official long ago.

When we got to Ziyi's building in the south of Taichung near the old train station, Ah-Ma led me into a compound of sorts through wide double metal gates. We stepped into a large courtyard that was in the middle of two buildings. Ah-Ma headed to the three-story one on the left.

"Ziyi lives here all by herself?" I glanced around, incredulous. The courtyard was lush with well-maintained plants and flowers, and the building to our right appeared to be some sort of office, at least on the first floor.

"No. This is her family compound. Her parents owned it, and relatives still run their business here. She lives in the apartment on the first floor with Ah-Ji." Ah-Ma led me into the building, and we paused in front of the door. She unlocked it with a key, then stepped aside to let me in first.

I walked into a big sparse room filled with what looked like antique wooden furniture. "I feel like we just went back in time." The room was filled with dark wood with intricately carved designs, some with flowers, others with dragons, serpents, and cranes. Much of the furniture was inlaid with marble and mother-of-pearl, including a coffee table, the backs of several chairs, and a long settee with red fabric cushions. Scrolls with mountains and birds, goddesses and flowers, hung on the walls, and one wall was taken up by a huge painting of ancient times.

"Ziyi," my grandmother called out. "We're here."

"Come in, come in," a voice called from a room in the back.

When we walked into Ziyi's bedroom, she was struggling to stand up from where she was seated on the side of the bed. My grandmother walked to her and said, "This is my granddaughter, Liv."

I reached out to shake her hand, but she beckoned me closer and then hugged me. "Oh, Liv. It's wonderful to meet you." Her grip was surprisingly strong, and I stayed in her embrace for a moment.

"So happy to meet you too," I said in English, even though she'd spoken in Mandarin. I smiled at this petite woman who, even though age had taken her youth, still shone with beauty and goodness. Her hair was all white and cut short to frame her face, and her smile was so warm I felt as if I were basking in sunlight. Despite the scars marring her face, I could see she'd been a beauty once.

"For you." Ziyi slipped a red envelope into my hand.

I flushed, accepting it with a bow of my head. It was tradition in Taiwan for the older generation to give the younger one a red envelope filled with money for luck. Ah-Ma had warned me not to turn them down, so just like I'd done with Mei-Mei, I thanked Ziyi and tucked it away in my purse.

"Help me up. Let's sit in the living room. Ah-Ji is making tea." She waved us over, and my grandmother and I helped her from either side.

"Ah-Ji." I nodded. "Your housekeeper, who now helps you out . . ." I trailed off, not wanting to remind Ziyi of what she'd been through.

"Yes. When my husband banished me to the country, he let Ah-Ji come with me." Ziyi's eyes were clear but had a defiant glint. "She's almost a decade younger than me and still as spry as ever."

"I'm so glad you had her," I said, even though I wondered what she meant by her husband banishing her. I looked over her head at my grandmother, who nodded, as if to say I would know more soon.

We settled Ziyi on the cushioned settee, and that was when I noticed a figure in the kitchen. I hadn't seen her when we came in because I'd been looking around. She came out with a tray and set it on the coffee table in front of us.

"I'm Ah-Ji," she said, beaming at me. She was taller than both Ziyi and my grandmother and looked much younger than her seventy-some years. "It's an honor to meet Yi-ping's granddaughter." She reached out and clasped my hand in hers for a moment.

My grandmother poured the tea and passed around the plate of delicate wafers with a strawberry cream in the middle. Ah-Ji sat down next to Ziyi, and there was silence for a moment as we sipped our tea. Then I filled them in on what had happened at Clare's place.

Ah-Ma turned to Ziyi. "I didn't want to bother you, but we might need your help posting on social media."

"Yi-ping." Ziyi's voice was firm. "You can bother me anytime you need. We've been searching for your daughter all these years. Why would you think I wouldn't help you now that you finally have a clue?"

"Oh." I didn't realize I'd said that out loud until Ziyi turned to me. Ziyi's dedication to my grandmother reminded me of the way Amy and I always had each other's backs. I wanted to embrace Ziyi for being so loyal to my grandmother.

"You really are the exact image of Yi-ping when she was your age." Ziyi spoke in perfect English.

"You speak English," I said, not able to contain my surprise.

"I do." She nodded, her eyes twinkling with mischief. "I speak many languages."

"That's wonderful." I looked back and forth between my grandmother and Ziyi. "I just think it's amazing how your friendship has lasted all these years."

My grandmother put her teacup down with a clatter. Her hands were shaking. "It didn't. We lost touch for many years. Over twelve years." When she turned to me, I was shocked at the grief etching her face. I also sensed another emotion, perhaps guilt?

"Yi-ping," Ziyi chided gently. "Stop that. I know you're blaming yourself again. I told you that I don't have regrets. Does she know?"

I looked back and forth between them, wondering what they were talking about, what I did or didn't know. I wanted to ask but held my breath instead, because my grandmother looked like she was in so much emotional pain.

"No." Ah-Ma shook her head.

Ziyi patted the couch next to her. "Come, Liv. Sit here."

I got up and walked to her side. When I sat down, she studied my face, as if trying to memorize every feature. I held still when she touched my cheek gently. "What I do, everything I stand for, is so that young people like you may have a better future. I know things are different in America, and I'm glad you can live life the way you want."

I stared at her, mesmerized by her timeless beauty.

"You and me, we're connected by your grandmother," Ziyi said. She took one of my hands and held it. "Yi-ping has told me so much about you over the years. It's an honor to finally meet you."

I glanced at my grandmother briefly, not wanting to say out loud that I hadn't known Ziyi existed until a few days ago. "I'm so honored to meet you too," was all I said. I knew this moment was important, but I didn't know why.

"I'm glad you're in Taiwan." Ziyi's hand in mine was warm. "To understand our story better, I'll tell you what happened to me after I helped Yi-ping leave Taiwan." She stopped and pressed her lips together for a moment. "But it is not a pleasant story." She looked over at Ah-Ji, who patted her on the thigh. "Please don't feel sorry for me. Or condemn me. I survived, and Ah-Ji and I did what we had to."

I felt my stomach drop, already anticipating something terrible.

"Are you sure, Ziyi?" my grandmother asked. There was a hint of warning in her voice, and I turned to her.

"I trust her, just like I trust you." Ziyi looked into my eyes, and I saw that was true. "But are *you*?" She pointed to me. "Are you sure you want to hear it? I have been keeping a dark secret for many years, and the only one who knew was Ah-Ji." She looked over at my grandmother. "And then Yi-ping, when we reconnected."

I looked at each of the three women, and for some reason, my skin tingled, a harbinger of whatever doom was about to be spoken aloud. The room filled with a heavy silence as they studied me, and I knew whatever Ziyi had to say, I wanted to hear it. I gave her a slight nod.

Ziyi let go of my hand and leaned back against the cushion. "Yi-ping said that she told you some of my story."

"Yes." I waited, not wanting to rush her.

"I helped Yi-ping get a passport and visa to leave Taiwan when Winston left for Stanford."

"Yes," I said again, remembering what my grandmother had told me.

"About a month after Yi-ping was safely in California, my husband found out I was the one who'd helped her escape." Ziyi smiled at Ah-Ji when her companion once again patted her on the leg. "My husband almost killed me that day."

14
ZIYI

October 1979, Taichung

I had many acquaintances, friends even, but I didn't trust most of them. There were only two people in the entire world that I would trust with my life: Ah-Ji and Yi-ping. When Yi-ping came to me, asking for my help, of course I said yes. She wasn't asking for much, since I'd done the same for many others, but this favor for my friend would alter my life forever.

Yi-ping and I were walking arm in arm down the street of a crowded market. We were heading for a shaved-ice shop because, even though it was fall, it was a brutally hot day. Sweat trickled down my back and dampened my shirt, and all I could think of was that first bite of cold, cold ice, sweetened by the brown sugar water drizzled over it.

"I have to go," she said.

"Go? Where?" I looked around, wondering if there was a store she wanted to visit.

She gave a slight shake of her head. "Leave Taiwan. Leave my husband."

I stopped walking to stare at her for a moment. "You mean . . . divorce Po?" I knew she was unhappy in the Wang household, but she'd never said anything about leaving Po.

She shook her head vehemently, tears pooling in her eyes. She quickly swiped a hand over them and kept walking toward the shaved-ice shop, now in view. She didn't say anything more until we'd settled at a table in the back corner, sitting next to each other with a large mound of shaved ice between us.

"Po would never agree to a divorce," she said in a low voice before putting a spoonful of ice and tapioca pearls into her mouth. She chewed and then said, "No one in their family has ever gotten one. He'd be disgraced."

Now I understood why she'd wanted to walk in the heat to get ice. I'd said no, not wanting to go out into the street, where the pavement felt like it was baking any humans who dared to walk across it. Whenever we needed to talk in private, we did it out in public, never in our homes. We didn't know who was listening, even in the places that were supposed to be our sanctuaries.

"Then what do you mean? Where would you go?" I asked again, the ice forgotten for a moment as my eyes searched her face.

She swallowed and then looked me in the eyes. "I mean, just leave. Disappear one day. I've stayed all these years because of my children. But now they're all grown and spread out across the United States. I don't even have a dog. It's time for me to go."

I sat back and clapped my hands together softly. "Good for you. You've finally grown a backbone."

She flushed and looked down at the ice, stabbing her spoon in to catch a mound of grass jelly this time. "I can't stay. I've never forgiven Po for giving Yili away. I'm nothing in that household. They treat me well enough, especially Mei Mei, but I can't do what I want."

"What do you want?" I asked. Yi-ping was usually reserved, always doing what was expected of her. I was happy to see her asserting herself.

"Independence." She looked up at that. "I'm only forty-one years old. I still have at least half of my life left, if I'm lucky. I don't want to stay in the Wang household for the rest of my life, under their control." Her voice grew stronger as she stared off at a spot above my head. "I want to be near my children and help raise my grandchildren when they start coming. I want to do and say what I want, without worrying about repercussions from the Wangs."

I looked at my friend with pride. She'd always been the more timid of the two of us, and I'd often had to coax her to step out of her comfort zone. I never in a million years thought she would find the courage to talk about leaving her husband.

"Good for you," I said again softly, but she wasn't listening to me.

"Lun-Shan said I can live with them." Her oldest, now twenty-four and out of college, had gotten married two years ago and had recently bought a house in California with her husband.

"You've thought this through." Again, I was surprised. But I shouldn't have been. I'd always known my friend had an inner core of strength and that it would come out one day. It appeared this was the day.

"I have." She turned to me, and I was glad to see the determined glint in her eyes. "I've always wanted to go to America, ever since Lun-Shan left for university." She grasped my hands in hers. "I can't stay here, waiting for Yili. She's never coming home."

"Is that what's been keeping you here?" I gave her a gentle squeeze.

"That and because I had to stay until Winston was grown." She let go of my hands and took another spoonful of ice. "I had to stay here in case she somehow found her way home."

"We wondered if they'd gone to America. The woman in the medicine store said they left Taiwan and were never coming back." I remembered the hopeless look in Yi-ping's eyes when she told me what the woman had said, and her fear that if they left the country, Yi-ping might never see her daughter again.

Yi-ping's eyes went glassy. "Maybe I'll see her in America." She paused and then said, "When Po refused to name her with Lun as the first part of her name, I should have known he had no intention of keeping her." It was a tradition in a lot of Taiwanese families to name their children with the same first part of their given name. Yi-ping had named Yili after herself.

"Maybe you will." Miracles did happen, after all. I finally picked up my spoon and took a scoop of the ice. It was so cool and refreshing that I dug in for another bite. I was relishing the cold treat, so I didn't realize something was worrying Yi-ping until I looked up.

She was biting her bottom lip, chewing at it in a way that told me she was contemplating whether to speak her mind.

"What is it?" I reached out and touched her hand briefly.

She seemed to be battling with herself, and I waited for her to speak. "I need help getting a passport and visa. My husband will never agree to get me one." She bit her lip harder after she said that.

"I see." And I did. "You want me to ask my friend in the embassy."

"Forget it." A flush rose on Yi-ping's face, and she swatted at the air in front of her as if there were an annoying insect. "I'm sorry I even brought it up. I know you can't."

I knew she was thinking about what had happened the last time I'd asked my old schoolmate for help in getting a visa for someone. I rubbed my ribs, which still ached sometimes, a reminder of my husband's wrath.

"I'll figure it out," Yi-ping said before I could say anything. Her cheeks were bright red, as if she'd taken a shot of whiskey. She tried to change the subject. "What are you going to do for Weili's birthday? I think you should—"

"Yi-ping." I held up a hand to stop her flustered words. "I would do anything for you. Of course I'll ask my friend."

"Ziyi, I'm sorry. I'm being selfish." Her face was scrunched with guilt. "You can't risk making your husband angry. I won't let you."

"I was young and stupid back then. I met my friend in public, where anyone could have seen us." I gave her a grim smile. "And they did, and of course reported to my husband." I tapped the side of my head. "I'm wiser now. How do you think I've gotten passports and visas for people who needed to leave the country since then?"

"You . . ." She stared at me with her lips parted. "You did?"

I'd never told her about my work getting women and children out of the country after their husbands had been persecuted. But I had thought she'd known, if only because we knew each other so well.

"We can do this." My mind was already working on her dilemma. "Get you out of the country and to your children." I knew how much she missed them as, one by one, they left for university in America, instead of staying here in Taiwan. She'd wanted them to go, to get away from the political instability and the fear our country lived under.

"No. I can't put you in that kind of danger again." Her voice was firm. "Forget I said anything."

"No, Yi-ping. I can help you. Trust me."

She looked at me, her eyes wide, and we didn't speak for a few seconds. "Are you sure?" she asked in a soft voice.

"Yes. I won't get caught. I haven't all these years." I lifted my chin. "And even if there's a chance that I do, I would still help you. You know that."

We stayed like that for a moment until she said, "And I would do anything for you too."

I nodded and focused back on the ice. "We need to eat this before it melts."

"I'll miss you." Yi-ping said it so softly that I almost didn't hear it.

"We will always be friends, no matter where we live. Distance can't change that. But you deserve to have a life."

"Thank you, Ziyi. I owe you." Yi-ping's face was filled with gratitude.

I brushed aside her thanks, not realizing that in three months, I would trade my freedom for hers.

January 1980, Taichung and southern Taiwan

I didn't see his fist coming. I'd just returned home from visiting our daughter Weili, who'd just had her first child, my first grandchild! I was humming to myself as I unlocked the front door, still smelling that perfect baby scent in my nose, remembering the happy gurgles coming from my granddaughter. I closed the door softly behind me because my husband hated it when anyone slammed a door. I turned, and my cheek connected with his fist in a loud crack.

My hands flew to my face as I fell, and then he was kicking me, stomping on me with his heavy boots. I didn't make a sound at first, as I was used to this, but then a soft cry escaped my lips when I saw him pick up a lamp.

"How dare you," he said as spittle flew from his lips, his eyes dark and hard. "You helped Po's wife leave Taiwan without his permission. You have disgraced my friend."

My eyes opened wide, and I wondered how he'd found out. I had thought I'd been so discreet. I'd covered my tracks, making sure there were no records, nothing to tie me to Yi-ping's disappearance. We'd even stowed her bags at the home of a neighbor who'd been out of town and asked me to water her plants, without my husband's knowledge.

My husband continued to rail at me, calling me names as he pummeled me with his fists, with his feet. The lamp crashed on my head, and then everything went black.

When I came to, I found Ah-Ji hovering over me. I could barely open my eyes, and only tried because she was calling my name so urgently.

"Ziyi. He's gone, you're safe for now." Ah-Ji was sobbing, her hands fluttering lightly over me. I moaned because even her light touch sent shock waves through my body.

My entire being ached, inside and out, and sharp pain pierced me every time I took a breath. I couldn't lift my left hand, and my head hurt so badly I had to close my eyes again.

"He's gone?" I managed to get out.

"For now. I stopped him from killing you. But he's sending you away." Ah-Ji's sobs grew louder. "He won't let me take you to the hospital."

"Where am I going?" My voice was slurred, and I wondered at that.

"Somewhere south, to a remote village. He said he can't stand to look at you."

"He can't send me away." I let out a sigh, wishing I could go to sleep.

"Ziyi, open your eyes. You have to stay awake." Ah-Ji shook me gently by the shoulders, making my head spin.

"Stop." My eyes fluttered open again, only to find her staring at me in fear. "He'll calm down; he always does."

"I don't think so." Her eyes filled. "You didn't hear what he said—"

She broke off as the front door banged open and my husband appeared. Ah-Ji shrank back away from me and stared at him, fear making her entire body tremble.

My husband strode to my side and gave me a kick in disgust. I curled around my middle, trying to protect myself. "The car will be here soon. If you try to come back, I'll kill one of our children. If you try to contact Po-wei's wife in America, I will find her and have her killed. Do you understand me?"

I forced my eyes open to look at him, but I didn't say a word. I wouldn't let him see how I was trembling inside.

"I never want to see you again. I'll tell everyone you've fallen ill and had to go away." He turned, and that was when I called out in desperation.

"You can't do that. No one will believe you." My words came out garbled. I tried to sit, but everything spun, and I slumped to the ground.

He whirled back at me. "Oh, they'll believe me. You're going down south, far away, and if you try to come back or contact our children, you'll live to regret it."

For the first time, real fear hit me like a hammer. He knew our children were everything to me. He knew how happy I was that our daughter had had our first grandchild, and how I looked forward to spoiling her. If ever there was a way to punish me, this was it. But did I believe him? Would he really harm one of our own children, just to get back at me?

We stared at each other for a few moments, the only sound in the room coming from Ah-Ji's ragged breathing. And that's when I saw the truth in his eyes: He was cruel enough that he would do just that, if only to hurt me in the worst way possible. He wasn't wired like a normal person. He could and would do terrible things to his own flesh and blood, and to Yi-ping, just to get back at me. I saw the moment he realized I knew he'd spoken the truth. A small smile curved his lips, so evil and smug that I wished I had a gun. I would have shot him between the eyes without hesitation.

"She needs a doctor," Ah-Ji said softly. "She can't travel that far in her condition."

My husband glared at her. "Then you can go with her and take care of her. The car will be here in half an hour." He turned to me and stooped down so he was at my eye level. "Remember what I said."

I stared back at him defiantly, not looking away or flinching, even though my vision was blurred and there seemed to be two of him. I wouldn't let him see my grief, or my pain, or my fear about where he was sending me. He might own me, but he wouldn't defeat me. I glared at him until he gave me a light slap across the face, stood, and then was gone with a loud bang of the door. Only then did I collapse back on the floor, the grief overpowering me at the thought of not being able to see my children again, or watch my granddaughter grow up.

Ah-Ji was by my side in seconds. "I'll go with you. I'll take care of you." She had no family; she was an orphan whom my husband's family had brought in as a maid when she was only a teenager.

"Go pack a bag for us," I whispered. "You know what we need."

She pulled away to comply, but I reached out and grabbed a hand. "Thank you." We stared at each other, and then she was gone.

The trip down south took over three hours, and the only saving grace was that my husband had sent a small van used to transport groups of people, so I was able to lie down in the back seat. Everything hurt, and Ah-Ji had cleaned me up as best she could. I suspected my wrist was broken as well as a rib or two. I probably had a concussion too, and my face was so swollen I felt like a balloon. When I started coughing up blood, Ah-Ji made a sound of distress.

"You need a doctor," she said, stating the obvious.

I was so tired and full of pain that I couldn't speak. My eyelids felt as heavy as rocks, and I drifted on and off. Every once in a while, Ah-Ji would yell at me to stay awake. I knew she was afraid that if I went to sleep, I wouldn't wake up.

I wondered about the driver as we bumped along. He had barely looked at me when he strode into my home and picked me up to carry me to the van, Ah-Ji hovering close by. He was surprisingly gentle for such a big man. He'd laid me on the back bench and then gone to the driver's side without a word to either of us. I wondered what he thought of my state, as he didn't seem surprised. Perhaps he was hired to take away battered women all the time.

Finally, finally, we reached our destination, a remote village in the middle of southern Taiwan. I didn't even know what it was called. The streets were unpaved, and the driver pulled up to a little shack in the middle of nowhere. Silently, the driver unloaded the bags that Ah-Ji had packed, with clothes, prized possessions, food, and a first aid kit. Then he carried me out of the van and into the house, depositing me on the threadbare couch that sat in the middle of the room. Without a word he turned and drove off, leaving us alone.

Ah-Ji looked around and found a wall switch, and we both sighed in relief when a light turned on. At least we had electricity. We were in a square room, with one end being a small kitchen and the opposite a living area where the couch and an armchair were. There was a table with two chairs, but other than that, it was bare. No televisions, no phones, no radios. I glimpsed a door on one side, which I assumed housed the bed and, hopefully, a bathroom.

Ah-Ji came to my side and knelt next to the sofa. "You need a doctor."

I heard her as if from a tunnel far away, and my eyes closed again. Someone was moaning, and it wasn't until Ah-Ji took my hand gently and started making "shh" sounds that I realized it was me.

"I won't leave you," she said. "I'll stay with you, make sure you're okay."

I wanted to protest, to say that she couldn't sit on the hard ground all night, but sleep pulled at me, and I moaned again in pain. My body felt as if it were on fire, knife strokes stabbing my flesh every time I took a breath or shifted my weight. I wanted to die, if only to end the agony. I drifted in and out, not sure what was real and what wasn't, my world condensed to the pounding of my head and the waves of sharp shooting pain that washed over me.

Hours later (or it could have been minutes), the front door banged open, waking me and startling Ah-Ji. It was our driver, accompanied by an old man with a long white beard. The old man came to my side and, with gentle hands, started to examine me. I protested, wanting to push him away, but I couldn't even move a hand to do so.

"He'll fix her," I heard the driver murmuring to Ah-Ji, and then he said a few more words I didn't catch.

"He's a healer?" Ah-Ji asked.

The driver's answer was unintelligible as I felt my eyes flutter shut, too weak to keep them open. I gave myself over to the man's ministrations.

The next few days passed in a blur. I found out later that the driver had gone to find this old man who practiced traditional Chinese medicine in the village and brought him back to our hut with his supplies. I never saw the driver again, but I wondered at his kindness, but also if he'd done this before: brought the healer to patch up someone my husband had beaten up. I felt sure that I would have died that night if he hadn't brought the old man, known by all as Lao Bo. I owed that driver my life.

Lao Bo made me drink some nasty fluids, placed compresses on me, and muttered over me as I slipped in and out of consciousness. I burned with a fever and my ribs hurt, and he set my broken wrist. Ah-Ji was always there, coaxing me to drink broth, helping me to relieve myself when I needed, and watching over me. Pain became a constant, always with me even in sleep, as I dreamed about my children and grandchild, thinking this was all a nightmare and that I'd awaken tomorrow back in my own bed.

But when I opened my eyes on the seventh day, my mind clear for the first time since arriving, I was confronted by the meager offerings of the simple hut. My heart sank as I looked around and knew that this was my reality now. I had no idea my husband apparently owned this place, but there was much I didn't know about him. I gave myself a moment to grieve, to feel sorry for my plight, and to wallow in pity. But then I took a breath and steeled my spine. I wouldn't allow him to win. I would bide my time, put my brain to use, and figure out how to get my life back. He couldn't keep me here forever. He couldn't keep me from my children and grandchild. He was going to learn that a mother's love was stronger than even the evilest of men.

It took twelve years. Ah-Ji and I adapted, once I finally healed, and lived a simple life in the country together, learning to make do with what we had. We taught the village children to read and write and were welcomed into the small community. I missed my children and grandchild every day, and prayed to the gods and goddesses that they were safe. I thought of my friend Yi-ping, so far away in America, probably frantic with worry that she couldn't get in touch with me. But I dared not even write her a letter because I believed my husband when he said he would have her killed if I contacted her. The KMT had reach in America, and I would not risk her life.

Even in this remote village, we heard about the massacre of a prominent pro-democracy politician's family less than two months after we were brought here. I had nightmares about the six-year-old twin girls of the jailed man who were stabbed to death, as well as his mother. What kind of country did we live in that they would murder innocent children and women? My heart bled for the third daughter, a nine-year-old who had survived. I longed to gather my children in my arms and protect my grandchild, but how could I, when I was banished here, and the very person who should be protecting them could very well harm them? I thought of Yi-ping often and wrote her long letters that I never sent. I didn't blame her because I knew if it weren't for what I'd done for her, something else would have set my husband off.

Over the years, Ah-Ji sometimes caught a ride back to Taichung with someone who was visiting our neighbors, and she was able to get messages to my daughter. I was afraid to contact my son, since I knew he would tell his father. Weili wanted to call me, for she'd been frantic with worry when I disappeared, but we didn't have a phone in the hut. I'd sent a note telling her to stay away, but she arrived out of nowhere one day about five years after I'd been banished. I was outside hanging our wash on a clothesline, and I dropped the basket when I saw her get out of the passenger side of a car. Her husband was in the driver's seat.

"Mama," Weili cried, and she rushed to me with her arms open wide.

I couldn't speak, but tears spilled out of my eyes as I held her tight. I thought I'd never see her again. "How did you get away without Baba knowing?" For I remembered my husband's threat to kill one of our children if I ever dared to see them.

She pulled away and showed me her rounded stomach. "I'm pregnant again. Our third. I told Baba I had complications and needed to see a doctor down south. My husband backed me up and drove me here." He stood to the side, eyeing us with concern.

"This is dangerous." I looked around and quickly hustled them into our cottage, where Ah-Ji cried out in surprise at seeing them. We sat together on the couch, my daughter and I, holding hands. "If he finds out you were here . . ." I trailed off, wondering if anyone in the village was a spy for my husband. I wanted to enjoy this unexpected time with my daughter, but worry clouded our reunion, and I wanted her as far away from here as possible. My husband always found out. "You can't come again. I don't want anything to happen to you or your *di di*."

Weili's jaw tightened, and a stubborn look crossed her face. She'd always been a headstrong child, and this quality had stayed with her into adulthood. "How can he keep you away from my brother and me like this? I have a right to see you."

I looked at her, anguish filling my heart. What could I do? I had no rights. I had to make Weili understand that she needed to be careful. She believed her father would never harm her or her younger brother, but I knew different.

"Yi-ping has called me multiple times." Weili focused her gaze on me.

I caught my breath. "How is she?"

"She's good. But she's out of her mind with worry for you. She thinks something she made you do must be responsible for your disappearance." Weili pressed her lips together. "I didn't know where you were either at first, so we commiserated together. But then when Ah-Ji told me . . ." She looked away. "I hated lying to her, so I started avoiding her calls."

"Poor Yi-ping." I sighed out a breath. How I longed to let my friend know I was fine. That this wasn't a bad life, and that I was making a difference in the village children's lives.

Weili turned back to me, her eyes flashing. "Poor Yi-ping? Really? If what she said is true, she put you here." Her chest heaved with anger, and I laid a hand on her forearm.

"No, Weili. Your father put me here. It wasn't Yi-ping. Don't be angry at her." I didn't want us to argue in what precious time we had together, so I changed the subject.

We had a few hours together, and she showed me pictures of my granddaughter and grandson, making me cry again at missing his birth.

She gave me a photo album and then, with reluctance, embraced me one last time before getting into the car with her husband. I told her not to come again, but she did a few more times, spread out over the years. I never knew when she'd show up, and each time, I was sure my husband would discover the truth and carry out his threat. But nothing happened for years, and I was buoyed by these infrequent trips of my daughter's, who filled me in on what was happening back in Taichung. I thought we'd found a way to see each other without my husband knowing.

Until one day, twelve years after Ah-Ji and I left Taichung, a car roared up to our hut, and a young man jumped out. He pounded on our front door, and when I flung it open, I stared at him. He was panting as if he'd just run a race.

"Weili's in the hospital," he said once he'd caught his breath.

I gasped, and my hands flew to my mouth. I knew then my husband had found out that Weili had been visiting me. "What happened?"

"Your husband hurt her. He was kicking her in the side when Weili's husband came home unexpectedly. He fought off your husband and called an ambulance. He sent me to tell you." The young man took the glass of water Ah-Ji offered him with a grateful nod.

He spoke more words, but I didn't hear them. Ah-Ji met my eyes over his head, and I knew it was time. I'd stayed away to protect my children and grandchildren, but I always knew what I'd have to do if he ever harmed any of them. He could beat me, hurt me, almost kill me, but I wouldn't allow him to hurt them. It was time to put an end to his tyranny.

15
LIV

I looked from Ziyi to my grandmother, to Ah-Ji, and then back to Ziyi again. I knew my mouth was hanging open, but I couldn't help it. When I finally got my lips working again, I choked out, "What did you do?"

Ziyi and Ah-Ji looked at each other before Ziyi focused back on me. "Are you sure you want to know?"

My heart skidded in my chest, and I drew in a sharp breath. Did I? By their reaction, I feared the worst. In my gut, I already knew the answer, but Ziyi was giving me an out. No one spoke, and I looked at these three women, each strong in her own way, and couldn't imagine a world such as they'd described.

"We don't need to go into details." Ah-Ma stood suddenly and jolted me out of the trance I'd fallen into. "Who wants more tea?" She picked up the teapot, but no one held out their cups.

"How did you do it?" I didn't realize I'd spoken out loud until all three turned to me.

Ziyi held my gaze for a moment, and I didn't look away. She gave a small nod and then said, "The medicine man, Lao Bo, who saved my life. He didn't ask questions." Ziyi spoke quietly, and one hand smoothed the hair away from her face. "He said to me, 'I'm a healer, not a killer.

But I remember the state you were in when you arrived. Whatever you need this for, I know you think you have no other choice.'"

"But how . . ." I wasn't sure what I was asking. How had she done it? How could she have done it? Never in a million years did I think that this was what Ziyi was going to tell me.

"He hurt my child. I had to protect her, and my grandchildren, as he'd go for them next. I had to protect my son-in-law, who'd stepped in to protect his wife." Ziyi's voice was quiet but fierce, as if she'd taken my question as an attack on her morals.

"Ziyi did what she had to." My grandmother spoke up. "Don't judge her until you've been in her shoes."

"I'm not judging." I held up both hands. "I'm just . . . shocked." I blinked a few times, as if that would clear my head.

"I was still friendly with some of the household staff," Ah-Ji said. "Her husband didn't care about me. He didn't even recognize me when he saw me talking to one of the staff outside on the street." Ah-Ji gave a mirthless laugh. "It was easy. His quest for anything that would make him heathier, stronger, was well known in the household. I told the staff the powder was for improved virility and health, so expensive that it was only for the man of the house. No one ever suspected, not even the person who gave him the tea. We didn't want them to have his death on their conscience."

"But . . ." I thought back to what Ah-Ma had told me. "He died of a heart attack."

"He did." Ziyi was still holding my hand, had been holding it through her entire tale, and now she gave it a light squeeze. "There was never any question."

"I'm sorry, Liv." I could see the worry lines on my grandmother's forehead. "We shouldn't have told you—"

I cut her off. "No. It's okay." I had wanted to understand what had happened. It was more than I'd bargained for, but really, what was I going to do? Turn an eighty-eight-year-old woman and her companion in for killing her husband over thirty years ago? I had no proof, only the words they weren't exactly saying, and the old healer must be dead by now.

I'd always thought I had a good sense of right and wrong, and never imagined that I would have thought it was "okay" to kill someone, even if he had done horrible things. My brain tossed around phrases like "self-defense" and "premeditated murder" and "moral dilemma" and "moral compass" until I wanted to squeeze my head and make the thoughts stop.

"I blame myself for what happened to Ziyi." My grandmother's voice broke into my whirling thoughts. "If she hadn't helped me, none of this would have happened. It was selfish of me to ask for her help."

Ziyi made an impatient sound with her tongue. "And I've told you it's not your fault. If it weren't for what I did for you, it would have been something else sooner or later. He was a time bomb just waiting to go off, and I never knew what would set him off." She shook her head and brushed one hand against the other. "What's done is done. I can't change the past, and neither can you. But we can try to change the future for you."

"Is this why you became so involved with human rights and women's rights in Taiwan?" Ah-Ma had told me Ziyi worked tirelessly to get laws changed, to protect women and children and those who couldn't defend themselves. She also worked with victims directly, getting them medical and mental help when they didn't have access, even taking in people herself who were fleeing a violent situation. There were often grumblings in the government about her, but because she'd been the wife of a high-level officer, they mostly left her alone. The compound where she lived had been vandalized once, someone splashing pigs' blood on the gates outside, then throwing feathers all over it so it resembled a poultry massacre.

"Yes. We were powerless back then to stop what was happening to us, but things are changing. They are slower to change here in Taiwan than they are in the United States." She gestured to Ah-Ji. "Can you get my laptop, please?" She turned to my grandmother. "You should have come to me as soon as you thought you saw your daughter."

I blinked at her sudden change in topic. I guessed our conversation about what had happened to Ziyi's husband was over.

Ah-Ma pressed her lips together. "You've done more than enough for me. What you've been through, Ziyi."

Ah-Ji came back with the laptop and handed it to Ziyi. Ziyi opened it and went to her Facebook.

"What did the woman look like?" she asked, all business now.

Ah-Ma described the woman as best she could, including what she was wearing and the heart-shaped birthmark behind her left ear.

Ziyi posted the description to several pages and then looked at us. "Done. Now we wait and hope someone knows who this is." She gave a great yawn, covering her mouth with a hand.

"You're tired." Ah-Ma went to Ziyi's side. "Let's get you back to bed."

"I could use a nap." Ziyi didn't protest as Ah-Ma helped her to stand.

I stood also and followed behind as they walked back to the bedroom. Once Ziyi was settled in bed, I leaned down to give her a hug. "I'm so glad to have met you." I looked into her eyes, and I didn't see a murderer. I saw a woman who had been through terrible things, who loved her children and grandchildren and would do anything to protect them.

She patted me on the cheek. "Thank you, dear Liv."

Ah-Ma and I closed the door behind us gently, and after saying goodbye to Ah-Ji, we went out to meet Mr. Thomas. My phone dinged right as we got into the car.

"It's Simon." I typed a message back and then looked at Ah-Ma. "He wants to meet us at your place. Is that okay?"

"Of course." Ah-Ma and I exchanged a look, and I knew she was thinking about Clare's reaction when she'd found out who my grandmother was.

As we pulled into the street where Ah-Ma lived, I could see Simon standing in front of the building. My heart gave a skip, and a glow lit up in my chest. I leaned toward the window, drawn to him as if by some invisible force, yearning to be next to him, but also feeling too fragile and broken to even think about starting anything with anyone. But I couldn't help the way my body was reacting. As soon as the car stopped, I opened the car door and hopped out.

"Simon. You got here fast." I stopped in front of him, and we stared at each other for a moment. His mouth was tilted in a crooked smile, and I longed to run my hands through his dark hair. I took a step toward him, forgetting about Ah-Ma and Mr. Thomas behind me. We would have touched, but then a loud bang came from somewhere on the busy street perpendicular to the one we were on.

I immediately crouched down, my arms over my head. My breath quickened until I was gasping for air and blood rushed to my ears, deafening me. I couldn't breathe. My vision darkened and panic gripped me, making me immobile. It was as if I knew I had to move, get out of there, but my body had become locked, frozen in place. I felt arms around me and a voice in my ear. My teeth were gritted together so hard my jaw ached. I was going to die.

Slowly, I realized it was Simon talking to me, much like he'd done at the airport. Slowly, I realized I'd given in to my panic again, just when I thought I was getting better. And even more slowly, I realized I'd humiliated myself again in front of this man I was so inexplicably drawn to. My arms came away from my head when I could finally move, and I lifted my face to meet his eyes. I took in a deep breath and released it in a sigh. Dimly, I saw Ah-Ma and Mr. Thomas hovering just behind Simon, gazing at me in concern.

"It was just a car backfiring," Simon was saying to me. He stroked a hand down my hair, and when he saw I was coming out of my panic attack, he drew me against his chest, wrapping me in his arms. I leaned into him, so grateful to have his arms around me, his solid presence and firm chest literally holding me together.

I wanted to stay like that forever, but too soon, he let go and stood. He helped me up, and I looked at Ah-Ma sheepishly. "I'm sorry."

"Liv, don't be sorry." She reached out and took me in her arms. "I didn't know you were still suffering like this."

I blew out a breath. "I thought I was doing better. I've been able to go out with you and Simon in crowds." I shook my head and pulled away. "I'm so embarrassed."

"You have nothing to be embarrassed about." She held both my arms in her hands so that I had to look at her. "Okay, now?"

I nodded. She turned to Mr. Thomas to reassure him everything was fine, and with a wave, he got back in the car and drove off.

"I was going to see if I could take you both out for dinner," Simon said, shifting from one foot to the other. "I wanted to talk to you."

Ah-Ma looked at me and then turned to Simon. "I think maybe Liv should stay in."

I couldn't imagine going out where there were a lot of people and was grateful my grandmother understood this. "I'm sorry. I can't."

"Why don't I go pick up some food then, and bring it back here?" Simon suggested.

"Perfect." My grandmother and Simon debated on what to get, and then he took off as Ah-Ma and I went inside. I sank onto the couch, grateful for the quiet and the walls enclosing me, keeping me safe.

An hour later, we sat around Ah-Ma's table as we finished the *orh ah mee sua*, an oyster and vermicelli soup, that Simon had brought back from one of my grandmother's favorite stands.

"I'm so sorry about Clare." Simon made a face as he spooned the last of his thick soup into his mouth. "I tried to get her to change her mind, but she refused."

"It's okay." I looked at Ah-Ma, who nodded. "We understand. Ziyi posted in the various groups she belongs to for us."

Simon nodded and then got up to help Ah-Ma put the leftovers in the fridge. I stayed seated at the table, my body suddenly feeling as if it weighed a ton. It'd been a day, with Clare's reaction, Ziyi's revelation, and my most recent panic attack. The thought of going through my nightly ritual before getting in bed was too much. Simon must have noticed my fatigue because he gestured to the door.

"I'll get out of your way. You look like you need to go to bed." He came to my side, and I leaned into him, our bodies pressed together. "You okay?"

I nodded, reaching out to take his hand. "Thank you again. This is becoming a very embarrassing routine. Me freaking out, you talking me out of my panic."

I could feel him looking at me, even though I didn't turn to meet his gaze.

"Have you talked to someone?" His voice was low, so only I could hear. "A therapist?"

I pressed my lips together, wondering if he was talking as a psychotherapist, or as my friend. "No. They gave me a name, but I never called."

He hesitated for a breath. "Maybe you should."

A spark of irritation lit inside me, which I knew was irrational since he was only trying to help. And maybe it was my humiliation rearing its ugly head, but I felt as though he was analyzing me like a patient. I shook my head, not daring to speak, because I wasn't sure what would come out.

He took his hand from mine. "Okay. I won't press." He leaned down and gave me a quick kiss on the cheek. "Get some rest. I'll talk to you tomorrow?"

I nodded, still unwilling to speak. I felt like a child who was angry at her parent because she'd been reprimanded, no matter how gently. I knew it was childish, but I was drowning in mortification. I, someone who was usually so strong and independent, had succumbed to my fears in front of a man I was starting to have feelings for. Twice. I refused to look at him, and after he said goodbye to my grandmother, I heard the front door open and then shut. Only then did I let out the breath I didn't know I was holding and sank into the chair, my entire body vibrating with a nervous energy that I didn't know what to do with.

16
LIV

Two days later, Ah-Ma and I were in her kitchen, tackling more recipes from her old cookbook. She had given me the okay to tell our audience about her search for her daughter, and I'd taped myself updating everyone. I told the camera that we had decided to make the *lo neng* and *khong bah png*, stewed egg and braised pork belly over rice. It would take some time for them to stew, and since we had nothing planned for the day, it was the perfect time for this recipe. I had my camera set up on a stand to videotape the entire procedure.

"These are ready." Ah-Ma took the pot of eggs off the stove and drained it before filling it again with cold water. I helped her peel the eggs.

"Do you stew the eggs with the meat at the same time?" I was looking at the cookbook as I worked, wishing I could read it.

"No. We'll make the sauce next, and then let the eggs cook in it until they turn brown." Ah-Ma had placed soy sauce, star anise, cinnamon, shallots, garlic, and rock sugar on the counter and now started putting them into the pot. "I also like to add cooking wine." She looked at the camera. "Since it simmers for hours, the alcohol cooks off, so don't worry about giving this to your children."

"You perfected this recipe with Yili in mind?" My voice was gentle.

My grandmother nodded. "She wasn't old enough to eat this before she disappeared." She bowed her head, and even I could see the emotion emanating from her.

I grabbed the cooking wine out of a cabinet and held it up close to the camera, giving Ah-Ma time to compose herself. "How much should I add?" I started to pour some in, and Ah-Ma looked up, letting me know when to stop.

I picked up my phone so that I could videotape the inside of the pot. I stirred everything together with one hand while holding the camera with the other, until the sugar had melted and the mixture had thickened. Ah-Ma took the eggs and gently slid them into the sauce.

"We have to keep stirring them so that they get evenly coated and don't stick to each other." Ah-Ma nodded at my technique. "Just like that. Ever so gently, letting every part of each egg soak up that sauce."

I continued stirring, switching hands when one got tired, until Ah-Ma was finally satisfied with the shade of brown of the eggs. The sauce was thick, and I leaned down to inhale it, remembering the scent from my childhood, when my grandmother used to stew a large pot.

"I had no idea this took so much work." I'd seen Ah-Ma making this for us back when I was in high school, but I always had homework and swim team practice and friends and boys on my mind. I'd never stopped to consider how she made all those delicious meals.

"That's why I thought today would be a good day for this." Ziyi's posts on Facebook hadn't yielded anything, and we had no new leads. We were at a standstill, so this was the perfect distraction.

"Do you always use pork belly for this?" I asked.

"Yes." Ah-Ma took the meat out of the fridge and looked at it for a moment. "My grandfather was the one who taught me this recipe. He loved to cook, while my grandmother hated it, so he made all our meals." She put it down on the counter. "It's time to take the eggs out. Then we marinate the pork."

I used a slotted spoon to gently extract the eggs from the pot. Ah-Ma placed the pork belly inside until it was submerged in the sauce.

"I'm also going to add the smoked dried tofu that you love so much." She sent me an affectionate look. "They can go in now to soak up the sauce. And then we put the eggs back in over the pork belly."

"You don't add the carrots?" I gestured to the ones I'd sliced into large chunks.

"No. I like to wait until the pork belly is almost done before adding them." Ah-Ma filled a measuring cup with water and slowly poured it into the pot until all the eggs were submerged. She placed the lid on the pot, leaving it ajar so that steam could escape. "We'll stir it every once in a while, but basically it just stews now for at least an hour, maybe longer."

"I can't wait." My mouth was already watering at the smells wafting out of the pot. "When do you add the seaweed bundles?"

Ah-Ma froze, and I saw her swallow hard.

"Are you okay?" I was by her side in seconds.

She nodded. "Yili used to love seaweed." She blew out a shaky breath. "I'm sorry. I don't have any, but you can add it now if you have it on hand."

I reached to turn off the camera, thinking she needed a break, but my grandmother stopped me.

"How long you stew this depends on if you like the meat firm or tender." Ah-Ma smiled at me. "You and your father always wanted the meat to fall apart, while your mother and brother liked it a bit firmer."

She spoke more, and then I picked up my phone to stop the video. As I was looking over the footage, my phone dinged with a text. I let out a gasp of surprise when I saw it was from Chef Wu.

"What's the matter?"

"Nothing. It's my old boss." I opened the message and read it silently before looking up. "He says he has some leads for restaurants looking for an executive chef, if I was interested. Not in New York City, though."

"Isn't that the head chef?" My grandmother lifted her eyebrows.

"Yes." Exhilaration and terror warred within me. This had been my dream ever since I'd decided I wanted to cook for a living. To be the executive chef of a restaurant, where I was the one in charge, making decisions about what was on the menu and overseeing the entire kitchen. But now it was the last thing I wanted to be.

"How wonderful, Liv." My grandmother knew how much I had wanted this.

"It's not." My heart sank because I knew I wasn't ready to go back to work in a restaurant. Would I ever be ready? The second full-blown panic attack had made me realize I wasn't as healed as I thought I was. How could I be in charge if the thought of being in an enclosed space like a commercial kitchen made my knees tremble? What kind of executive chef would I be if a panic attack could grip me at any time, my staff seeing me cowering on the floor, whimpering? At the back of my mind, I heard Simon suggesting I see a therapist. But I pushed the thought aside, because just thinking about talking to someone about what had happened was enough to send me headlong into a panic.

"Is this not a good thing?" My grandmother searched my face.

"No—" I broke off and shrugged helplessly. "I couldn't return to 852. I don't know if I want that lifestyle anymore." I walked to the stove and lifted the lid, gently stirring to make sure that the eggs, tofu, and pork belly were all submerged in the sauce. Then I looked at my phone again, staring at Chef Wu's message. "What should I tell him?"

"Thank him and ask if you can think about it for a day or two." Ah-Ma came to my side. "I'm sure he doesn't expect an answer right away. He just said he has leads, right?"

"Right, you're so wise." I was glad my grandmother was here to be the voice of reason, since all rational thinking had flown out of my brain.

I fired off a message to Chef Wu and then looked at the videos I'd made of us cooking. I started to edit them, splicing them together so that I could post something to YouTube. My thoughts spun the entire time, wondering what I was going to do with my life if the dream I'd always had was no longer something I wanted.

The next morning, I woke early but didn't get out of bed. My mind was still swirling with so many thoughts about what I was going to do once I returned to New York. Who was I if I wasn't a chef? Was I really going to let what had happened chase me away from the dream of having my own restaurant? On top of that, I kept hearing Simon suggest I see someone, and even though part of me wondered if he was right, the other stubborn part of me didn't want to open myself up to those feelings of terror. It was easier to push it out of my mind, to the back of my thoughts, than to confront them. Which was why I had been kind of avoiding Simon for the past few days. Whenever he suggested we get together, I made an excuse, even though I wanted to see him.

As if sensing I needed her, my phone rang with a call from Amy.

"*Xin chao,*" she said as soon as I said hello.

I recognized the Vietnamese greeting. "You're in Vietnam?" My eyes widened, knowing she'd been missing the country where her father grew up. She'd visited often when she was a child. "You know you're getting closer and closer to me. Is Taiwan next?"

"Maybe." There was a teasing note in Amy's voice.

"Yes!" I sat up, excitement swirling through my body. "Come see me and Ah-Ma. I miss you so much."

"Me too. It's been months since I saw you. And even though I just had an excellent meal with excellent company, it's not the same without you." Amy's voice was wistful.

"When can you come?" I was literally bouncing up and down in bed at the thought of seeing my best friend.

"Tomorrow, if that's okay. But I can only stay a day or so."

"What? Why?" I asked, my body deflating. I'd hoped to have at least a week to show Amy around Taichung.

Amy blew out a breath. "After I see you, I'm going back to New York to pack up my apartment. I'm moving here. At least for a year or two."

My heart stopped for a moment before it picked up again. "'Here' as in Vietnam?"

"Yes."

"Oh." I didn't know what else to say. The thought of my best friend so far away from me once I returned to New York made my entire being freeze up.

"I know," Amy said, her voice soft. "This whole thing, what happened to you and Cat at 852, it's really put everything into perspective for me. I've met so many interesting people on this trip. That couple from South Africa I was traveling with? Turns out he was diagnosed with a terminal illness and so they're finally seeing all the places they'd been saving for." Amy paused for a moment and then went on. "I met this older woman last week. She was imprisoned for ten years for a crime she didn't commit. She just got out and is busing tables at the restaurant where I had dinner. You'd think she'd be bitter, but Liv, she was the happiest person I'd ever seen. Life is short. We need to grab our happiness now."

"And your happiness isn't in New York anymore? With me?" I couldn't help the pitiful tone in my voice.

"Liv, of course not. If I was being selfish, I'd make you move to Vietnam with me." Amy's voice got stronger as she spoke. "You know I've wanted to get to know my family in Vietnam better." Her father was Vietnamese, while her mother was from China. She knew her mother's side of the family better because most of them had moved to the States. "I kept putting it off because I was busy with my career in New York. But I think now is the time. I want to be here. I'm going to help my uncle and aunt with their bakery. They want to expand, make it a café." She stopped again and then said, "I feel like I'm supposed to be here now."

I nodded, even though Amy couldn't see, because my throat was suddenly clogged, and I could feel tears gathering behind my eyes. Then I took a deep breath, not wanting to make this about me. This was about Amy.

"I'm happy for you." And I was. But sad for me that I would be losing my best friend.

As if she could read my mind, she said, "You're not losing me. We'll just be farther apart for a few years. That doesn't mean you're going to get rid of me that easily."

I let out a dry laugh and then coughed, trying not to sob. "I'll visit you."

"Of course you will." Amy sounded so confident that I smiled through my tears. "I'll look into flights to Taiwan later. I'll keep you posted."

"Okay."

"I can't wait to meet Simon," Amy said, her voice teasing.

I let out a laugh. "Well, I might have screwed that up." I told her about my second panic attack and how I'd been avoiding Simon ever since.

"Do you like him?" she asked.

"I do." I stopped for a moment. "But I'm not the same person I was before. I'm a mess, Amy. He's seen me at my worst, twice now. I'm so embarrassed."

"Exactly." Her voice was firm. "He's already seen you at your worst, and yet you say he keeps contacting you."

I was silent as I thought that over, knowing she was right. I was an idiot.

"You're an idiot," she said, making me smile. "Gotta go. I'll let you know when my flight arrives."

"Thanks, Ames." We said goodbye, and I looked up at the ceiling, thinking how well she knew me, even as my heart was aching to know we wouldn't be living in the same city for the first time since college.

Suddenly, I heard Ah-Ma cry out from the kitchen area. I bolted upright and jumped out of bed, wondering if everything was okay. I rushed out of my room to see Ah-Ma seated in front of her laptop at the dining table.

"Liv! I got my DNA results back!" She looked up, her eyes sparkling.

"Oh!" I went to her side. "I can't wait to see who you've matched with." I peered over her shoulder, and we both waited as the page loaded. When it finally did, Ah-Ma ran a finger down the possible relations list. "Do you recognize anyone?"

She nodded. "Some cousins. My sister." Her finger lingered over a name, and I wondered if it was the sister who had passed away last year. "But look. Liv." She turned to me, and I saw that her hand was shaking.

I followed her finger and gasped when I read "Parent/Child," with a name listed. "Ah-Ma. Is that her?"

"I don't know." The name next to this relationship was Hsu-Min Chen. "They could have changed her name, but I was told her surname is Ong."

"Maybe it's her married name?" I suggested. I pulled out my phone. "Let me do a Google search." I put the name into my phone and then shook my head. "Not many matches. There is a Facebook account, though."

"Let me see." I showed my grandmother and then took the phone back to open the Facebook app, where I added the name in the search bar. Only one result popped up, but the profile picture was of a flower. And the account was private, so I couldn't see any of the posts. "Well, this isn't helpful."

"Oh." I could see the disappointment on Ah-Ma's face.

"I'm going to friend her. See if she responds." I hit the friend request button and looked at my grandmother. "We'll find her, even if we have to stalk her." I turned back to my phone to take a closer look at the search results from Google. But I got distracted by a notification from TikTok.

"Oh wow. Ah-Ma, look at this." I clicked on TikTok and showed her the views and likes from the video I'd uploaded yesterday.

"What? What am I looking at?" She searched my screen, confused.

I pointed to the numbers. "Our video from yesterday has over one million views. And over thirty thousand likes."

"Is that good?" Ah-Ma peered at me over her glasses.

I laughed. "Yes, that's really good." I clicked on YouTube. "And it's doing just as well on YouTube." I slung an arm around Ah-Ma. "People love us."

"I still don't know why anyone would want to watch an old woman cooking and talking about finding her daughter." Ah-Ma wrinkled her nose.

"Because you're fun and amazing." I looked through the comments and read some out loud to Ah-Ma. "'I wish I had a grandmother like Ah-Ma.' 'You two are so cute together!' 'My heart breaks at what you've been through.' 'I hope you find your lost daughter.'"

Ah-Ma didn't say anything, but she had a doubtful look on her face. She turned back to her screen, where her matches were listed.

"We're so close to finding her." I sobered immediately, realizing my grandmother couldn't give a hoot right now about internet fame. "I mean, a parent/child match can't be any clearer. Unless you have children that you didn't know about?"

"I think I would have remembered that." Ah-Ma gave me a wry look.

"The best outcome is that the woman responds to my friend request. Worst-case scenario, we have a name now. We can hire a private investigator if needed." I tapped Ah-Ma's computer screen. "And now that your match has shown up, maybe she'll see it and reach out to you."

"I hope so." She looked at her fingers and muttered something to herself.

My phone dinged and I jumped, hoping it was a Facebook alert, but it was a text from Simon. "Simon wants to see me. Take me out for lunch."

"Go ahead. I'll be fine by myself. We have all that leftover *lo neng* and *khong bah png* from yesterday."

"No." I shook my head, even as Amy's words echoed in my mind. I knew I had to talk to Simon, but now wasn't the time. I was here to help find Ah-Ma's daughter, and this was the first real lead we'd had. "I'll stay with you. I'm going to search more for this woman on my laptop. And maybe she'll respond to the Facebook request."

"You sure?" Ah-Ma studied me. She knew I was holding something back. Sometimes it didn't work in my favor that she knew me so well.

175

I nodded. "I want to work on more recipes with you. You said we'd make *zha jiang mian* today. Let's try it with ground chicken, and I want to add more vegetables to your original version."

My grandmother frowned at me, but then she let the subject of Simon go. "You always loved those fried bean noodles. We'll make it for lunch. You can tweak it however you want."

I nodded, eager to get started. I gave my grandmother an impulsive hug. "Thank you for helping me find the passion to cook again."

She squeezed me back. "We should write a cookbook together." She let out a laugh.

I pulled back to stare at her. "We should." My mind raced with all the possibilities.

"I was kidding, Liv." My grandmother was still chuckling.

"I'm not." My mind was flooded with ideas. "We can do a Taiwanese cookbook influenced by modern times. Make some of the recipes lighter, not use as much pork and red meat." I turned to Ah-Ma, my enthusiasm bubbling over. "I think we can do great things together, and I already have a good platform." I'd heard colleagues talking about how hard it was to find an agent for cookbooks, unless you had a big platform.

"Are you serious?" Ah-Ma finally stopped laughing and looked at me, her eyes wide.

"I think we should definitely explore this idea." I cocked my head at her.

She thought for a moment and then nodded slowly. "Let's talk about it over breakfast." She looked at her laptop one last time and then rose from her chair and headed for the kitchen.

"Perfect." I was about to follow her when my phone dinged. I looked at it and then froze in place. Hsu-Min Chen had accepted my friend request.

17
LIV

"Look." I rushed into the kitchen once I could finally move. "She friended me."

"Yili?" My grandmother whirled around to face me, her skin pale.

I was already opening her page and showed it to my grandmother. "It's mostly pictures of flowers. She must love them." I scrolled through her feed until I came to a profile picture. "This seems to be the only picture of her. Is this the woman you saw?" I held out my phone.

She took it from me and put her glasses on to peer at the picture. "It's kind of fuzzy, and she's turned away from the camera. It might be her?" She looked up at me, her face both hopeful and disappointed. "I don't know. I can't tell."

"I'll message her." I took my phone back and opened Messenger.

"What are you going to say?" I'd never seen my grandmother so nervous. She was tapping her fingers on the countertop, and her left eye was twitching.

"I just told her we're looking for a woman named Yili and asked if that was her, or if she knew anyone by that name." I showed my grandmother what I had typed, and when she nodded, I sent the message.

"Do you think she'll respond?" Anxiety made my grandmother's voice break.

"She accepted my friend request when she doesn't know me." I shrugged. "Maybe?"

My grandmother twisted her hands together. "Oh my. I'm so nervous." She reached out to grip my arm. "Liv, what if this is her? What if this really is Yili after all these years?"

"It would be a miracle." I put my hand over hers, which was holding on to my arm so tight I had to stop myself from wincing.

Ah-Ma finally let go of my arm and started pacing around the small kitchen. "My daughter. My lost daughter. Could it be her?" she muttered to herself, and I wanted to reach out and hold her, but I knew she needed to move. "Yili. After all these years." She looked over at me. "Do you think it's her? Do you?" Her eyes pleaded with me to say yes.

"I don't know. I hope so." Her anxiety was making me stressed, and I kept looking at my phone, willing the woman to answer. So far, nothing. "Okay. We need to distract ourselves. We need breakfast. Staring at the phone isn't going to make her respond faster."

"I couldn't possibly eat anything." My grandmother looked at me as if I'd just suggested she eat cockroaches.

"Then you can watch me. We're going to do what we planned today and make *zha jiang mian* after breakfast." I went to the fridge and pulled it open, checking its contents. There was some leftover vegetable fried rice we'd made last night, and I pulled it out. I scooped some of the rice into a bowl and stuck it in the microwave. "You sure you don't want anything?"

My grandmother didn't answer and instead resumed her pacing and muttering. When the microwave dinged, I took my food out and sat down at the table, my phone in front of me. I tried scrolling through my emails and other social media, but I kept returning to Facebook. Nothing. Then an email made me put my bowl down with a thunk.

I looked up at my grandmother. "Someone wants us to film a cooking show together."

"What?" Ah-Ma was distracted, her head stuck in the fridge as she rummaged within.

The adrenaline kicked in. This was a legit production company. It was small and mostly shown on streaming sites, but it was a real opportunity. A producer in Taiwan was the one who'd seen my YouTube channel and reached out to me.

"Look." I got up and showed my grandmother the email and then waited while she read, my toes tapping the floor. If we did this, that would mean I'd have to stay in Taiwan for at least a few weeks, probably more. I had no idea what taping a show would entail, but I was already thinking ahead, and I didn't hate the idea of staying in Taiwan longer.

Ah-Ma handed me back my phone. "They're really interested in my story?"

"Yes. As are hundreds of thousands of people." Even I hadn't realized that Ah-Ma's search for her daughter would resonate with so many people. "What do you think? Should we do this?" I was excited, but I wouldn't agree unless Ah-Ma was 100 percent on board.

She nodded slowly. "Who would have thought that at eighty-six years of age, I'd get a chance like this?" Her eyes looked at me, lit up with hope. "And maybe there will be a happy ending to this story."

"The producers want to meet with us. Whenever we're free." I held my grandmother's gaze, and I could tell she was as excited as I was.

"We have nothing to lose by meeting with them." Her eyes sparkled, and I was glad something was distracting her from waiting for Hsu-Min Chen to respond to our message.

"Okay, I'll email him back." I'd just looked down to do so when suddenly, Messenger lit up with a notification. I wanted to read it before getting Ah-Ma's hopes up, so without saying anything, I opened it.

I'm sorry, I don't know who that is. But that's funny, recently, someone called me by that name on the street.

"Ah-Ma." My voice trembled with excitement.

She turned to me and then rushed to my side at the look on my face. "What is it?"

"It's her. The woman you saw at Yizhong Shopping Street. Look." I held my phone out to my grandmother.

She read the short message, her eyes scanning over my phone, and then looked at me, her eyes filled with emotion. "It's her. I knew that was Yili."

I gave her a tremulous smile, not quite daring to believe we'd really found my missing aunt. "What do you want me to say to her?"

"Ask her if we can meet her. That you have something important to tell her."

"Okay." I typed out the message and sent it, expecting her to answer right away. But then, nothing. No reply. The minutes ticked by as Ah-Ma and I both stared at my phone, willing a reply to come through.

"Oh no." Ah-Ma collapsed into a chair at the table. "We scared her away. Maybe we shouldn't have said we wanted to meet her."

"No, no." I was quick to reassure Ah-Ma. "She's probably doing something right now. Maybe she's at work and hasn't looked at our reply yet. Don't think the worst."

"Liv, I . . . this is just . . ." Ah-Ma struggled to find the words.

I got up and put an arm around her. "I understand. But you've waited this long. We'll see her somehow. We'll figure this out." I let go and sat back at the table, suddenly ravenous. "Let's stick to our plan and cook this morning. I'm sure she'll reply soon."

To distract ourselves, Ah-Ma and I made the noodle dish with the fried bean sauce, using ground chicken instead. I'd suggested that we should sauté the onions with the chicken (Ah-Ma usually added raw onions at the end to the sauce) to give it more flavor. *Zha jiang mian* was traditionally served with thinly sliced cucumbers on top, but I'd found radish and carrots in Ah-Ma's fridge and had sliced a bit of both to give the bowl more color. I videotaped the whole process and then took a photo of the final dish, wishing I could send scents through the internet, because it smelled so good.

While we were cooking, we both kept waiting to hear the ding from my phone that would tell us I had a Facebook notification, but by the time we sat down to eat the noodles, there was still nothing.

"I can't." Ah-Ma pushed her bowl away.

I looked at her helplessly. Why didn't that damn woman answer us?

I took a bite of the noodles and let out a sigh. "Oh, but this is delicious, Ah-Ma. We're going to be so good if they pick up our show." I'd made an appointment for us to meet with the producers for the day after tomorrow.

She gave me a weak smile.

"Look." I tried to be optimistic. "Even if she doesn't answer, we have a name and a profile. Ziyi can ask in her groups if anyone knows her."

Ah-Ma perked up at that. "I'll call Ziyi right now."

"Forward her the Facebook profile." I went back to eating as Ah-Ma spoke to her friend on the phone. I was checking my phone yet again when the door buzzer went off.

Ah-Ma gestured for me to answer it, and I got up to go to the intercom. "Hello?"

"Liv. It's Simon."

Ah-Ma raised an eyebrow at me. She knew I'd been avoiding Simon, but she hadn't asked why. Biting my lip, I pressed the buzzer and then waited by the door to greet him.

"Hi." I tried to sound casual, as if I hadn't been ghosting him. "Are you hungry? We made *zha jiang mian*."

"I already ate." He came in and stood by the door. "It smells good, though."

"It is."

And *he* looked good. He was dressed in khaki shorts with a light-blue short-sleeve polo shirt that showed off his tanned skin and ropelike arms, and the sight of him made me forget why I'd been avoiding him for days. I was embarrassed at the way I'd acted, like a petulant child instead of a grown woman. Feeling awkward, I shifted from foot to foot, wondering how I'd explain to him all that I'd been feeling the last few days. Ah-Ma waved at Simon and then went into her bedroom to finish her call with Ziyi.

"Sorry for just showing up like this, but you weren't really answering my texts." He didn't sound angry or hurt, but I could feel my cheeks heating. "Can we talk? Go for a walk?"

"Now?" I asked, looking back at my bowl of unfinished noodles.

"Are you free?" His voice was low, confident.

Maybe a walk would be good, instead of staring at my phone, waiting for the woman to respond. And we did need to talk. I nodded. "Let me just tell Ah-Ma where I'm going."

Five minutes later, we were strolling down a side street near Ah-Ma's apartment, filled with family-owned stores and little restaurants. We passed a barbershop and then a store that sold sewing notions. Simon pointed to a shop on the corner that sold everything from plastic step stools and brooms to dishes and bowls and electronic equipment.

"You can get everything you need in there." He chuckled at how crammed the tiny store was, filled from floor to ceiling with household items.

I smiled too, surprised by how relaxed I was with him. I'd thought things would be awkward, but everything was fine. Which just spoke even more to his character.

"Why have you been avoiding me?" Simon didn't look at me when he said this. "Did I do or say something to offend you?"

I shouldn't have been surprised that he was getting right to the point. It was one of the things I liked about him. He didn't beat around the bush or try to figure something out in a roundabout way. He just went right to the heart of the matter.

"I'm sorry. I've been rude." I looked everywhere except at him. "I guess . . ." I hesitated for a moment, trying to figure out how to put into words my feelings of humiliation and my growing attraction for him. "I like you. A lot. And it's hard for me to . . ." I trailed off again, circling one hand as if it could conjure up the words I couldn't quite get out. "I feel like such a hot mess. You've talked me out of two panic attacks. I probably remind you of your patients. And not someone you'd be interested in."

Simon stopped walking and moved off to the side of the street so that we weren't in anyone's way. "Liv. You're not a hot mess. And I don't see you as a patient. I don't know what you've been through, but you're obviously dealing with PTSD in some form." He reached out and touched my cheek briefly. "You're so strong. Despite what happened to you, you still flew all the way out here to help your grandmother. I think that takes a lot of guts."

I gave him a small smile and nodded because he was right. Despite the shooting, despite how low and a mess I felt now, I knew I had an inner core of strength. Ah-Ma's influence all my life had helped shape me to be the woman I was today. Perhaps that Liv was still in me somewhere. Amy was right: Simon had seen me at my worst, and yet here he was, still wanting to get to know me.

"Can I ask you a question?" When I nodded, he continued. "Do you have something against therapy? Is it your family?"

"No. It's not that." I twisted my fingers together. "It's just that every time I think of talking about what happened, it makes me feel like I can't breathe. I don't want to relive it. I'm not ready."

Simon reached out and pulled me into his side in a gentle motion. "I get it. But at the same time, it's not good to keep it all bottled in. I hate seeing you suffer."

I tilted my head slightly so that my ear gently brushed against his chest. It was reassuring, his arm holding me to him. Even though there were people all around us, mopeds and bicycles whizzing by and kids running and shouting up and down the street, for that moment, it felt as if it were just Simon and me, alone in the world.

I finally spoke. "I know. I just can't. Not yet."

He nodded. "I'm here, as your friend or more if you want."

We were silent, tension crackling between us as we stared at each other. Then he turned so that he was fully facing me at the same time that I leaned into him. Our bodies met, and the warmth radiating off him wrapped around me like a hug. One of his hands went to my face, and he cupped it gently. And then I was reaching up and he was leaning down, and our lips met in one perfect moment. My eyes closed and our kiss deepened. I didn't care that we were standing in the middle of a street with people all around us. Everything fell away except for Simon.

It didn't last long, and when we pulled away, he wrapped me into a hug that had my eyes closing as my head rested against his chest.

"I've been wanting to do that for a long time." His voice rumbled against my ear.

"Me too." I liked him way more than I realized. He was a friend, but there was so much more. Maybe that's why I'd been avoiding him. Because I couldn't admit how much this man was affecting me. Not when my mind and life were still such a mess.

"I never thought our first kiss would be in the middle of the street, though." His voice rumbled again.

I let out a laugh, tightening my arms around his waist. We stayed like that for a few more minutes until he pulled away to look at me.

"If something is bothering you, just talk to me, okay?"

I nodded, and then he let me go so we could continue walking. Except now, he took my hand in his and we linked our fingers together.

"Oh, I forgot to tell you. We found the woman that Ah-Ma saw on the street." I told him about the DNA results and how we'd found the woman on Facebook.

"That's amazing." Simon's eyebrows raised. "Did you reach out to her?"

"That's the thing. When I asked if we could meet her, that we had something important to tell her, she went silent." I checked my phone with the hand that wasn't holding Simon's. "Still nothing. Ah-Ma thinks we scared her away."

"Let me see." He let go of my hand.

I gave Simon my phone and kept walking, taking a few steps before I realized he'd stopped and was staring at my cell. I turned back to him.

"What is it?" He looked like he'd seen a ghost. His eyes were wide, his brow furrowed.

He looked up. "Liv, I know her."

"What?" I closed the gap between us. "You know her?"

Simon stared at me some more, and I felt my heart rate quicken. His next words stole the breath from my lungs.

"This is Ang-Li's daughter. My friend Ken's aunt Sue."

PART 2

18
Ang-Li

March 1961, Taichung

When my wife, Jin, appeared one day with an eighteen-month-old toddler and said she'd found a *shim-pua* for our second son, my heart went out to the woman who had just lost her baby. *Shim-pua* marriages were still common then, even though there were those who spoke out against the practice, saying it wasn't natural for two children who grew up together to be married later.

The little girl had stared at me with wide eyes and asked when she could go home. Something about her was familiar, as if I'd seen her before, but of course I hadn't.

Jin crouched down in front of her. "This is your home now." Her voice was gentle.

"Not." The little girl stamped her foot. "Want Mama and Baba. My *jie jies* and *di di.*"

I met my wife's eyes over her head, and I narrowed my eyes. *Where did you get this toddler from?* Jin looked back at the girl without acknowledging my question.

"You're safe with us. I promised your father we'd take good care of you." She gestured to me. "This is your baba now."

She refused to call us "Baba" and "Mama." The girl cried and asked to go home for many days. Our oldest daughter, who would change her name to Clare when we moved to America only a few months later, was the only one who could console her. Clare was only seven, but she snuggled the smaller girl against her and told her fanciful stories that eventually made her stop crying. Jin and I were thankful for Clare, as Jin had her hands full with our two little boys, George, who was four, and Henry who was three and had been blinded by an illness soon after he was born. George was full of energy, tearing around the house and neighborhood, not paying much attention to a new little sister, while Henry tended to stay by our sides, learning how to navigate life without sight.

Jin insisted that we change the little girl's name, which made me even more suspicious. My wife claimed a family had needed to adopt her out, but something about the way she wouldn't meet my eyes told a different story. I loved Jin and had always gone along with whatever she wanted. I knew she didn't love me as much as I loved her. That had been the way it was from the moment I'd laid eyes on her, and I'd accepted it when I married her. It weighed heavy on my heart, but I didn't allow myself to dwell on it often. We had a good life together.

A few days later, I was determined to ask Jin more about the little girl when I got home from work. I was a journalist and wrote articles for a local paper, most of which were censored by the government. I knew I was under scrutiny by the very definition of my job, but I always toed the line carefully, never really giving them a reason to arrest me.

"Yili." Clare streaked past me as I opened the front door. "Where are you?"

I watched as Jin rushed after Clare into the girls' bedroom. "I told you not to call her that," Jin scolded our daughter. "Her name is Hsu-Min now."

"Yili." The girl popped out of the closet and looked at my wife in defiance. "Home?"

"We're your family now." Jin reached out to stroke her head, but the little girl pulled away and ran to Clare.

"No," she said in a pitiful voice, and I could see she was about to cry. Clare took her hand. "You're so lucky you get to have a new name. It's like a game. We can pretend you're a character in a book."

Hsu-Min looked at my daughter with curiosity. "Pretend?"

"Yes." Clare nodded vigorously. "You're a beautiful goddess named Hsu-Min, and a dragon has captured you. But he turns out to be a good dragon, and you take care of him."

I gave my daughter a grateful smile, marveling at the bond between the two girls, and started to back out of the room. But then I stopped, because there was something about the way the light was catching the two of them in profile that made me pause. What was it? I stared at them, trying to puzzle out what it was that had set something off in my memory. But the vague thought floating in my mind refused to coalesce. After a moment, I shook my head. I had more important things to worry about, like what was happening to our country. I was troubled by the rumblings in the neighborhood about people being arrested randomly. I also had to find out what my wife was up to, since she wouldn't tell me. And I knew just who to ask.

"Dinner will be ready in half an hour." Jin threw me a harried smile as she hurried back to the kitchen.

I nodded and looked around for my boys. Henry was on the couch, but I couldn't find George anywhere. He was probably at one of our neighbors' apartments playing with his myriad of friends. The girls were occupied, so I took Henry's hand and walked down the street to the corner medicine shop. Wong Tai Tai greeted me as we entered the store.

"Here for Henry's herbs?" She handed my little boy a lollipop, which he held up in front of him as if he could see it.

"Yes." Wong Tai Tai and I were old friends, having grown up together in this neighborhood. She'd learned everything about herbs and Chinese medicine from her late husband, who'd been considerably older than her, and ran the shop alone these days. She'd helped us so much when our Henry was recovering from the terrible fever that took his sight.

"Here." She handed me a package, and I did a quick survey of the store with my eyes.

Only two other people were there, an elderly man inspecting the ginseng root and a woman who I knew had a son Clare's age. They were both at the other end of the store, but I leaned closer to Wong Tai Tai just the same.

"What do you know about the little girl?" I whispered. Wong Tai Tai kept a careful eye on the neighborhood and somehow always knew what everyone was up to. I could count on her to tell me the truth. She doted on my children, especially Henry, since she didn't have any of her own. I'd often catch her looking longingly at them when she thought no one was watching. But she always looked away in embarrassment when she caught my gaze, so I'd never broached the subject with her.

"You mean where she's from?" Wong Tai Tai too kept her voice low.

"Yes." A twinge of guilt plucked at my heart for going behind my wife's back, but I knew Jin would never tell me the truth. And I had a bad feeling that I wasn't going to like whatever it was that she'd been up to.

Wong Tai Tai's eyes shifted around the store before focusing back on me. "She's from a KMT family. I first saw the man way down there—" She broke off to point to the main street that was perpendicular to the side street that our neighborhood was on, which you could see from her shop. "He was with Jin. They looked friendly. Too friendly."

I sucked in a breath. There was only one man that my wife would have been too friendly with. My thoughts spun even as my heart dropped. It was just as I suspected.

"He walked by my shop once, on his way to the pub across the street. He had two drinks in there and then left. I thought maybe he'd been stood up." Wong Tai Tai's sharp eyes caught mine. "I think Jin and the man . . ."

She didn't have to say it. "Does he have a mole? Here?" I pointed to my right cheek.

Wong Tai Tai nodded, and her eyes filled with sympathy.

I closed my eyes and winced at the pain in my heart. I thought Jin had put that part of her life behind her. I thought we both had. If he was who I thought he was, how long had this been going on?

I felt a hand on my arm, and my eyes snapped open.

"Are you okay?" Wong Tai Tai looked at me with a mixture of concern and pity.

I drew myself up to my full height of five eight, my pride unwilling to accept her pity. "I'm fine." My words were clipped, and I knew I'd hurt her feelings by the way she snatched her hand back. But it couldn't be helped. "Are you sure the little girl is that man's daughter?"

"Yes." That was all she said. I didn't question her, even though I wondered how she knew. Because she always knew, and she was never wrong.

Henry tugged on my hand. "Baba, can I have this?" He held up the lollipop.

"Of course." I was glad for the distraction, if only to look away from Wong Tai Tai's knowing eyes. I took the wrapper off for Henry and handed it to him. Once he was happily occupied, I turned back to Wong Tai Tai. "Let me know if you hear anything else."

"I will. I'm sorry." She pressed her lips together, and I knew there was more she wanted to say. But I couldn't take any more.

"Me too." She didn't know the half of it. I turned to the door so she wouldn't see the wounded betrayal on my face. "Thank you," I threw over my shoulder. My brain was an angry buzz, but I didn't know if I was mad at Jin or at *him*.

I pounded a fist against my thigh once Henry and I were back on the sidewalk. I wanted to yell and scream, punch a wall, hit something. Someone. But I didn't want to scare Henry, so I took a deep breath and then blew it out. I'd thought Jin and I had been happy these past seven years, that we'd finally put our university years behind us and had an understanding. Even loved each other. When Jin had agreed to marry me during her first year at university, I was sure she would eventually forget about Po-wei. We hadn't seen him since we'd moved to the Beitun District. I'd been relieved, glad he was out of our lives, no longer a temptation for Jin now that she was my wife. I gave a bitter chuckle, causing a woman walking by me to look at me askance and move away from us. I was a fool. Po-wei had somehow wormed his way back into our lives. For some reason, he'd given his daughter to my wife. And I was determined to find out why.

May 1961

Two months later, I was walking home from work when Wong Tai Tai ran out of her store. I'd gotten out early because it was Clare's eighth birthday, and she'd made me promise to be there for her birthday dinner. Jin had made a strawberry cake that morning, and I held a small bouquet of bright flowers to present to Clare.

"Ang-Li. They got Jin." I'd never heard Wong Tai Tai so frazzled before.

I stared at her blankly, noticing absently that her hair was wild around her head and her face was unusually pale.

"Who got her?" My mind was still on the birthday celebration we had planned for the night, complete with games and presents that Jin had wrapped last night while the children slept. I thought Wong Tai Tai was referring to one of the children.

She leaned in and whispered in my ear, making it tickle: "The police. They just went to your place. I saw them dragging her down the street, your children crying and trying to get to her." Wong Tai Tai's voice shook, and that's when my blood froze in my veins.

The flowers dropped from my hand, and a thundering noise filled my ears. "No." Why would they take her? She wasn't under suspicion.

If anything, we were worried that *I* was the one who could be taken. I'd been so careful, making sure I kept my writing as neutral as possible, not criticizing the government or writing anything that could be conveyed as controversial.

We stared at each other in horror as I tried to understand what was happening. So many men had been arrested, some never to be seen again, but a woman? Why would they take Jin? She wasn't involved in anything political and wasn't outspoken in any way. She didn't even work. This made no sense.

"Come inside." Wong Tai Tai motioned to her store. "I'll tell you what I know."

"I can't. I must find her." I looked wildly down the street toward our building. "Where are the children?" I needed to sprint home, find Jin, and take care of them. Instead, my eyes were drawn to the flowers I'd dropped, petals scattered across the ground like the remnants of funeral wreaths left behind after a body's been taken away.

"They're with neighbors. Come." She opened the door and ushered me in. "This is important." She turned the "Closed" sign around on the door before locking it behind her.

She strode to the back room, and I followed, my body numb but my mind sharp. I had to save Jin. I had to. My heart was pounding so loud I was surprised Wong Tai Tai couldn't hear it.

She cut right to the chase as soon as we were in her office. "You know Jin was having an affair with that man. Wang, his name is." Her voice was low, even though we were alone.

I pressed my lips together tightly but didn't answer. Yes, I knew.

"I heard he was the one who had Jin arrested. For sedition and spying for the Communists." Wong Tai Tai still spoke in a whisper.

"What!" The word burst out of my mouth, and my hands went up to frame my head. "How can that be? Why would he do that?"

I started to pace the tiny office, my mind filling with so many memories from university. Of me, Jin, and Po-wei, friends despite being on opposing sides of the political divide. I knew Po's father was a KMT officer, and he knew my family had been in Taiwan for years before the Nationalists came over after they lost the civil war in China. So had Jin's family, but unlike some of our classmates, we hadn't let politics get in the way of our friendship. I'd fallen in love with Jin the moment I saw her, sitting under a tree on campus reading a book. She had a tiny frown on her face, a little crease between her eyebrows that I longed to smooth away. I'd asked what she was reading, and she launched into a long description about how Lungshan Temple in Taipei was dedicated to the goddess Kuan Yin and how most of it had collapsed during an earthquake and then been rebuilt, only to have termites and typhoons damage it, along with the Second World War bombings and . . .

I smiled now at the memory. She'd been so lovely, her short hair framing a face with a pointed chin, her eyes flashing as her hands waved in the air. But I soon found out she was with an older student, Wang Po-wei, who was two years older than me and four years older than Jin. I loved Jin so much and wanted her to be happy, so I swallowed my own desires and became the third wheel in their triangle. We spent a lot of time together, the three of us, but I didn't interfere with their love affair. Po had loved her too once, or so I thought. How could he have turned on Jin and had her arrested?

"I don't know why, but it was definitely Wang." Wong Tai Tai's words snapped me back to the present, the musty odor of herbs and incense from the shrine in her office filling my nose.

"This doesn't make any sense." I ran a hand through my hair, knowing I was missing something. Po had broken Jin's heart when he'd met Yi-ping. I was there to pick up the pieces as Jin fell apart, wailing to me that she would rather die than live without Po.

She'd hiccuped and slumped to the floor in defeat. "I'm all alone now. No one will ever love me again." I gathered her up and held her as she sobbed, her tears soaking my shirt.

"You have me. I love you," I blurted out, desperate to stop her pain, yet at the same time wanting to find that bastard Po and punch him for breaking Jin's heart. "You'll always have me."

"No, I won't." Her voice rose. "You'll meet someone and get married and forget all about me. Just like Po did."

"No, I won't." I gripped her arms and held her away from me so that she had to look into my eyes. "You don't understand. I love you, Jin. Marry me." The words had popped out before I realized I was going to say them. "You'll never be alone again. Marry me and have children with me. We'll be a family."

She stopped crying and stared at me for so long that I was sure I'd scared her away forever. I berated myself in my head: *Stupid, stupid, stupid. Why would you tell her you love her when Po's just broken her heart?* I knew she was going to turn me down, or even worse, laugh at me, because she'd only ever seen me as a friend. I gritted my teeth, anticipating her rejection.

But she surprised me. "Yes."

That was all she said, and we stared at each other for what felt like an eternity. Me because I was too stunned, wondering if I'd imagined her saying yes, and her because later she told me she was shocked that she'd accepted my proposal. And then the spell broke, and she threw her arms around my neck. I picked her up, not quite believing she'd just agreed to be my wife, and we laughed and cried, cried and laughed some more.

We had a happy marriage, or so I thought. The day she said yes to marrying me, Jin vowed that she never wanted to see Po again. I was relieved, because even though he was my friend, I wanted Jin more. I'd thought they'd had no contact at all for the last seven years. When had they reconnected? Was it only recently, when I'd felt Jin pulling back a few months before she'd brought Hsu-Min home? Or was it even before that, when I'd been happily living my life with Jin, oblivious to the fact that my wife was in contact with the very man she'd sworn she never wanted to see again?

"What are you going to do?" I looked up to find Wong Tai Tai studying me with sympathy and curiosity. She took a step closer to me, and suddenly, the air in the room shifted.

I'd always known she wanted more from me, something that my marriage wouldn't allow me to give to her. Her husband had passed away when she was only twenty-two, and I knew she'd been lonely, running the store that had been in his family for generations by herself. She was five years older than me, in her midthirties, and I'd always admired her. But I loved my wife and had never given Wong Tai Tai any reason to think that I had feelings for her. Had something changed between us now that she knew my wife had betrayed me?

I took a step back and cleared my throat. "I need to find her, once I make sure my children are okay." I let out a shaky breath, my heart filling with dread at what was to come. "I must get her out. This is a mistake."

I'd find Po, demand he have her released. I wanted to believe there'd been a miscommunication somewhere, and that my old friend couldn't possibly have had Jin arrested. Even though we were no longer friends, I couldn't imagine the Po I knew doing something like this. We'd shared many good moments, able to talk to each other about life and what we wanted, despite our different political views. He'd brought me medicine and soup when I was sick, and we'd gotten drunk together and shared a smoke when we'd both gotten really bad grades on an exam. He'd treated Jin well when they dated, and I couldn't think of a single reason why he would betray her like this now.

Wong Tai Tai shut her eyes briefly, and then with a determined nod she stepped back, creating space between us. I saw in her eyes that she understood what I was telling her. I would stand by my wife, no matter what she'd done.

"Go to her." She looked away from me, and I was sorry for hurting her.

I turned to leave but then stopped. "What do you know about the mother? Wang's wife? Did she give away the child willingly?"

Wong Tai Tai kept her face averted. "I don't know anything about her. But she must have known what her husband had done. Maybe they have too many children?"

"Or maybe she's heartbroken and has been searching for her daughter." It wasn't uncommon for a child to be wrenched from their mother without the mother's permission. I shook my head, not wanting to imagine this scenario. I knew nothing about Yi-ping, but I knew Po-wei could be ruthless when he wanted something. But what could he possibly have gained from giving Jin his daughter?

Wong Tai Tai's next words made me look up sharply. "Be careful. They could come for you next."

The room spun for a moment when I realized she was right. My very profession already put me under KMT scrutiny, and now with my wife arrested for espionage, it was only a matter of time before they came for me.

Wong Tai Tai bit her lip. "Can you get out of the country somehow?"

My forehead scrunched as I thought. Our country was still under martial law, and the only way to travel was by taking a business trip or by studying abroad. My local journalist job didn't require me to travel, so that was out of the question. My mind raced at the other option. I was only twenty-nine, and a couple of years ago, I'd applied for a master's program in Georgia, near where one of my sisters and her husband lived. I'd had the daydream of moving our family there, away from everything happening in Taiwan, a new start. But Jin had put an end to that idea, and I'd had to defer my acceptance. She'd refused to leave Taiwan, and now I wondered if it was because of Po.

I looked at Wong Tai Tai. "Yes, one of my—"

She cut me off. "No, don't tell me. In case someone comes asking."

I nodded because she was right. My sister's husband worked for the government. Maybe he could help me get all my children out of Taiwan. But in the next breath, I realized I couldn't leave. There was no way I'd leave Jin in jail. I knew what they did to political prisoners. They could be torturing her right this minute, doing unimaginable things to her. My stomach roiled at the image, and for a moment, I thought I was going to be sick.

"Are you okay?" Wong Tai Tai must have sensed my distress.

I swallowed back the nausea and took in a gulp of air. "I have to go. I need to find Jin."

I rushed out of the room without looking back. As I let myself out of the store and hurried toward my children, a sick dread started in my stomach and spread to every part of my body until I felt as if poison ran through my veins. I knew our lives would never be the same again.

19
Liv

Simon and I took a cab to Clare's apartment as soon as we realized that my grandmother's missing daughter was Clare's sister, Sue. We'd stared at each other in disbelief when he'd recognized Ken's aunt's Facebook profile.

"How is this possible?" I'd asked, my mouth hanging open.

Simon only shook his head. "Sue, or Yili as you know her by, is the youngest of Ang-Li's children. Clare's the oldest, Ken's father George is next, and then another boy named Henry. I think Sue was adopted, but I'm not positive."

"We need to go ask Clare," I said, adrenaline pumping through my body.

Simon nodded. "She must have recognized your grandmother's name. And for some reason, she doesn't want your grandmother to find her daughter."

"This is unbelievable." I shook my head, trying to piece together everything we knew. "I wonder what happened."

"I have no idea." Simon looked as stunned as I felt.

"Is Sue here too for Ang-Li's funeral?" I asked.

"Yes. But she's staying at Ang-Li's apartment with her family."

I nodded, connecting the dots. "And that's why Ah-Ma saw her recently after all these years. She must live in the States?"

"Yes. She lives in New York City."

I'd stared at him, trying to comprehend that Ah-Ma's lost daughter had lived in the same city as me all this time.

We sat now in the cab, both still too dazed to speak. As soon as we got to Clare's building, we went up the elevator, and then Simon let us in with his key. Clare and Genevieve were inside, along with a man I assumed was Genevieve's husband, George. Ken's father.

I rushed into the living room, my gaze zeroed in on Clare.

"Clare. Who is Sue, really?" I blurted out without even a greeting.

"Liv." Simon was at my side, a hand on my forearm. He gave me a warning squeeze.

"What?" Clare was sitting on the couch, flipping through a magazine, and paused to look at us, her face twisted in a frown.

"We just discovered some surprising news." Simon's calm voice smoothed over some of the tension my question had raised in the room. "About Sue."

"Sue. Who is she?" I couldn't help myself and pressed on despite the warmth from Simon's hand telling me to slow down. "Did her name used to be Yili?"

Clare turned pale and dropped the magazine into her lap. "What . . . where did you hear that name?"

Simon gestured to me. "Yili is Liv's missing aunt."

"I'm sorry. It's just, my grandmother has been searching for Yili for so long. If Sue is her, it's a miracle." I looked around the room, finally embarrassed at my outburst. "I'm Liv," I said to the man I assumed was Ken's father, George.

"I'm George, Sue's brother." The wiry man came to our side and shook my hand. "What's all this?"

My hands waved in the air. "Long story short, we traced my grandmother's missing daughter to a woman named Hsu-Min Chen."

He turned to Clare. "Do you know what they're talking about?"

Clare had a look of indecision and something else I couldn't decipher on her face.

"Clare?" Genevieve came out of the kitchen and walked to her sister-in-law's side. "What's going on?"

Clare pursed her lips and shook her head. "I promised my father that I would always protect Sue. I'm the only one who knows Sue's true story. Even Sue doesn't know everything."

"Then Sue really is Yili? That was her name before?" I tried to tamp down my impatience, but it took everything in me to stop from leaping across the room and shaking the truth out of her.

Clare's gaze settled on George. "Ba did everything he could to protect Sue. That's what our mother wanted."

"What are you talking about?" George asked, his brows knitted together.

"You and Henry were too young when Sue came to live with us to really understand what was happening." Clare looked back at me, her eyes flashing with an emotion I couldn't name. "At the time, we thought your grandmother threw away her daughter."

"What? No." My voice rose in indignation. "She was devastated when Yili disappeared." I walked to Clare and sat next to her on the couch. "My grandfather gave Yili away at their son's one-month celebration. My grandmother had no idea what happened to her fourth daughter all these years. She's been searching for Yili her entire life. All she knew was that she was given away to a family named Ong."

"My father changed our last name to Huang to protect us after the KMT executed my mother." Clare spoke softly, almost to herself.

I gasped and heard a similar reaction from George. Apparently, he hadn't known that their surname used to be Ong either.

"My grandmother didn't give Yili up. She's been grieving her lost daughter all these years." I touched Clare on the arm. "Please, tell us what you know."

Clare looked at George again, and then back to me. "Yes, Sue is Yili. That was the name she came to us with. She was only a tiny thing, a toddler."

I let out a long sigh. Finally. We'd found my grandmother's missing daughter. Simon came to my side and sat next to me, taking my hand in his.

"Thank you. My grandmother is going to be so happy." I turned to Simon. "We need to go get her, bring her here."

"Wait." Clare reached out to take my arm. "I need to explain to Sue first. She doesn't know any of this. It's going to be a shock."

I looked at Clare and nodded. She was right. "Where is Sue now?"

"She went to tend our father's grave," George said. He had a stunned look on his face and kept shooting his older sister looks that she was ignoring.

I turned back to Clare. "Sue has no idea that she was adopted?"

"No, she knows she was adopted. But I don't think she remembers anything about her previous family. She was too young." Clare shook her head. "When my mother was taken by the KMT, my father made preparations to leave Taiwan just in case they came for him next."

"Why did they arrest your mother?" I'd never heard of a woman being persecuted during the White Terror.

Clare started to answer, but then my phone rang. "It's my grandmother. Can I at least tell her we found Yili?" When Clare nodded, I picked up the call. "Ah-Ma, we found Yili!"

Ah-Ma sucked in a breath and then said, "It's her? That woman is Yili?" Her voice was so full of emotion that it made tears spring to my eyes.

"Yes. Hsu-Min Chen is Yili."

"Oh, my goodness." I could tell my grandmother was crying by the way her breath hitched. "Where is she? I need to see her."

I looked over at George, who'd been on his phone trying to reach Sue. He shook his head. "She left a few hours ago. I don't think the cell reception is very good at the grave site. She might not get my messages until she comes back to the city."

I told my grandmother what George had said and shot Clare a pleading look.

Clare's jaw tightened, and then she said, "Tell her to come here. When we find Sue, I'll explain everything to her before she meets your grandmother."

I sent Clare a look of gratitude before saying into the phone, "Tell Mr. Thomas to bring you here. Her older sister and brother are here. They can tell you more while we wait for Sue."

Ah-Ma was openly sobbing now. "Thank you, Liv. You have no idea what this means to me." She let out a breath. "I'm on my way."

Twenty minutes later, Ah-Ma was seated next to Clare on the couch. "What is she like? What does she do?"

Genevieve had left the room to get her laptop so she could show Ah-Ma pictures of Sue. George still hadn't gotten through to his youngest sister, and I knew the suspense was torture to Ah-Ma.

"She was a diplomat and traveled all over the world. But in the last few years, she worked mostly out of the UN in New York City." Clare's voice was clipped, as if it pained her to tell my grandmother these details. "She loved her job and was good at it. People trusted her, and she often brought peace to areas where people were at war with each other."

"A peacemaker." There was a faraway look in Ah-Ma's eyes. "I always knew that's what she would be." Ah-Ma turned to me. "All this time, she was in the same city as you. I could have run into her on the street when I came to take care of you."

Clare looked at me in question. But now wasn't the time for my story. Now was for my grandmother to hear about her lost daughter.

Genevieve came back and sat down on the other side of Ah-Ma. "This is Sue from a few days ago."

Ah-Ma accepted the laptop and traced a finger over Sue's face. "I was right. The woman I saw at Yizhong Shopping Street." Ah-Ma turned to Clare. "She has a heart-shaped birthmark behind her left ear."

Clare nodded, and Ah-Ma's hand came up to her cheeks. Tears streamed down her face, and I longed to wrap my arms around her, but Genevieve comforted her by drawing her into her side. I brought a fist up to my mouth, tears prickling in my eyes. We were all silent until Ah-Ma had regained her composure.

"Did she . . ." Ah-Ma cleared her throat and tried again. "Did she ever marry your brother? The one who's blind?"

"No." Clare held up a hand. "They were too close, like a true brother and sister. They weren't blood related, since Sue is your daughter with Po, and Henry was my mother and father's child. But they were bonded. Sue used to guide Henry and pick things up for him or do things for him that he couldn't. When they grew up, they fell in love with other people. They're all here in Taiwan for our father's funeral."

George spoke up. "Sue and her husband have a daughter, your granddaughter, Francesca."

"I'm so sorry for what you went through." There was regret in Clare's voice as she addressed my grandmother. "We didn't know that your child was taken from you." She sighed and leaned back into the couch. "It was a terrible time. We were so scared when they took my mother. I still remember it." She shuddered, and Ah-Ma placed a hand over one of Clare's.

"I'm sorry." Ah-Ma's voice was barely a whisper, but Clare didn't seem to hear her.

"These men just grabbed her as soon as she opened the door and dragged her down the stairs. My sister and brothers ran to her and clung to her, but I held back. I knew they were bad men, and I didn't know what to do. I couldn't stop them."

"I don't remember any of this." George's voice was anguished.

"Baba came home soon after and took care of us. He tried to visit her, but they wouldn't let him see her." Clare squeezed her eyes shut and then opened them to look at Ah-Ma. "They killed her two months after they took her. My father was finally able to see her before she was executed in July of 1961."

Someone gasped, and I realized no one else present had known any of this. My heart hurt for Clare and her father and mother.

"Why didn't Ba ever tell me this?" George looked like he was going to collapse, and Genevieve quickly shoved a chair in her husband's direction. He sank down on it as if his legs could no longer support him.

"He didn't want the three of you to remember that terrible time. I'd just turned eight, so it was different for me. I remember how scared he was when he applied to get our visas and passports. He was sure we were going to get denied because of what had happened to our mother. But our uncle knew someone in the Ministry of Foreign Affairs . . ." She trailed off.

George shook his head. "I can't believe I never knew any of this."

"It was better that way. Ba feared that the KMT would come after us, even in the States. He told no one in America that his wife had been executed. He was very paranoid, but he had a right to be." Clare looked from him and then to my grandmother. "My father kept a journal. Even I didn't know the whole truth until I read it when I'd just graduated from college."

"Do you still have it?" Ah-Ma asked.

Clare nodded. "My father gave it to me after I found it. I was saving it, thinking I'd give it to Sue one day, but I never did."

"Can I see it?" The hope in Ah-Ma's voice was too much to bear.

"Are you sure you want to?" Clare bit her lip, suddenly looking nervous. "Your husband . . ." She trailed off.

Ah-Ma drew in a breath. "Po? He was involved somehow, wasn't he?" She looked at me before turning back to Clare. "I need to know."

Clare nodded again, her eyes filling with tears.

20
ANG-LI

June 1961, Taichung

We lived in fear, my children and I, for the month after the Taiwan Garrison Command took Jin. I was afraid my children or I would be next, so I kept the older two home from school. I feared they'd come for me at work, but if I didn't show up, they'd fire me, and then what would become of us? Every day I awoke with the sick dread that today would be the day. And every night when nothing happened, I'd gather them close and thank the gods that we were still together.

No one would tell me what had become of Jin. I went to the police, asked everyone I knew, but they all shook their heads. How could they have just taken a woman, a mother at that, without any explanation? I knew she was innocent of whatever she was being accused of, and for the first two weeks, I went to every government agency, every police station I could find. I even went to Po-wei's family's office, but they wouldn't let me in. It was as if she'd vanished, and no one who knew would tell me what they'd done with her. It wasn't until a month after she'd disappeared, when I'd stormed Po's office again, that I finally got answers.

"You tell Po-wei to come out here and face me like a man!" I shouted at the receptionist, who stared at me with cool eyes, not intimidated at all.

She was about to speak when an older man with gray-streaked hair came out of nowhere and walked toward us, guided by a younger man. I drew in a breath because I knew the older one was Po-wei's father, a powerful KMT official. He didn't bother to greet me. The younger man took me by the arm and marched me back to a room before closing the door behind us with a sharp click.

"She's in a facility. She's fine." Po's father's words were clipped, his tone devoid of emotion. He might as well have been talking about the weather.

"She's in prison," I bit out. "She's not fine. You took her from her home, from me and her children, for no reason. She's innocent." I faced him, not willing to show him that I was trembling inside, even though I knew he was blind, sure that he'd have me arrested at any moment. The younger man didn't say a word.

"Go home. Take care of your children." Po's father spoke quietly, and I wanted to punch him in the face. "There's nothing you can do."

I seethed in silence for a moment, trying to frame my thoughts. "I need to see Po-wei. Man to man. I need to know why he did this to my wife. To a friend of his."

"That's between them." He gave me a cold stare, and then he gestured with his head and the younger man rushed to his side. They left the room before I could say anything else.

That was when I knew Po would never face me and tell me what he'd done. To him, I was just someone he'd once been friendly with at university, who'd had a crush on the girl he was seeing. I was nothing to him, and he didn't owe me any explanation. That realization hit me like a blow to my gut, and I bent over, heaving for a few breaths before I could get myself under control.

I don't remember walking out of that building. I don't remember getting home and hugging each of my children, including Hsu-Min, to me. For she was just another pawn in whatever game her father was playing. I vowed that, as soon as I figured out how to get Jin out of wherever they were holding her, I would get us all out of Taiwan. The university that I'd been accepted at was willing to take me starting that fall. My sister and her brother were working on getting my children out too. And Jin. I refused to acknowledge that we might have to leave her behind. I would get her out of jail, cleared of whatever charges they were holding against her, and we would all leave for America and start over. This was the dream that held me together for the next month as our children cried for their mother and I mourned for what my beloved wife was going through.

July 1961, Taichung

It was a typical hot, sweltering day. Our apartment was unbearable, every window open to catch whatever breeze there was, but they let in flies and other insects that settled on our food and our skin. The children were irritable and bored, stuck all day in our small apartment. I wouldn't let them leave except at night, when I took them outdoors, one at a time, so they could get some air. I paid a neighbor to look in on them when I was at work, but I knew we couldn't keep living like this.

"Why can't I go to school?" Clare whined. She missed her friends, even though I allowed her to play with the ones in our building. But only if they came to our apartment.

"It's too dangerous." I was putting out a breakfast of *mantou*, a white steamed bun that we ate with pork floss and pickled radishes layered in the middle.

My heart was heavy because I missed my wife. I still had no idea where she was, and I wondered if she'd been transferred to Green Island, a small volcanic island about twenty miles off the coast of Taiwan, where they'd been keeping political prisoners. I couldn't sleep at night, imagining all the ways that they were torturing her. My Jin, the love of my life, who didn't deserve whatever they were doing to her. She wasn't a spy, wasn't even involved politically in any way. I sighed as I looked at the breakfast I'd laid out, missing the meals Jin had prepared for us. I knew our children felt her absence to the depths of their souls.

Henry was already eating, and Hsu-Min, who sat at his side, helped him pick up the pork floss that fell out when he bit into the bun. I stopped to watch them for a moment because they were so sweet together. He was older than her, but she treated him like a little brother, always watching out for him when he ran into furniture and guiding him when I couldn't.

"Nothing's happened." Clare glared at me and crossed her arms over her chest. She didn't pick up her *mantou*. She was usually so good, and I knew being cooped up and missing her mother was chipping away at her. "I want Mama."

Her lower lip stuck out, and I felt a pang again at how her birthday party had been spoiled by the imprisonment of her mother. I'd tried to make it up to her a few days later, arriving home with a cream cake from the local bakery, but she'd only pushed the piece I'd cut for her away, staring listlessly out the window.

"I'm sorry." I felt so helpless, wondering if I was being paranoid and should let them go back to school. I didn't know how to do this. Jin was usually the one to soothe the children, always knowing just what to say to calm them. But Jin wasn't here. Hadn't been for two months, and our family was drowning. I was trying to figure out what to say to Clare when a knock sounded at the door.

I turned to it with my heart thundering in my ears. I was afraid, but the knock had been too soft and timid to be that of the police. I opened the door to find a young boy on our doorstep.

"Wong Tai Tai says you need to go to her shop now." He was panting slightly after running up three flights of stairs.

My stomach dropped, as did my heart. "Why?"

He shrugged. "I don't know. She just said it's important." He turned away to go back down the stairs.

"Stay here. Don't leave. Please." I sent a pleading look at Clare, who must have caught the urgency on my face because she nodded obediently.

I ran down the stairs after the boy. When we got to the street, I saw that Wong Tai Tai was waiting for me outside her door. I quickened my pace, already expecting the worst. When I saw her face, I knew my nightmare was coming true.

I'd barely stepped foot inside her store before her words pierced my heart.

"She's going to be executed. Tomorrow." Her voice trembled. "They'll let you see her. If you go now."

I squeezed my eyes shut, not wanting to believe her words. But Wong Tai Tai had never been wrong, and the look on her face told me this was true. I shivered, grief and disbelief coursing through my body. Not my Jin. How had it come to this? Why had Po done this to us?

When I finally opened my eyes, I realized Wong Tai Tai was holding both my hands, tears brimming in her eyes.

"Thank you for letting me know. Where is she?" My heart was breaking, but I was so thankful to my friend that she'd given me the opportunity to see Jin again.

As soon as she gave me an address, I turned and ran out of the store.

When they brought Jin into the room where I waited, my breath caught at her appearance. She was too thin, her body encased in a blue uniform, her eyes dark hollows in her skull. There were cuts on her face, and her jaw looked swollen. She walked stiffly as if in pain, and I rose from my seat, meeting her halfway. I'd heard the stories about what they did to prisoners, punching and kicking them, forcing them to drink their own blood, hanging them upside down while forcing salty water into their mouths. I died a little inside, seeing what they'd done to her. When the guard who accompanied her closed the door behind him, I took her in my arms gingerly, afraid I was going to hurt her.

"Ang-Li," she choked out, burying her face in my chest. "I thought I'd never see you again." She sobbed for a moment and then lifted her face to look me in the eyes. "I'm so sorry for what I did. Please don't hate me." The last came out in barely a whisper.

"I could never hate you." I looked deep into her eyes, wanting her to know I loved her, no matter what she'd done. "What happened? Why did Po do this to you?"

Her breath hitched, and then she shook her head slightly, as if gathering strength. "I ran into him at the library about eight months ago. I hadn't seen him since you and I got married. I kept my word to you." Her eyes pleaded with me, and I gave her a slight nod. "I meant it when I told you I never wanted to see him again. But then he was there, sitting at a table, and I dropped all the books in my arms." She looked down at the floor. "He helped me pick them up."

She didn't say more, but I could imagine what happened next. She'd been so in love with him at university, and so devastated when he told her he was marrying Yi-ping. I'd hoped time and distance from him would make her forget and learn to love me, but I realized now she never had. She may have cared about me, but her heart had always belonged to Wang Po-wei.

My own heart felt as if someone had physically reached into my chest and ripped it out, but I refused to acknowledge the pain. I was here for Jin, and I would hear every word she had to tell me. "It's okay," I reassured her. "I understand."

"Don't understand." Her words were tortured. "Ang-Li, be angry at me. Tell me you hate me. I slept with him again, betraying our vows, not caring about his wife. I thought he'd finally realized he loved me, and not her." Tears ran down her face, and I wanted to wipe them away, but I couldn't.

"If that was the case, then why did he have you arrested?" I made my voice as neutral as I could, not wanting her to know how each word she spoke was a knife wound in my flesh.

She hung her head as if too ashamed to look at me. "Because I wouldn't let him go. I kept calling him, wanting to see him, even after he told me it was only a fling. I got angry, threatened to tell his wife. I couldn't believe he'd been with me after all these years, only to throw me aside once again."

Her words hurt me, but now I finally understood why she'd been so distant these past months. Why she'd turned her back to me every night, feigning sleep when I wanted to touch her. Why she had missed many dinners, saying she was going out with friends, or had to visit her parents in Taipei. My heart shattered, and I wanted to crumble to the ground, but I couldn't. I had to stay strong for her.

"I'm sorry, Ang. So sorry." She covered her face with her hands, and I couldn't help but gather her against me. As much as her words cut to my very soul, I also couldn't stand to see her suffer. "I've lied to you all this time."

"It's okay," I murmured into her hair. "I forgive you." I had to, because they were going to kill her tomorrow, and I wanted her to leave this world knowing she was loved.

She pulled away from me. "No, you don't understand."

"What?" I was confused by the ferocious look on her face.

"Clare, she's not your daughter. She's Po's." She held her breath and stared at me as if waiting for me to strike her. "I was pregnant when he broke up with me."

My mouth fell open even as I realized I wasn't surprised. I'd always wondered, but I loved Clare so much and hadn't wanted to know the truth. And now it made sense, why I'd felt like I'd seen Hsu-Min before when she first came to our household. She looked like Clare, and also like Po. I stared at my wife because words escaped me.

"Hsu-Min, she's Clare's half sister." Jin let out a sob but then continued. "When Po heard about Henry, he asked if I wanted his daughter as a future wife for Henry. I thought he was joking and said yes. I didn't realize he was offering me his daughter because he couldn't give me what I wanted. Himself. He thought it was a fair trade."

I shook my head because I still couldn't speak. My wife was telling me she wanted Po, not me. At the same time, my mind was still trying to process that my suspicion about Clare's paternity had been confirmed. Emotions warred in me, hurt, anger, humiliation, and grief. For I loved Clare as if she were mine, and to know for a fact that she wasn't was the last dagger to my already-butchered heart.

"You need to protect them." Her voice turned fierce, and she gripped my arm with one hand. "Both of them, Clare and Hsu-Min. If Po could do this to me, throw me in jail and have me executed just to get me out of his life, he'll come for them next."

"No." The word left my mouth as if I'd blown it out. "He can't have them."

"Promise me." Her grip on my arm tightened until I could feel her short nails digging into my skin. "Protect them with your life. Get them out of Taiwan. I'm so sorry for what I did to you. You need to know this. I do love you, but my obsession with Po kept me from fully loving you as a wife should a husband."

"I just don't understand why Po did this. He cared for you, loved you back in university." Something about this situation didn't sit right with me. Why would Po be this vindictive?

"It was a mistake." Jin let out a bitter laugh and let go of me to sit down in one of the chairs. "He came to see me a week after the Garrison Command took me. He said he'd only wanted to scare me, to teach me not to cross him and to leave them alone. But somehow, my paperwork was mixed up with another woman's, and they thought I'd been jailed for spying for the Communists. There are two other women here with me, who used to work for the Post, Telephone, and Telegraph Administration, and they thought they'd been sent by the Communists to infiltrate the office's institutions."

"But if it was a mistake, surely Po or his father could have set them straight?" My heart bloomed with hope. Po had been our friend. He would fix this and get Jin out.

She shut her eyes and tears leaked out. "Po told me he tried. But his father refused. He believed I was in the wrong and trying to sabotage his son. There's nothing Po can do."

I stared at her in horror. Po's father had the ability to save her, but he had basically signed her death sentence. She would be executed tomorrow morning by firing squad, and no one could stop it. Even if I tried to grab her now and escape, we would be shot before we even made it out of the door. Our old friend, the object of Jin's infatuation, was responsible, and yet he could do nothing. Hatred exploded in my chest, and I had to clench my hands hard, not wanting Jin to see my rage. I wouldn't allow her last view of me to be one of anger. I smiled at her, my mouth trembling.

Her eyes glistened as she stared up at me, and I wanted to hold her in my gaze forever. Even now, beaten and tortured, probably sleep deprived and not getting enough to eat, she was beautiful to me. My eyes blurred, and the image of her as a schoolgirl the day we first met merged with the prisoner in front of me, about to be executed. I didn't want her to die, even though she'd betrayed me. I wanted more than anything to grab her and help her escape this hellhole and take our whole family somewhere where innocent women weren't persecuted. But I couldn't, and that realization felled me to my knees. This was the last time I'd ever see my wife.

"I love you." I whispered the words, leaning close to put my head in her lap. Her hands stroked my hair, her fingers tracing down my cheek, around my ear. "I will always love you, no matter what you did. And I will protect our children with my life. You have my word."

We stayed like that for a long moment, knowing we didn't have much time left. I finally lifted my head, and we stared at each other before she nodded, her tears spilling over. "Thank you, Ang-Li. I didn't deserve you."

The guard knocked on the door, making us both jump. Our time was up. How did I say goodbye to this woman who was flawed and had hurt our family because of an obsession with another man? How would I walk out of here and back home to our children, and tell them their mother was never coming home? I drew her to me and held her tight, aware of how slight and bony she felt in my arms, wanting to absorb every moment of our last time together. But all too soon, the door opened, and the guard gestured with his head that I had to go.

"I love you, Jin. Be brave." I gave her a last kiss on the lips.

"I love you too, Ang. I'm so sorry."

"Don't say that." I traced a finger over her lips. I didn't want her last words to me to be ones of sorrow.

She understood and nodded. "I love you."

And with those words ringing in my ears, I turned away from her and walked to the door, not looking back because if I did, I believed I would have died right there on the ground in front of her. But I had to stay strong because our children needed me.

Choking back a sob, I walked out, ignoring all the people shouting around me. All I could think was that this was Po's fault. That if he hadn't swept Jin back into his web, none of this would have happened. I wanted to kill him with my bare hands. I wanted to hunt him down, that smug Wang Po-wei, with his slicked-back hair and privileged air. He wasn't normally someone I'd have befriended, but he'd been with Jin, and I was besotted. My body trembled with anger, and it was all I could do not to run out of the building and find Po.

But I knew I couldn't. If I killed a KMT officer, I'd be as good as dead. And then what would happen to our children? They were so young and so innocent. I couldn't abandon them, make them orphans, all to get revenge on a man who had destroyed our lives. Po's life wasn't worth that of my children's. Jin had made a fatal mistake, hooking up with him again. I wouldn't let their actions and repercussions have even more power over our lives. I wouldn't stoop to their level, obsessing about how to kill him. I knew I had to leave Taiwan, take my children, and start over somewhere new, a place where no one would know about my wife's tragic passing. Because if I stayed, I knew I would eventually hunt Po down and kill him.

21
Liv

Ah-Ma looked up from the journal that Clare had given to her, eyes red and tears threatening to spill. But there was anger also, snapping in her eyes, and she closed the book with force. Simon, George, and Genevieve had left soon after Clare gave my grandmother the journal. I'd risen to leave too, but Ah-Ma had asked me to stay. I sat now next to her, wondering what she'd read, since I couldn't make sense of the characters. Ah-Ma and Clare locked eyes, and I sat impatiently, waiting for someone to speak.

"You're my stepdaughter." The words were so soft that I wasn't sure if I'd heard correctly. But Clare was nodding her head.

"What?" I looked between them in confusion.

Ah-Ma turned to me. "Your grandfather had a relationship with Clare's mother before he met me. Clare is his child." She gave me a brief overview of what she'd just read, ending with Jin's death. I couldn't help the gasp that escaped.

"How horrible." One hand went to my mouth, and I watched as Clare shifted in her seat across from us, her hands folded primly in her lap.

"Sue and Clare are blood related," Ah-Ma said.

"I was shocked too when I found out." Clare let out a dry laugh. "When my mother was arrested, we only knew she'd been taken away by the government. But my father never told us why or about Po's involvement with my mother."

"My husband did a terrible thing." Ah-Ma's voice was heavy with sorrow. Her eyes met mine, and I knew she felt worse about Jin's fate than that her husband had been unfaithful.

Clare nodded. "I was so angry, so confused when I read my father's words. I yelled at him, asking why he hadn't told us. I didn't want to know the truth, that my biological father had basically sentenced my mother to death. And I was so sad that my father wasn't my real father."

Ah-Ma stood and went to sit at Clare's side. "I'm so sorry for what my husband did."

"My father took all the anger and hurt I threw at him." Her words were calm, and I could see Clare had had years to absorb the news, even though her eyes were storm clouds of turmoil. "What I didn't realize at the time was that he'd lived through a period where no one was safe. Innocent people like my mother were being thrown in prison, sometimes for no reason at all. He couldn't trust anyone, and even in America, the KMT had reach. Professors, known pro-democracy advocates were assassinated on American soil. He couldn't risk anyone finding out what had happened to my mother and put a target on our backs."

"What did you do when you found out?" I couldn't imagine finding out that my father wasn't who I thought he was. My heart was breaking for Clare.

Clare gave me a small smile. "I decided to move back to Taiwan. I was supposed to start work as an assistant at a publishing house in New York, but I couldn't. I didn't think things through. My father begged me to take the job, let time pass, and formulate a plan if I really wanted to come back here, but I refused. I just wanted to get as far away as I could. I lived with his parents down in Kaohsiung for a few months before finding a job and my own apartment in Taichung." She made a face. "I think deep down, I had the idea that I was going to confront my biological father and make him pay for what he did to my mother."

"Oh, my dear Clare." Ah-Ma patted one of Clare's hands, but Clare snatched it back, her demeanor suddenly changing.

"I hated you for so long," Clare confessed in a low voice. "There you were, living with the man who'd killed my mother and threw away your own daughter. I didn't know he'd taken her from you until years later." She gripped her hands together and dropped her gaze to the floor. "I spied on you for years after I came back to Taichung, until I heard you'd run off to America. I'd stake myself outside of your building and watch you and your husband, coming and leaving. I was so angry." Her face twisted with loathing. "I was twenty-two years old, about to start my adult life with my first job and the first time living by myself, and I longed for my mother to guide me. I saw the way you were with your son, who was a teenager then. I wanted someone to look at me the way you looked at him. The more I saw, the more I hated that you lived, and my mother hadn't."

"I had no idea." Ah-Ma's voice trembled, and she reached out to lay a hand over Clare's clasped ones. This time, Clare didn't pull away. "I'm so, so sorry. If I'd known, I would have welcomed you to the family."

Clare nodded, her chin trembling. She took in a breath and then turned her hand around so that she was holding Ah-Ma's. I wanted to leave, to let these two women finally say what they needed to each other. But I couldn't. My grandmother wanted me here. Besides, I was riveted to my seat, unwilling to break the emotions that were swirling in the room by getting up and walking out.

"When Liv said your name the other day, I was so shocked." Clare glanced at me briefly. "I couldn't believe your granddaughter was standing in my apartment, asking me to help you find Sue. The years of hating you automatically made me shut down, not want you to find Sue. I'm sorry. I shouldn't have kept what I knew from Liv."

Ah-Ma pressed her lips together and shook her head. "I might have done the same if I were in your shoes. I don't know what kind of coincidence it was that Liv and Simon met at the airport, but I believe it was meant to be. And I'm so glad I've found you."

Clare tried to smile despite the emotion welling in her eyes. She was about to respond when her phone rang, and she picked it up.

"Hi, George." She listened to her brother as Ah-Ma and I exchanged a look.

Ah-Ma rose and hovered anxiously in the space between Clare and me.

"Okay. I'll meet her in the lobby. Explain everything to her before I bring her up to my apartment." Clare nodded a few times and then hung up. "Sue's on her way. She got George's message on the drive back from our father's grave."

Ah-Ma's face paled, and her hands came up to her mouth. I stood quickly and moved to her side in case she was going to fall. But she only took my hand and pressed her lips together, her breath coming out jagged and fast.

"It's going to be okay." Clare stood but didn't come to us. "I have to explain to Sue first, but I know she'll be happy to meet you."

"Do you want me to leave?" I asked. This felt like a moment that should be between the three of them, but my grandmother's grip on my hand tightened.

"No, Liv. Please stay." Her voice was unsteady. "I need you." She gestured to the journal with her chin. "Sue should have that. But I hope you'll share it with me when she's read it."

Clare nodded. We stood like that for a moment before Ah-Ma broke away from me to go to the window. She stayed there, looking out at the traffic fifteen floors below, while I texted my mom and brother and told them the latest. They both responded immediately, and I was occupied answering their questions for the next few minutes. And then I got a text from Amy that she was arriving in Taiwan the next morning. I had so much to tell her once I saw her again.

I looked up and noticed Clare was checking her phone too, while Ah-Ma stayed in front of the window, motionless. We all jumped when the door buzzed, and Clare moved to the intercom to let Sue into the building.

"I'll be right back," Clare said, going to the door. With a nod of encouragement at my grandmother, she was gone.

The silence while we waited was so thick that I could have cut it like a piece of pie. When we finally heard the soft knock on the door, Ah-Ma turned from the window.

It opened, and a petite woman with mostly white hair pulled into a low ponytail walked into the foyer with Clare. Ah-Ma and I stood motionless, focused on the two women only fifty feet away, but it felt more like fifty miles. I couldn't see Sue's expression from where I stood, but we heard her sharp exhalation when she caught sight of Ah-Ma. Clare's voice murmured, and then they finally made their way into the living room until they stood in front of us.

It was as if there was no one else in the room except Sue and Ah-Ma. Clare and I held still, and I watched the way Sue stared at Ah-Ma in wonder. Her lips were slightly parted, and I didn't miss the way her eyes roamed over Ah-Ma's face. Tears spilled out of Sue's eyes, but she seemed oblivious, her entire awareness reserved for my grandmother. And then slowly, so slowly that I didn't realize they were moving at first, the two gravitated toward each other until they were face to face.

"Yili." Ah-Ma's voice trembled, and her arms reached out. Sue walked into them, and then they were hugging.

I couldn't stop the tears in my own eyes as a sob choked my throat. Ah-Ma was rocking Sue back and forth in her arms, her eyes squeezed shut and a look of utter anguish and joy marring her features. Sue had her face buried into Ah-Ma's shoulders, and her weeping was audible as she struggled for air. Her hands clenched around Ah-Ma as if she never wanted to let go. Both were crying, their tears mingling, and I realized I was full on sobbing, my heart so joyful to see the reunion my grandmother had waited sixty-three years for. She never lost hope, and now she held her lost daughter in her arms again.

I wrapped my own arms around myself. I could see Clare was just as affected by this reunion as I was, and her eyes were wet too. I pulled my cell out of my pocket. I took several pictures, knowing Ah-Ma might want them later. It was miraculous that they'd found each other all these years later.

When they finally pulled away, Clare rushed forward and led them to one of the couches. She handed them a box of tissues after taking some and handing the box to me. Then she and I perched on the other couch facing Ah-Ma and Sue. No one spoke for a moment as we dabbed at eyes and blew noses with a loud honking sound from Ah-Ma. That broke the tension, and we laughed, looking at each other in wonder.

"I had these dreams." Sue was the first to speak, her voice hesitant. "It was always the same woman. She was kind, with gentle hands. She smoothed my hair away from my face when I was sick with a fever and caught me when I ran at her full speed. She was beautiful, and I longed to know who she was." She blew out a breath and looked at my grandmother. "I was too young to remember anything of my time with you, but your image, your presence, stayed with me." She gave a sad smile. "I knew I was adopted, but I knew nothing about the family I'd been born into. My father never told me, and it wasn't our way for me to ask."

"He did it to protect you. To protect all of us." Clare was quick to jump in, and I loved that she was defending her father's actions. "Even though we were in the States, there was a chance Wang could have tracked him down and come after my father, maybe taken you." She looked at Sue, her eyes full of love. "We love you so much. I knew the first day I saw you that you were mine."

Sue nodded, her chin wobbling. "This is . . . a lot to take in. Especially on the heels of Ba's death." She stopped and swallowed, the grief showing on her face. "I wish he were here right now. It . . ." She stopped again and took a breath. I could see she was trying to control her emotions, and I longed to reach out to her, much as I was sure Ah-Ma wanted to comfort her. But how did you comfort someone who'd just found out at the age of sixty-five who her biological mother was?

My grandmother held out an arm then, and Sue moved closer until she was resting against Ah-Ma's side, her head on her mother's shoulder. My grandmother stroked her daughter's hair, and I bit my bottom lip at the beautiful scene before me.

"My daughter. My Yili." I could hear the words that Ah-Ma murmured, almost as if they were coming from my soul.

"Mama." Sue closed her eyes, and a look of peace crossed over her face.

Clare cleared her throat. "I'm sorry for never telling you the truth after I read Ba's journal. He left it up to me to tell you or not." Clare shook her head. "As time went on and it became safer to do so, I should have. But I just . . . didn't."

Sue sat up and looked at her sister. "I don't know what I'd have done in your shoes. We're too old to hold grudges. After all these years, to know that we're related and to find my mother—" She broke off, her hands clasped at her mouth. "I never really had one."

Ah-Ma reached out and touched her on the cheek. "I have longed for you, dreamed of you, hated my husband for giving you away." Ah-Ma's voice was strong. "I never gave up hope that I'd see you one day, but in the last few years, I was prepared to die without ever seeing you again. But here you are."

"Here I am," Sue repeated softly. "I think in the part of my mind that I don't scrutinize too much, I must have longed to know where I came from, which was why I did that DNA test a few years ago. But there weren't any matches that were close, and I forgot about it."

"And I saw a commercial for a DNA test months ago and wondered why I'd never thought to do one before." Ah-Ma looked over at me and gave me a smile full of joy. "Liv helped me find you."

"Liv," Sue said, with a questioning look at me, as if just realizing I was in the room with them. "Oh."

"My granddaughter." Ah-Ma gestured for me to come to their side. "Your niece."

I stood in front of Sue, suddenly shy and at a loss. What should I say to her? Before I could figure it out, Sue stood and hugged me to her.

"More family I never knew about." Sue's voice was muffled.

"Hi, Aunt Sue," I said as I pulled back. For some reason, this made everyone laugh, which helped to lighten the mood.

"You have three older sisters and a younger brother," Ah-Ma said. "And a whole bunch of nieces and nephews."

"And you have a granddaughter, Francesca." Sue turned to me. "Your cousin. My husband Momo and I only have one child."

"Clare said they're all here? In Taiwan?" I asked.

She nodded and then turned to Clare. "We need to organize a reunion. A dinner. Something." Her face came alive. "I've just found my birth mother after all these years. And found out we're blood related. We need to celebrate."

Clare nodded and pulled out her phone, her face still emotional. "So many of our family is here right now. This would be the perfect time."

"Is tomorrow too soon?" Sue looked at us hopefully. "Can we pull this off?"

Ah-Ma nodded, and Clare, the no-nonsense woman I'd first met, took over. "I can make it happen. Let's do it." She reached out her arms, and then we were all hugging, four women spanning three generations, connected in ways we could never have imagined just a few hours ago.

22
Liv

The private back room of a restaurant near Clare's apartment was full and buzzing with conversation. It was mostly Clare and Sue's relatives, since Ah-Ma and I were the only ones from our side of the family who were in Taiwan. But Ah-Ma's youngest sister-in-law, Mei Mei, was there with her husband, along with Ziyi and Ah-Ji. And Amy, who had landed in Taiwan earlier this morning. When Mr. Thomas pulled up at the front of Ah-Ma's building, I'd been waiting. As soon as Amy opened the car door and stepped out, I'd swooped in on her, pulling her into such a tight hug that she yelped. But then she hugged me just as hard and started cackling her Amy laugh, which made me laugh so hard that I cried. And now she was here in the restaurant with us, celebrating Ah-Ma's reunion with her daughter. The seven of us formed the Wang side of the family, while the Huangs plus Simon numbered around twenty.

Ziyi hugged Sue to her for a long embrace when they were introduced. Then she pulled away and said softly, "We've searched for you for so long." Ah-Ma hovered next to them, gratitude for Ziyi shining in her eyes as Amy grabbed my hand, squeezing hard at the tear-inducing scene in front of us.

Clare presided over the gathering, giving out orders to the waitstaff and ushering people to their tables. Once everyone was seated, she stood and held up her water glass.

"Ni hao," she said as everyone turned to look at her. "Tonight, we are celebrating the reunion of Yi-ping and her fourth daughter, Hsu-Min Chen, who was named Yili before she came into our family."

Sue's husband, Momo, a husky man with a big smile, let out a cheer and patted Sue on her shoulders. Their daughter, Francesca, clapped, and everyone else joined in. Amy and I had met Francesca when we'd first arrived, and I was immediately drawn to her bubbly personality.

"No way. You're both chefs? That's amazing." Francesca looked at me as if I'd said I invented the oven or something, but it'd been a while since I'd felt pride at my chosen profession, so her comment made me stand up a little taller. "I'm a huge foodie, but I can't cook a meal to save my life." She looked over at Sue, who nodded but gave her an affectionate smile. "Mom tried to teach me, but she gave up after I burned water."

"How do you burn water?" I asked, sure she was exaggerating.

"By leaving a pot on the stove and forgetting about it until there was no water left, and the pot started to smoke and set off the fire alarm." She gave a self-deprecating shrug, and Amy and I burst into laughter.

"Okay, that is bad," Amy said.

"Yup." She grinned at us. "I just don't have the attention span to cook. There's always so many other things I need to take care of. Besides, living in San Francisco, we have such a diverse food scene that I don't need to waste time trying to make it myself."

"You're right." I was about to ask what she did in San Francisco when she plowed ahead.

"Do you two work in a restaurant? Or as a private chef? What's it like?" She fired off the questions faster than I could process them.

"Yes. Well, we did." Amy and I exchanged a look. I chewed my lip before glossing over our time at 852 and then telling her how Amy was moving to Vietnam, and I was staying in Taiwan for a while to write a cookbook with Ah-Ma and, hopefully, film a TV series if everything went well at our meeting tomorrow morning.

"That's so amazing! And how fun to be doing that with our ah-ma." Francesca's face was lit up with admiration.

I was taken aback when she addressed my grandmother as "ah-ma," but then I realized that Ah-Ma was Francesca's grandmother too. Her mother was Ah-Ma's daughter, just like mine. I decided then that I'd do a family tree for Ah-Ma for her birthday, which was coming up in a few months, adding in this new branch of the family.

Once the applause had died down, Clare continued speaking, bringing me back to the festivities. "This is truly a momentous occasion. Yi-ping has been searching for her lost daughter for sixty-three years, and because of a chance encounter between her granddaughter Liv and Simon, who's like part of our family, at the airport, we were able to reunite them."

Clare continued to speak, but Simon took my hand in his, and I didn't hear another word. He was seated next to me, with Ah-Ma on my other side and Amy next to Simon. Even though we were surrounded by people, for a moment, it was as if I were alone in the room with him. The smile he aimed at me, the warmth of his hand in mine, the way my body was drawn to his; I'd never felt like this before. And added to that the emotions of having witnessed Ah-Ma reuniting with her daughter yesterday, and having my best friend here with me, and I felt as though anything was possible in that moment. I was so filled with hope and joy, it was a wonder I didn't suddenly burst into song and start dancing around the room. Simon's hand in mine kept me anchored, and all I could do was smile back at him as everyone clapped at whatever Clare was saying.

The night was full of laughter and chatter, and I met more of Sue and Clare's relatives, including Henry and his wife. Amy chatted with Simon, telling him embarrassing stories from our time in college. Mandarin, Taiwanese, and English all melded together, and everyone kept toasting Ah-Ma and Sue. My grandmother's face was flushed, with rosy spots on her cheek from the whiskey she'd thrown down as if she did shots all the time. It was so great for me to see my grandmother in her element, and I FaceTimed with my mother and brother for a few minutes so they could see how happy Ah-Ma was. My mother was already planning to fly out to New York once Sue returned. She and her older sisters and Winston had a Zoom call planned with Sue for the next day.

Many courses appeared, from platters of sushi and sashimi on elaborate boats to cold dishes like spicy cucumbers, tofu with bonito flakes, cold noodles with a sesame sauce, and sea urchin and sliced abalone. Then a giant tureen of seafood soup arrived, followed by more entrées than I could count—everything from a whole fish cooked to perfection with ginger and leeks to clams in black bean sauce, sizzling sliced pepper steak that smelled heavenly, long noodles filled with vegetables, and so much more. When Ah-Ma got up to talk to someone on the other side of the table, Francesca plunked herself down in her chair.

"I just looked up your YouTube channel. You and Ah-Ma are so good together." She held out her phone, and I could see she was playing back the video of us making Taiwanese scallion pancakes. There was flour on the end of Ah-Ma's nose, but she was oblivious as she instructed me on how to get numerous layers in the light and crispy pancakes. I was laughing but trying to keep a straight face on the screen until Ah-Ma stopped and put her hands on her hip, demanding to know what was so funny.

Simon smiled as he watched the video. "There's something almost hypnotic about the two of you together."

Amy nodded. "You guys have been going viral."

I blushed. "People love Ah-Ma." I'd known our videos were getting many views, but I hadn't really watched them again after I'd posted them.

"Don't sell yourself short, Liv." Amy gave me a mock frown. "You've always been so good on camera. That's why you have such a large following."

I smiled at Amy's loyalty, knowing she was right. I needed to give myself more credit for everything I'd achieved.

"And the way you wove in her story about her lost daughter with each recipe." Francesca put a hand to her heart. "That was what did it for me."

Simon leaned back in his chair and looked at Francesca as the waiters cleared away our dishes. "When do you go home?"

"Tomorrow. I wish I was staying longer. But work calls." She rolled her eyes.

"Yeah, I know," Simon said. "I leave in three days. Wish I could stay longer too." He glanced at me out of the corner of his eyes. "Liv and I are going to Sun Moon Lake tomorrow after she and Ah-Ma meet with the producers." He looked over at Amy. "Want to come with us?"

Amy cackled, which made Simon and Francesca grin. "No, I don't want to go on a romantic date with the two of you to Sun Moon Lake. Besides, my plane leaves tomorrow afternoon for New York."

"Short trip," Francesca remarked.

"I know. I wish she could stay longer." I was looking forward to Sun Moon Lake with Simon before he had to go back to New York, though. I turned to Francesca. "What do you do for work?"

"I'm a lawyer, of course." Francesca smirked. "Typical Taiwanese overachiever, specializing in intellectual property protection and licensing." She yawned as she said this. "It's so boring it puts me to sleep just talking about it."

I burst into laughter, not only at her words, but the look on her face. "Love your job?"

"Love it." She gave me a knowing look. "But I have a five-year plan. I'm going to stick it out for another five years, then I'm getting married, having kids, and becoming a stay-at-home mom."

"That's nice." I nodded. "You have a boyfriend?"

Simon snickered as Francesca pealed in laughter. "Nope. But I'll find one."

"She will." Simon gave us a serious look. "Francesca has always gotten everything she sets her mind on. It's really scary."

"Oh, you exaggerate." She swatted Simon on the arm and then jumped up when Ah-Ma and Clare approached us. "Here you go, Ah-Ma. Sit." She gestured to Simon. "Come with me. You've barely spoken to Big Auntie all night. You know she's going to be offended if you don't do your duty."

Simon groaned and leaned over to whisper in my ear, "She's a big gossip. I know she's going to grill me about you."

I tried not to smile, but the look on Simon's face was so pitiful I couldn't help the big grin that spread over my face. Simon allowed Francesca to lead him away. Clare, in the act of sitting down with us, knocked a bowl off the table with her elbow. I saw the bowl fall, knew I wasn't in danger, but flight took over in my body and I slid off my chair, cowering down as the adrenaline revved up my heart. I could hear every beat in my ears, and my breath came in gasps. All I could think was, *No. Run. Get away. He has a gun.* It was as if I were floating somewhere above myself, watching the panic attack happening while trying to tell myself I was okay, that I was safe here and not back at 852. But the panic won out over logic, and I was left a gasping mess. Gentle hands touched my shoulder, my back, and then Ah-Ma and Amy were by my side, lifting me up and practically carrying me out of the crowded dining room.

When I became aware of my surroundings again, the first thing I noticed was that I'd dug my nails into my palms so hard that I'd almost broken skin. The second thing I thought of was defeat that once again, I'd let panic take over. I blinked, wondering where I was.

"We took you into a side room. It wasn't being used tonight," Amy said, reading my mind as usual.

"Oh." That was all I could manage as I saw Amy, Ah-Ma, and Clare hovering over the chair they'd placed me in.

Ah-Ma handed me a glass of water, and I took a sip, grateful for the cool liquid, even though my hands shook so hard that the water almost sloshed out.

"Liv." That was all my grandmother said.

I met her eyes and pressed my lips together tightly before answering. "I know. I need help."

"Has this been going on since the shooting?" Clare still had ahold of my arm, even though I was safely in my chair. "I hope you don't mind—your grandmother told us what happened."

I nodded, too ashamed to say anything else.

"Liv, honey." Clare sat in the chair next to mine and scooted it closer. "There's no shame in asking for help. If a bowl breaking on the floor can elicit such a reaction of terror from you, you need to address it."

It was exactly what Simon had said to me. Looking around at the three pairs of concerned eyes, I was embarrassed, but something else was lurking on the edge of my consciousness. Ah-Ma and Clare had gone through things that were unimaginable to me, yet they were still here, stronger for not having given up in the face of adversity. Was I really going to let something like a panic attack prevent me from living my life when I could get help?

"I thought I could ride it out, that it would go away by itself." My mouth trembled, and I squeezed my lips together. "I guess I was wrong." I looked at Clare. "I'm sorry for disturbing the celebration."

"You have nothing to be sorry for." Clare patted my hand. "We all react to situations differently. But I hope you'll think of getting help. For your own peace of mind."

"Are you okay to stand?" Amy asked. When I nodded, she said, "Come on. I'll take you home." She turned to Ah-Ma. "You stay, enjoy your night. I'll take care of Liv."

And then Amy put an arm around me, and with my best friend's help, I rose on shaky legs, giving Ah-Ma and Clare one last hug before we left the restaurant.

Hours later, I couldn't sleep, my mind filled with the events of the past two days. Amy was softly snoring in the bed next to me, having conked out soon after we got home. Francesca and I had exchanged contact information and promised to stay in touch. Thoughts of Simon filled my mind, and then I'd think about Ah-Ma and Yili again. It was as if my brain had decided to play hopscotch, jumping around instead of resting. I pounded my pillow impatiently, willing sleep to come. But damn, it wouldn't, and I sat up abruptly, completely awake.

Deciding to find a midnight snack, I got out of bed, closing the door softly behind me so that I wouldn't disturb Amy. As I passed Ah-Ma's room to make my way to the kitchen, I saw a light under her door. I'd heard her get home about an hour ago. Could she not sleep either? I imagined she'd be filled with all sorts of emotions after finding Yili. I shook my head. I meant Sue. It was going to be hard to think of her as Aunt Sue.

I decided to knock on my grandmother's door. Maybe we could keep each other company. "Ah-Ma? Are you awake?"

"Liv?" I heard through the door. "What are you doing up?"

"Can I come in?" I waited until my grandmother assented before pushing open her door.

She was sitting in bed, two pillows behind her and with something on her lap. As I moved closer, I saw that it was a book, but it was upside down.

"Reading?" I teased.

She held the book up with a sheepish look. "I couldn't sleep, so I thought I'd read. But I can't stop thinking about Ang-Li." Her face sobered. "I feel terrible for what Ang-Li and Jin went through. And all because of my husband." She patted the space next to her. "Come."

I took a running start and jumped into the bed with a breathless laugh. I used to do this when I was young, rushing to my grandmother's bedroom when I woke before anyone else in the house. I knew she'd be up, for she was an early riser like me. She always smiled when she saw me, which was my invitation to get into bed with her. She'd pull her comforter over me, and we'd snuggle together as I'd tell her what I was looking forward to that day, or what was bothering me. It was our special time together, before the rest of the household woke up.

"Did you read more of the journal than what you told me before Sue showed up?" I wished again that I could read it for myself.

My grandmother nodded.

If I stayed in Taiwan, I was going to take a Mandarin class while working on the cookbook with Ah-Ma. And there was that possibility of filming a show. The producer had said he wanted to weave in the footage I'd shot with the new program. He was interested in filming a few episodes to see how they'd do. I was excited for our meeting. But for now, I wanted to hear more about Ang-Li.

"I wish I'd known him," Ah-Ma finally said, a wistful look on her face. "Or that I'd gotten a chance to thank him for taking such good care of Yi . . . I mean Sue." She shook her head in regret. "It's a shame he passed away right as I found my daughter. And that he thought I was a monster."

"He really thought that?" My forehead crinkled.

"Yes. For a long time he did." Ah-Ma looked down at her hands and was quiet for a moment before she began to tell me what she'd read in his journal.

23
ANG-LI

August 1961, Taichung

I made the final preparations to leave Taiwan and was relieved I'd put the wheels in motion months ago. It was no easy task to get myself a passport and visa to study in the United States, much less to get ones for all my children. I had to go through many checkpoints, including clearance from the Taiwan Garrison Command, the same secret police unit that had captured Jin. But for some reason, I'd gotten mine without any problems. I wondered if Po had had anything to do with it, his way of making right what he'd done to Jin, but I wouldn't acknowledge that thought. I had more important things to dwell on. Like how I was going to convince the government to let me take all four children with me. No matter how I fought, they wouldn't budge.

"They're all under eight," I'd argued, "and their mother is dead." I didn't elaborate on Jin's death. "What am I supposed to do, leave them to fend for themselves here?"

"Send them to live with relatives," was the answer I got. No matter what I said, I was always rejected. It wasn't until my brother-in-law in the States, who had a friend who was a US congressman, got involved by sending the Taiwanese government a letter that the KMT finally granted all four children permission to leave Taiwan. Po had given Jin official papers for adopting Hsu-Min, so she was included as one of my children. I breathed a sigh of relief the day I got their passports.

Everything was in place. The children had helped me pack up the clothes and belongings they wanted to take to America, and I'd given away everything else to neighbors and friends. I had my acceptance letter from the university in Georgia, and my sister had booked us plane tickets. I'd spoken to my parents, who lived down south in Kaohsiung, and said goodbye. I'd wanted to visit them before I left, but with Jin's execution, I was afraid to make the trip. And my father had just had knee surgery, making it difficult for him to travel. My heart ached, and I wondered when I'd see them again.

The day we left, I stopped in to say goodbye to Wong Tai Tai. She sat behind the glass counter on her high stool and watched me as I made my way back to her. She didn't move until I was in front of her, and then she finally got off the stool and came around to stand in front of me. She spoke before I could.

"The mother, she was just here, looking for her little girl." Wong Tai Tai's gaze didn't waver.

"What?" I felt ice in my veins. We were so close, and yet, on the very day when we would leave Taiwan, Po's wife had found her way to Wong Tai Tai's store? "What did she want?"

"They showed me the girl's picture. Wanted to know if I knew the Ong family who had adopted her." I couldn't read the expression on Wong Tai Tai's face.

"'They'?" Had Po been with her? He knew I had his daughter. Why would he be asking about her?

"No, not him." Wong Tai Tai shook her head. "It was the mother and a friend. I didn't tell them anything, but I overheard their conversation. She said that she 'threw her daughter out like garbage.' That she didn't love her and wished that she'd died."

"No." I'd just been starting to feel sympathy for Yi-ping, that perhaps she really hadn't known what Po had done to their child, but at Wong Tai Tai's words, my heart hardened. "How could any mother say that about her own child?" I wanted to run home and gather Hsu-Min in my arms and hold her tight, reassure her that no one would ever throw her away again.

"I don't know. I wasn't close to them, so I only heard certain words, but . . ." Wong Tai Tai trailed off and shook her head. "I have a bad feeling. If she hadn't wanted the girl, then why were they here, asking about her?"

"We're leaving. Today." Wong Tai Tai didn't know our plans, for she'd told me not to tell her any details. In case she was ever brought in and questioned, it would be better if she didn't know where we were going. I closed my eyes for a moment, wondering what kind of world we lived in where a woman who'd only ever done good had to be worried about being tortured for information.

"It's for the best. Safer for you and for the girl." She nodded, and I saw her breath hitch. She blinked a few times, and I realized I was going to miss her. She'd been a steady part of our days, someone we could rely on to help make us better when we were sick. She knew everything and was generous with her time, looking out for everyone in the neighborhood. Even though I didn't have romantic feelings for her, I cared about her and was sorry that I wouldn't see her after today.

"Goodbye." My words were formal, but I didn't know how else to express my gratitude. She'd been a good friend, and without her help, I'd probably not have gotten to say goodbye to Jin. "Thank you for everything."

She cleared her throat and tried to smile, but tears filled her eyes, and she ran the back of her hand over them. She opened her mouth, but nothing came out. So, I did the only thing I could. I took her in my arms and held her close, saying everything I wanted to say with my embrace.

When we pulled away, she finally spoke. "Take care of the children. And yourself. If the woman comes back, I won't tell her anything."

"Thank you."

"I'll miss you all." Her voice was gruff, and she scowled, but I knew she was covering her true feelings.

"We'll miss you too." I gave her one last look and then turned and went out the door. I had a feeling I might never see her again.

When I got back to our apartment, our suitcases and bags were lined up by the door. I gave Clare a look of thanks, for she must have placed them there. It was time to go. I looked around the apartment I'd shared with Jin and eventually the children for the past seven years. Every space was filled with memories, and I didn't want to let them go. I'd been comforted by our home the last month because Jin had touched that chair, slept in our bed, and left behind that shirt that still smelled like her. But now all of it was packed up and gone, and we were leaving.

Clare came to my side and slipped her hand into mine. "We'll be okay, Baba."

I nodded because I couldn't speak. Unable to bear it any longer, I reached down to pick up two of the bags and started transferring them to the ground floor. We hadn't packed much because we didn't want to attract attention. I paid someone to drive us to the airport in Taipei, and the children were surprisingly good in the car, as if they sensed the gravity of what was happening. Even George, who would normally be peppering me with questions about where we were going and if there would be a boy his age to play with since Clare was so boring and no fun, was silent for most of the trip.

The children were still quiet when we entered the airport, the crowd and chaos holding their attention. Their heads turned at the announcements over the loudspeakers, and they watched as people hurried by. I had a moment of panic when I realized I was leaving the only place I'd ever lived, and I had no idea where to go in this airport. Taiwan was my home, and I suddenly berated myself for not making the trip down to say goodbye to my parents. I'd almost lost it and bawled like a baby during that last phone call to them.

"You'll be fine, ah?" my mother had said. I'd been holding it together those past months ever since Jin had been taken and executed, because I needed to be a rock for my children. But for just a tiny amount of time, I was the child again. Tears leaked out of my eyes, and I muffled the phone with a hand, not wanting my parents to know.

"I'm sorry about your wife. You're doing the right thing. *Jie Jie* will take care of you once you get to America." My father was referring to my older sister.

I'd nodded, still unable to speak.

I squeezed my eyes shut now, not realizing how much I wished I could see my parents again before heading off to the unknown, a single father going to a land where everything would be different, from the language and the culture to the food. What was I doing, taking four young children all the way across the world to a country that I'd only seen in pictures? I knew some English, but would it be enough to get by and get through school? How would I make a living once we'd gone through the small savings that Jin and I had?

Just as I was about to usher all the children out the door and find a ride back to our apartment, Clare pointed ahead. "There. That's our airline." She headed toward it, and I let out a breath and then followed her.

Unlike my older sister, who'd left for America as soon as she could, I didn't long to explore different countries. Taiwan, as imperfect as it was, was my country. Now that the time had come to leave, I realized I didn't want to. I vowed that one day, I'd come back when it was safe and make Taiwan my home again.

But for now, America was about to be our new reality. I took a deep breath and said goodbye to my country as we headed for our gate. I gathered my children ahead of me, bringing up the rear. I didn't dare look back for fear I'd lose my resolve and herd everyone out the door, running all the way back to a place that was no longer our home.

※

June 1963, Georgia

America was kind to us. My sister, who'd gone by Emily Chang ever since she married Joe Chang, found us a decent apartment close to their house. It only had one bedroom, but Joe had found an old bunk bed for the boys, and the girls slept together in a full-size bed. I slept on the couch in the living room. I was often up late studying after the children went to bed, so it worked out. I found that I liked my studies. The first year, I struggled to just learn English well enough to get by even as I nursed the Jin-shaped hole in my heart. Not a day went by that I didn't think of her. Sometimes it was the happier times, but more often than not, I tortured myself imagining the two months she'd spent in jail and what they had done to her. I'd wake in the middle of the night, my heart pounding and sweat drenching my shirt, because I'd dreamed once again of her execution and my frantic efforts to get her out. The nightmares woke me often and left me exhausted.

One day, I was in the library of the college, laboring to look up the definition of a word, all the English swimming before my eyes until it might as well have been written in Greek. I put my forehead down on the table because I was so tired. I needed to rest my eyes for just a moment.

Thank goodness I had Emily to help with the two younger kids while I was in classes. But my struggle to understand English and read the assignments made me work harder than the other students. Plus, at thirty-one, I was older than most of them. It was lonely, not having any friends at my new school.

A hand landed gently on my shoulder, causing me to jolt. I looked up to find an older woman with the darkest skin I'd ever seen and gray-streaked brown hair looking at me with eyes that shone of kindness.

"Do you need help?" Her tone was gentle, but I was afraid I was about to be yelled at for falling asleep at the library like a miscreant.

"Sorry. Not mean to sleep." I struggled to think of the right words, but she stopped me by holding up a hand.

"It's okay. My name is Mrs. Davis. I help many of the students who are learning English as a second language." She handed me a card. "I'm a tutor."

"Oh." I looked down at the card. ROSE DAVIS, ENGLISH TUTOR, it said.

"I see you're a hard worker. Always here at the library." She gestured to the textbooks and dictionary I had scattered in front of me. "Would you like me to work with you?"

I did a quick calculation of our finances, wondering if I had enough to cover a tutor. If we lived frugally, I might be able to manage it, and I had to admit I was in over my head. Emily had told me about a job bagging groceries at the nearby store on the weekends. It was minimum wage but would help supplement the savings I had.

"Yes. I need help." I hated to admit that, but I knew I would fail every one of my courses if I didn't start to understand English better.

She nodded and took the seat next to me. I looked at her in surprise, wondering what she was doing.

"No time like the present, right?" Her dark eyes twinkled at me, and I gave her a hesitant smile. It was seven at night, and Emily had all the children at her house until I could pick them up. Shouldn't this woman be home with her own family having dinner?

"You not go home? You family, um, wait for you?" I asked, my brows knitted together.

She shook her head. "It's just me. My husband passed away five years ago, and all my kids are grown with their own lives."

"Oh." I didn't know what to say to that. I wondered if she was lonely. But she didn't look it. She seemed quite content as she reached for my homework assignment and read it over before turning to me. "Shall we?"

Mrs. Davis was a lifesaver. She started working with me a couple of times a week, and then it went up to three or four times a week, sometimes in our home, when Emily couldn't mind my children. She refused to charge me for her work, claiming she'd been doing this on a volunteer basis ever since her husband passed away and she found herself with too much time on her hands. She introduced me to another Taiwanese family, also named Huang, causing her to ask me if all Taiwanese people were named Huang. I laughed and said no. But my George became good friends with the other Huangs' boy Steven.

Since Mrs. Davis wouldn't take payment, I cooked for her and the other Huangs instead, introducing Mrs. Davis to Taiwanese dishes that made the Huangs and me homesick.

"This is delicious, Ang," she said, digging into her bowl of noodle soup. "What's it called again?" She slurped up a long piece of noodle, causing Henry and Hsu-Min to giggle.

"Niu rou mien," Steven Huang said, slurping up his own noodles.

I smiled at them, proud they were all enjoying my cooking. I'd gotten better lately, by trial and error. Even George, the pickiest eater of the four, would generally eat the meals I made these days.

"It reminds me of Gullah cooking. Rich, thick, and so delicious." She'd told me she was from the Lowcountry of South Carolina and described her big family, some of whom still lived there. She'd moved to Georgia with her husband for his work and stayed because she loved it so.

Hsu-Min snuggled into her side, smiling shyly at her.

"Hello to you too, Miss Sue," Mrs. Davis said.

Hsu-Min giggled. "My name Sue," she said in English. And that was how Hsu-Min became Sue.

I'd been surprised at how fast Sue and Henry had picked up English. I let them watch cartoons on TV, knowing that immersing them in the language was the best thing I could do for them. George was a bit slower to learn, but I knew he missed Taiwan more than the younger two and was glad he had a friend in Steven. I'd found George and Clare huddled together one Sunday morning, crying over a photo of their mother. I'd had to swallow the giant lump in my throat, knowing there was nothing I could do to soothe their pain. How was I supposed to be both mother and father to our children? Some days, it was all I could do to drag myself up to face another day without her. But our children were what always got me up and going, because I needed to build a better life for them.

With Mrs. Davis's help that first year, I finally caught up to the rest of my class, and I eventually graduated with honors. She was there at my graduation with my four children, my sister and her husband, their two children, and the other Huangs. My English had improved so much that I'd gotten a job as a translator for a major company in Atlanta. Clare, who was twelve when I graduated, bought me a leather briefcase with Mrs. Davis's help and proudly presented it to me at dinner that night.

"Congratulations, Baba." She beamed at me, and my heart swelled with pride at how mature she was. We'd weathered so much together, and she was the only one of my children to have concrete memories of Jin. We had a special bond, and I was happy to see how Mrs. Davis had taken her under her wing, guiding her through the pains of her preteen years.

But try as I did to relax, to believe that our new home in Georgia was safe, I was haunted by what had happened to Jin. I couldn't let my guard down, and I knew I'd never tell my children what had really happened. Hsu-Min must never know what her father had done to my wife. And I would die before letting her know that her biological mother hadn't wanted her. I vowed, that day when I finally had a real job and was able to provide for my family, that my children would never know what had really happened. It was the only way I knew how to protect them.

24
Liv

The night after the celebration dinner, I sat on the balcony of Simon's and my hotel room overlooking the lake in Ita Thao while Simon took a shower. My flowered sundress fluttered lightly in the breeze, and my wet hair was wound up on top of my head and anchored with a clip. My grandmother had told me about Sun Moon Lake, a beautiful lake less than a two-hour drive from Taichung that was in Nantou County, right in the middle of Taiwan. It was considered one of the most beautiful places in Taiwan and was famous for its scenic bike paths, beautiful hiking trails, rich indigenous culture, and delectable aboriginal cuisine, with temples and pagodas and a street food market at the Ita Thao Shopping District. When Simon had suggested the morning of the celebration dinner that we go for an overnight visit, I was surprised, but also filled with anticipation.

"Isn't May a bad time to visit?" I'd heard that it could rain for days during this month.

"Yes, but I looked at the weather for the next two days, and we're in luck." He cleared his throat. "What do you say? I'd like to spend time with you. Alone."

My stomach fluttered because I wanted that as much as he did. I craved a chance to get to know him better and see if there was more than just surface attraction between us. Simon was going back to New York in two days, and this would be our chance to finally see if the pull between us was real.

Simon had driven us here after Ah-Ma and I had a successful meeting with the producers this morning. I talked nonstop on the drive about the show, and how the producers had offered us a contract that I was ready to sign but Ah-Ma had said she wanted to read over more carefully. Simon laughed at my enthusiasm, reaching over to squeeze my thigh briefly before returning his hand to the steering wheel.

"Are you okay, though?" Simon asked, knowing I was sad about Amy leaving soon after our meeting.

"Yes." I nodded. "At least we'll be on the same continent. I'm going to visit her in Vietnam as soon as she gets back."

"That's good," Simon said. "You'll also finally get a chance to really know Taiwan and learn the language, since you're staying for a while." His words were positive, but I heard a note of sadness in his tone.

I was wondering if that sadness meant he'd miss me if I didn't return to New York right away when Simon joined me on the balcony, dressed in khaki shorts and a white T-shirt that shone against his dark skin. My heart skipped a beat, and my hand reached out to him without a thought. He took it and moved the other chair on the balcony until it was right next to mine. He sat, keeping our hands linked.

"It's so beautiful here. Peaceful." I looked out over the serene water at the mountains rising in the distance, the horizon a beautiful shade of orange as the sun started setting. "It's exactly what I needed after the last few days."

"I'm glad you like it. I know you've been through so much lately." His body leaned toward mine, and I shifted so that our shoulders touched.

We'd explored different trails at Sun Moon Lake, walking into the greenery with tall leafy trees surrounding us on both sides. A monkey swung on a branch above us, and we saw birds and butterflies of every color when we walked along the lake. We visited temples and climbed up many steps, side by side, marveling at the view from the top, the blue of the lake spread out below us in every direction. We didn't hold hands, but he stayed close enough that I could feel the heat from his body. We were silent for most of it, taking in the beauty around us. It had been a comfortable silence, but now I wanted to know more about him. Amy's words to me before she left for the airport echoed in my head.

Get to know him. See if you're compatible. What do you have to lose? He's already seen you at your worst.

"Why aren't you seeing anyone right now?" *Smooth, Liv.*

"I was engaged once, right out of grad school." His voice was distant as he stared at the lake. "My sister didn't like her. Said she was too materialistic, focusing too much on status." He turned to me, a wry smile on his lips. "Looking back, I have to admit I was taken with her outer package and was too young to realize that that wasn't all you needed for a good marriage. She did us a favor when she broke off the engagement before we put down a deposit for a venue. I've dated since then, even a long-term one for about two years. But we parted when we realized we were more like good friends who lived together." He turned to me. "What about you?"

I shrugged. "I've never cared about being paired up. I think that was my grandmother's influence. She told me it was more important to find myself, to know what I want, rather than chase a relationship. If someone right came along, then I would consider myself lucky."

"And no one right has come along?" His voice was light.

"No." I gave him a small smile. "At least not so far."

His eyes held my gaze as my heart thundered in my ears. I was the first to look away, but he kept my hand firmly in his. Silence descended as we absorbed the breathtaking view in front of us. It felt so far away from the busy city streets of Taichung, as if we'd somehow been transported to a magical land where everyday problems didn't exist.

Without realizing it, I started to speak, to tell him about what I'd been through before I came to Taiwan.

"I'd never seen anyone die before. Never seen so much blood splattered all over like that, never seen the scene of a murder, except in movies." I stopped, not sure how to go on. .

Simon didn't say anything, but his quiet acceptance calmed my nerves. He looked out over the water, and somehow, that made it easier to tell him what had been on my mind ever since that night at 852.

"I can't get the pictures that are imbedded in my mind from that night out of my head. I'll be going about my life, trying to figure out how to live, and any loud noise or sudden movement will trigger the absolute terror from that night." I squeezed my eyes shut, not wanting to see that man pointing the gun at me. "I didn't know Cat well, and yes, I was so upset that she died, but at the same time, I was relieved it wasn't Amy."

"Was she supposed to be working that night?" Simon asked.

I opened my eyes to look at him. "Yes. But she had a migraine that day, and the new girl, Cat, who Amy was training, said she could handle the shift. It was a weeknight, so wasn't as busy as it would have been on the weekend."

"Ah." He nodded.

"I can't help being glad that Amy wasn't working that day." A shiver went down my spine. "But then that means I'm glad Cat died, and how can I be, when I saw her die?"

He reached out, his fingers skimming over the skin of my arm. I shivered again, this time because of his touch. "Being glad your best friend wasn't killed isn't the same as being glad someone else was. Don't beat yourself up for how you feel."

"I know." My fingers fluttered briefly over his before I let them drop. "And that's the problem. My head knows this, but my heart can't make sense of it. Amy isn't just my best friend. She's someone that gets me and lets me be me. She's my foodie partner and my travel partner, and even when one of us was dating someone, we always knew that if the other called, we'd drop everything to be there."

I smiled, remembering the time when we were freshmen in college, and Amy called because she didn't know what a blow job was and had blown on a guy's crotch, making him die laughing. She was humiliated, and I'd gone to her dorm room so that we could drown her misery in cheap beer and late-night pizza dipped in blue cheese.

"A friendship like that is a rare thing." Simon's fingers slipped away from my arm, and I missed his touch.

"It is, and we know it." I squeezed my eyes shut for a moment and then opened them to find Simon focused completely on me, his dark eyes compassionate. "I can't forgive myself," I whispered. "Even though deep down, I knew there was nothing I could have done to save Cat, I still feel responsible somehow, that I lived, and she didn't."

Simon reached over and drew my head against his shoulder. He stroked a hand down my hair, and I closed my eyes, comforted to be against him, his body warming my frozen heart. He didn't speak for a moment, and I was grateful.

"The heart doesn't always heed what the head knows." His voice rumbled against my ear, and my other hand reached across his chest in a loose hug. "It's survivor's guilt, and nothing will make you forgive yourself, except time. And the knowledge that Cat wouldn't have wanted you to blame yourself. There was nothing you or anyone else could have done to change the situation. All you can do is be grateful Chef Wu jumped the man before he shot you again."

I nodded against his shoulder because that was exactly what I'd been telling myself all these months. I'd resisted going to see a therapist because I knew this was what they would say to me, and I hadn't been ready to hear it.

"I've isolated myself, staying in my apartment, afraid to go out." This was the hardest thing to admit. But what the past few days had taught me was that holding things in, keeping secrets, led to misunderstandings. I didn't want that to happen to Simon and me. "I stopped answering my friends' calls and texts and didn't leave my apartment for two months after Amy left for her travels and my grandmother came back here."

This was the point where I knew Simon would either run away screaming or accept me for the mess I was. I was laying it out on the line, showing him the real Liv Kuo. I'd lived like a hermit since that night, and while my time in Taiwan had been a reprieve, I wasn't sure if I had the courage to live life the way I used to. And most of all, I didn't know if I had the courage to open myself up to a possible relationship with Simon.

He didn't speak, only drew me closer to him so that I was practically on his lap. He stroked a hand down my hair again, and I sighed. I didn't want to face reality, didn't want to think of all that waited for me back in New York.

"You'll be okay," he finally said. "I believe in you." He kissed the side of my temple and then drew my head against his chest. "I'm here for you, if you want me."

My heart thudded so hard I could hear it in my ears, and then I picked my head up to look at him. Then we were kissing, my arms wrapping around his neck, his hand cupping my cheek, and I knew everything that had happened had led to this moment with this man. He stood and I went with him in one fluid motion, and then we were moving back inside, onto the bed. He pulled away to look down at me, our legs entwined, my arms holding him close. I couldn't get enough of him, wanting to feel him against me. When I smiled, he let out a breath, and then his lips closed over mine again, and I knew I'd found the other half of my soul.

25
Liv

I woke with the knowledge that I wasn't alone in the bed. Before I opened my eyes or was even aware of where I was, a languid feeling spread through my body, making me smile and stretch my arms over my head. I was aware of a leg thrown over mine, an arm across my middle, and I snuggled a bit closer, knowing it was Simon but not quite ready to be fully awake and acknowledge what had happened between us last night. Because it had been the most magical night of my life. I'd had many boyfriends, and even more sexual encounters, but nothing had prepared me for what Simon and I had shared. It wasn't just physical attraction, which I'd always thought was important. It went way beyond that, and when Simon hovered over me, it was like looking into an alternate vision of myself, knowing I'd found the one person I'd been waiting for all this time. I saw in his eyes that he felt the same, and our union was unlike anything I'd ever experienced.

I didn't want to wake up now because I feared that, in the light of the day, it had all been an illusion. I wanted to stay in that dream world between sleeping and awake when anything was possible. I had such strong feelings for this man, and I didn't trust them, didn't trust myself.

Simon shifted in the bed, and I sensed he was awake. I didn't move for a few moments, but then the feeling of someone staring at me had my eyes popping open. He was looking at me with a smile on his face, and my lips curved too.

"Hi," he said, his voice husky.

I smiled wider but didn't speak. I didn't want to break the spell. I didn't want to leave this magical hotel and would always remember our time here together. We'd gone down to the street market after making love, both ravenous. We'd gotten so much food and stuffed ourselves, eating it in the street and grinning at each other. We then returned to our room and spent the next few hours tangled together, making each other laugh and then succumbing once again. I'd drifted off at some point, satiated and so happy, wondering when the other shoe was going to drop, because this kind of happiness always brought tragedy. That was the way of my family, never trusting a good thing, knowing something bad was going to follow.

My phone rang just then, making me jump. I grabbed it off the side table, frowning at the display. "It's Ah-Ma," I said. "I hope everything is okay." I sat up, bringing the sheets up to cover my chest as I answered the call.

"I did it," Ah-Ma crowed. "I'm amazing."

I chuckled and then said, "Of course you're amazing. But what are you talking about?"

"I just called the producers. I got them to give us six episodes by telling them four is an unlucky number."

I gasped. They had offered us only four episodes yesterday, and I didn't really think Ah-Ma could get them to up that number. "You *are* amazing."

"This is really happening." Ah-Ma's voice trembled. "They were so invested in our YouTube videos, but now that we found Yili, they said it's going to make for even greater TV."

"You're okay with that?" I didn't want Ah-Ma to feel like she was being exploited.

"Yes." Her voice was firm. "There's so much bad in this world. I want people to see that if you believe, good things can happen too. They want Yili to make an appearance, if she's comfortable."

"Then we're really doing this." My voice shook with excitement and a little bit of fear.

"We are. I'm so happy you're going to stay in Taiwan for a bit. Yili has decided to stay too." Ah-Ma's voice practically burst with happiness.

"Shouldn't you call her Sue?" I asked.

"She told me to call her Yili. It was what I named her, and she said it felt right."

"Oh, Ah-Ma." I was so happy for her. We chatted for a minute more and then said goodbye.

When I hung up, I found Simon studying me with a strange expression on his face. "You're staying in Taiwan."

"Yes." I reached out and touched him on the arm. Even though I was excited about staying and doing the show, I was sad that Simon was leaving the next day. Simon and I were so new. Would whatever was happening between us fizzle out before it even had a chance to begin?

Simon took my hand in his as his face darkened for a brief moment.

"What is it?" I asked.

He stared at me and then shook his head. "Nothing. Just a thought I had. I'll tell you later. Let's enjoy our time together and worry about what comes after when we get to it, okay?"

I wondered what he was keeping back, but I didn't want to dwell on it, so I nodded. We'd planned on heading back to Taichung after lunch, and I was looking forward to spending the morning outside, exploring more of the area. I turned and wrapped my arms around him, and he drew me close. It would be another forty minutes before we finally made it out of the bed.

Back in Taichung later that afternoon, I found Ah-Ma in her kitchen humming as she stirred something on the stove. Simon had dropped me off and said he had some things to take care of, but we planned to meet up for dinner later that night.

"That smells so good. What is it?" I followed my nose into the kitchen, still floating on a cloud from my time with Simon.

"*Rou geng.* Left over from last night." Ah-Ma turned to me, her face all lit up.

"How did it go?" I'd forgotten that Ah-Ma had had Yili and Clare over last night, finally cooking some of the recipes she'd saved for when she found her daughter again.

Ah-Ma's hand went to her chest. "It was exactly as I'd imagined." She looked at me, her eyes shining. "She wants to call me Mama."

"I'm so happy for you." My heart felt ready to burst, not just for Ah-Ma, but for how I was feeling about Simon.

"Are you hungry?" Ah-Ma turned back to give the pot another stir. "I was just heating this up for a snack."

"Sure. I'm not going out to dinner with Simon until later." It would be our last night before he went back to New York. I'd toyed with the idea of getting a hotel room so we could have one more night together.

"Oh." Ah-Ma nodded knowingly. "I'm glad."

As if he knew we were talking about him, my phone rang with a call from Simon.

"Livia, hi."

A little glow spread in my chest at his use of my full name. "I have an idea for tonight—"

He cut in before I could continue. "About that. I'm so sorry to do this, but I have to go to Taipei tonight. Work related."

"What?" The smile on my face slipped away. "What work?"

"The university I taught at before. They need help." I heard rustling on the phone, and then he came back. "I have to go. Catch a train. I'm so sorry, Liv, but I'll make it up to you."

"But you're leaving tomorrow." I tried to keep the emotion out of my voice, but I heard the tremor in the last few words.

"I know." His voice softened. "I'll make it up to you. I promise. I'll see you in the morning, okay? Mr. Thomas can drive you to me? Ten a.m."

"Yes." That was all I could muster.

He said goodbye and then disconnected the call. Disappointment flooded through my system, along with doubt. What was so important that he was rushing to Taipei out of the blue instead of spending his last night with me? Had our time in Sun Moon Lake just been a fling and hadn't meant as much to him as it had to me? I had the sudden urge to cry, but instead I sank onto a dining chair, staring off into space.

"Everything okay?"

Ah-Ma's gentle voice made me jump. I looked up at her, my bottom lip sticking out. "I don't know."

Ah-Ma studied me for a moment, and I knew I looked the picture of a dejected (or should I say rejected) person. She reached over and chucked my chin. "Everything will be fine. Come." My grandmother gestured, turning back to the kitchen. "Let's eat. *Rou geng* always made you feel better. And I think I have something to take your mind off Simon."

"What is it?" Despite my disappointment, I was curious.

I watched as Ah-Ma spooned *rou geng* into two bowls and then brought them over to the table, where I was still slumped in my chair. I knew I should have gotten up to help her, but the heaviness in my heart was making me immobile.

"Before I show you, have you heard anything more from agents for our cookbook?" Ah-Ma began eating the soup, while I just stared at it, not hungry anymore.

"I haven't checked my email today." I'd been too wrapped up in Simon. Now I wondered if I'd imagined the connection we'd had and read too much into his actions.

"Well, check." Ah-Ma nudged my phone toward me, and I picked it up. I scanned my emails, my eyes widening before I looked up at Ah-Ma. "When did this happen?"

Ah-Ma beamed at me. "You know Clare's an editor. She knows a lot of agents. I showed her our proposal and sample recipes yesterday, and she got really excited. She forwarded it to an agent she knows that was looking for exactly what we're proposing."

"And this New York agent wants a phone call with us." I dropped my phone to the table, my mouth hanging open for a moment. Then I jumped up and ran to Ah-Ma's side. "Do you know what this means?"

Ah-Ma nodded, a wide smile breaking over her face. "I think she's interested. I was skeptical at first, telling Clare we didn't want to use her influence, but she said it's what the agent has been searching for. She just made the connection."

"This is incredible, Ah-Ma." I hugged her shoulders from behind her chair and then went back to my place at the table, suddenly ravenous. I spooned a big helping into my mouth, relishing all the flavors of home that we would hopefully be able to share with the world soon.

"I'm so glad you decided to stay in Taiwan for a couple of months." Ah-Ma's eyes shone with so much love that I had to look down because I felt as if I was going to cry. She reached out and took my hand in hers. "Thank you. You have no idea what this all means to me."

I squeezed her hand. "I would do anything for you." We stared at each other, the love between us so strong that I no longer felt sad about Simon canceling our date tonight. I would be fine, no matter what. I was going to finally make an appointment to see a therapist and sign up for a Mandarin class for English speakers. Whatever happened with Simon, I knew I'd become an even stronger person just by being here in Taiwan for Ah-Ma.

Ah-Ma let go first, and then went into her room without a word. I looked after her but then shrugged, focusing back on finishing my bowl of soup. When I drained the last drop, Ah-Ma put down a stack of papers bound together in front of me.

"What's this?" I looked at the papers, written all in Mandarin.

"Yili brought it last night. She made a copy of her father's journal. She thought I'd want to read the rest of his words, to understand her life and what happened to their family."

"That's really great of her to do that." I flipped through the papers. "I wish I could read this. Maybe soon."

Ah-Ma's lips curved. "I wanted to wait to read the rest with you. You've helped so much, and you're just as invested in this. What do you say we get comfortable on the couch, and I can read it to you?"

"Yes. I'll make some tea." I stood to put our bowls away in the sink. "I wish you'd met him before he passed away."

"Me too." My grandmother picked up the papers and hugged them to her chest.

When the tea was ready, I brought the tray to the coffee table and then settled at Ah-Ma's side. She opened the journal to a page she'd marked and began to read Ang-Li's last words to me.

26
ANG-LI

May 1976, Georgia

The years passed, and my children grew and became more American than Taiwanese. Henry and Sue no longer spoke any Mandarin or Taiwanese, and George could understand it but only spoke English. Clare was the only one who held on to our language and spoke to me in Mandarin and Taiwanese. But when Sue turned ten, she asked if she could go to Chinese school. I remember how happy I'd been that day that one of my children wanted to connect to our past. She eventually became fluent in Mandarin.

I was so proud of Clare when she graduated at the top of her high school class and got a full scholarship to Cornell University. She loved to read and write and wanted to get her MFA. I fully supported her dreams, and when she graduated from Cornell summa cum laude and landed a job at one of the biggest publishing houses in New York City, I knew all my sacrifice had been worth it.

I never stopped looking over my shoulders, even after all these years in Georgia. I stayed vigilant, aware of anyone who looked at our family too closely, wondering if the KMT had sent them. I knew I was overprotective of the children, but I couldn't help it. I woke at night, terrified that Po had found us and was taking Sue back. Whenever I fell fully asleep, I dreamed of Jin the way I'd last seen her, a prisoner, tortured and beaten, and I'd jolt awake, unable to sleep. Our children were thriving in America, but I was dying a little inside every day, tortured by the events in Taiwan, always tired because I was afraid to sleep.

But I knew Jin would have been so proud of our oldest child. Our baby was going to take New York City and the publishing world by storm. The week after her graduation, I was treating the whole family to celebrate Clare's good news at her favorite restaurant in Atlanta. I had just gotten out of the shower and was knotting my tie when Clare walked into my bedroom.

"I'm almost ready," I said, focusing on my tie. She was always so punctual, and I knew she hated when I was late.

"Baba." Her voice was clipped, and my hands stilled at her tone. "How could you keep this a secret from me all these years?"

I turned slowly; my body was suddenly flushed with heat because I knew whatever it was that she was referring to was not going to be good. And when I saw what she held in her hands, my heart literally stopped for a moment.

"Where did you get that?" I couldn't breathe. I always hid my journal carefully in the safe in my closet, not wanting my children to find it. It was the only outlet I had to express all the fear and anxiety I had while trying to raise my children alone and survive in this country.

"It was between the back of the couch and the bottom cushion." She stared at me without blinking, her face pale.

I remembered writing in it a couple of days ago, sad that Clare was growing up and knowing I had to let her go. I'd been writing a letter to Jin, telling her about our amazing daughter, and wishing she were here to witness Clare's graduation. I hadn't been able to sleep after and had broken out the whiskey, which I kept only for emergencies. I'd had a few shots and must have fallen asleep on the couch, because I'd woken up the next morning to George sitting on me to wake me up as Sue and Henry giggled by my head. Had my journal fallen into the crack at the back of the couch? How had I not realized it wasn't in its usual spot in my safe?

"You're not my father." Clare's chin wobbled, and I knew she was trying not to cry. Even though she was all grown up, I could still read her every expression.

"I am your father." I walked to stand in front of her.

"No, you're not. My real father killed my mother." She was crying now, the tears streaming down her cheeks and her nose running. "Why didn't you tell me the truth? I thought we always told each other everything?"

"Oh, Clare. I couldn't." I didn't know what else to say. She'd grown up as an American, while I still lived in fear like I had in Taiwan. I'd learned that there were things you didn't speak out loud, because you'd be punished for it one day. But now as I stared at my daughter, who looked so betrayed, I wondered if I'd done the right thing.

"I hate you." Clare's chest heaved with emotion. "I wish we'd never come to America."

And before I could stop her, she ran out of the room, leaving me staring helplessly after her, wondering what I could do to fix our relationship.

We never went out that night. Clare refused to come out of her room. I didn't find out until a few weeks later that she had contacted my parents in Taiwan and made arrangements to stay with them. Clare wasn't the one who told me. It was my mother, when she called to ask me when Clare's flight would arrive. I hung up the phone with a heavy heart, knowing I was losing my eldest daughter and not knowing what to do. I went to find Clare in her old room, where she'd been staying before her move to New York.

"Why?" That was all I said, but I could tell by the look in her eyes that she knew what I was referring to.

"I need to go." She turned away so that I only saw the back of her head.

"It's not safe." My heart pounded with fear, just thinking about my daughter going back to the very place I'd fled from. "You can't contact him. You don't know what he'll do."

For I knew my daughter, and I knew she planned on finding Po. The red stain that spread across her cheeks told me I was right.

"Clare, please." I moved closer to her. "Promise me you won't contact him."

She turned to me, and I saw the anguish in her eyes. "I . . ."

"Listen to me. He did terrible things to our family." I sat on the bed next to her. "If you must go back to Taiwan, then go, but promise you'll stay away from him."

She didn't say anything for a moment, but then she gave me a slight nod.

"Thank you." I wanted to take her in my arms, but that wasn't our way. Unlike the Americans around us, we didn't often hug or kiss each other. I settled for patting her on the back. "I wish you'd stay here, start your new job like you're supposed to."

"I can't. I need to go back." Her voice was tortured. "I dream about Taiwan."

"You'll come back soon? It's just for a visit?" I didn't want her to throw away her dreams because of what she'd read in my journal. I kicked myself again for being so careless. But at the same time, maybe I'd been wrong to keep the truth from my children. I only wanted to protect them.

"I don't know." She stood then and pulled her suitcase out of her closet while I sat on her bed, knowing there was nothing I could do to make her stay.

She left us the next day, after saying goodbye to her sisters and brother. She never moved back to America. After a few months in Taiwan, she decided to make Taichung her home again. I didn't see her much after that, since I was afraid to return to Taiwan, and she only visited us in the States a few times. We wrote letters and sent each other packages, but it wasn't the same. It wasn't until 2017, when I learned that Po-wei had passed away, that I finally returned to my homeland for the first time in fifty-six years.

February 2017, Taichung

I was eighty-five years old when I saw Taichung again. It was surreal to walk down the same street that Jin and I had lived on all those years ago. My parents were long gone, but Clare had been there to welcome me home. She lived in a newer part of the city in a modern high-rise and had insisted I stay with her. I wanted to see our old neighborhood, and she'd accompanied me here today. In all the years since she'd moved back to Taichung, she'd never once returned to the street where she was born. In part because she didn't know the address and I hadn't given it to her, but also because it was too painful for her. She associated this place with her mother's death.

We walked slowly, since my joints didn't work as well as they used to. I had to look hard to recognize landmarks, for most of the buildings had been torn down and shiny new structures built in their place. A few old buildings still stood, the architecture as I remembered from years ago. When we got to the corner where Wong Tai Tai's store used to be, I was surprised to see that it was still a Chinese herbal medicine store, although the building looked like it had gotten a facelift. I paused, looking into the glass windows, thinking I could see the ghost of my old friend walking toward me. Wong Tai Tai would be around eighty-nine or ninety if she was still alive.

"Do you want to go inside?" Clare looked at me, and I could tell she remembered. "This was Wong Tai Tai's store."

I nodded and looked at the sign. It still read Wong's, except the sign was new. Had she remarried, and her children or grandchildren had taken over the shop? Clare guided me up the one step to the door, and she pulled it open to the tinkling of bells. I stood just inside, looking around. It smelled exactly as I remembered, but the displays were all new, and the place was brighter than I remembered. A young man came toward us, calling out a greeting.

"Do you know Wong Shei-Ming?" I asked when he was close enough, using her full name.

His eyes widened. "That's my grandmother."

Clare's grip on my arm tightened. "Is she still alive?"

I held my breath as I waited for the answer and then let it out when the young man smiled. "Alive and kicking, still bossing everyone around." He gestured to the back. "She's in there right now, making my father miserable."

My breath whooshed out, and I looked at Clare. I was so happy my old friend had finally had a child. Without realizing it, I started walking toward the back room, which had once been Wong Tai Tai's office. I vaguely heard her grandson saying something, but I was too focused to listen. My joints no longer hurt, and I felt as if I were twenty-nine again, the age I was the last time I'd been here and said goodbye to my friend. Taking a deep breath, I rapped my knuckles against the door.

"Come in," a voice called from within.

I pushed the door open and then paused.

A man somewhere in his fifties and an older woman turned to stare at us. My eyes went right to the woman, as if drawn by a magnetic force. She still had the imposing figure she'd once had as she presided over the shop, but her face was lined now, and there was a stoop in her back. Her hair was completely white, but I recognized my old friend and whispered, "Shei-Ming?"

She frowned and squinted at me, no recognition on her face. But then slowly her brows loosened, and her hand came up to her mouth. "Could it be?" she said softly. She used her cane to leverage herself out of her chair and walked toward me, until she was a foot away. "Ang-Li? Is that you?"

I nodded, and her mouth dropped open. She swayed on her feet, and her son came rushing over, even as I reached out to steady her. Then her arms opened, and I stepped into her embrace. Happiness flooded me to see my old friend again after all these years. When I pulled away, my cheeks were damp, and I saw that there were tears on Wong Tai Tai's cheeks too.

We spent many days together after that, catching up. She told me about Yi-ping's visit soon after we left for America. I could see the regret on my friend's face that she'd gotten the story so wrong. All these years, I'd thought Yi-ping was as bad as Po, when she'd been a victim too. I wanted to reach out to Yi-ping, tell her I was sorry and that her daughter had turned into an amazing person. But Clare told me Yi-ping was no longer in Taiwan. I thought of looking for her but ultimately decided to leave things alone. I'd spent most of my life hiding the truth, and I didn't want to open old wounds for her or for Sue.

And then I found out I had lung cancer, probably a result of all the years I'd smoked. Clare went with me to all the doctor appointments, and I decided to stay in Taichung, to live out my remaining days. After our years apart, it was nice to have Clare taking care of me.

One month ago, Taichung

I fought the cancer when I was first diagnosed, beating it into remission for years. Wong Tai Tai and I spent most of our days together; I'd found a small apartment to rent in our old neighborhood. Clare had wanted me to move in with her, but I needed my space, and I couldn't breathe in that modern monstrosity she lived in. Wong Tai Tai and I would sit outside her shop when the weather was nice, with mugs of tea in our hands, and talk about the people we'd known and what had happened on this street in the years I was gone.

I told her about my children and my grandchildren, and about the other Huangs in Georgia. My son George and the other Huangs' son Steven remained best friends, standing up for each other at their weddings. And then they each had a boy, only a few months apart. My grandson Ken became best friends with Steven's son, Simon. Ken and Simon used to spend hours with me after school when their parents were working, and Simon became another grandson to me. I showed Wong Tai Tai many photos of my grandchildren.

When Wong Tai Tai passed away five years after I returned to Taiwan, it was as if a part of my life went with her. She'd helped me reconnect with everything familiar to me: the food, the language, the sense of belonging I'd never really felt in Georgia. On the seventh day after her death, her family and friends gathered for a ritual where her spirit was thought to come back to her loved ones one last time to say goodbye. Through the haze of incense, I swore I could detect the powder she'd always used, a faint floral scent that brought a smile to my face. I felt her spirit in the air, and I bade farewell to my old friend, telling her I'd see her soon.

The cancer came back a few months ago, and this time, I was ready to go. I wanted to see Jin again. And my dear grandson Ken, who left this world too soon. I'd lived a full life and brought up my children as best I could. They'd given me many grandchildren to spoil, and I was back on this island, where I belonged. I don't regret not telling my children the truth, for it was the only way I knew how to protect them. But I told Clare it was up to her if she wanted to tell Sue. I knew she would do whatever she thought right.

I wanted to leave one last thing for Clare to give to Sue if she ever decided to tell her the truth. It was a letter Sue had written when she was in eighth grade. The assignment had been to write a letter to her mother telling her why she admired her, why she was grateful for her. Sue had come to me in tears, saying she didn't have a mother. I cursed the insensitivity of the teacher, for surely, Sue couldn't have been the only student who didn't have a mother. I told her the only thing I knew.

"Your mother lives inside you, deep in your heart, always. Even though she can't be with you, know that she is always with you when you need her most."

She'd stared at me, her eyes wide. "Which one?"

"Either. Or both."

She'd stared at me some more and then given me a nod. "I know what to write now."

She'd gotten an A+ on that assignment and then given the letter to me, telling me to keep it since she couldn't give it to her mother. I'd kept it all these years, and now I took it out of my drawer and tucked it inside this journal. When I'm gone, maybe Clare will finally decide to tell Sue the truth and give the letter back to her.

I'm so tired. I need to rest. I want to close my eyes and see Jin again as I first saw her, so fresh faced and innocent, neither of us knowing what was to come. But I would do it all over again, despite all the heartache, because our union gave me our children. Jin, my love, I'll see you very soon.

27
LIV

"Oh."

Ah-Ma's dejected tone made me look at her as she put the pages of Ang-Li's journal on the coffee table.

"What is it?" I peered at her in concern. "What's wrong?"

"Nothing's wrong." But her slumped shoulders said otherwise.

"Ah-Ma." I frowned at her. "I know you well enough to know that something's bothering you."

She stared at me for a moment and then muttered, "Maybe you know me too well."

I laughed at the disgruntled look on her face. "What is it? Spill."

"The letter." Ah-Ma's mouth twisted to the side. "That's what's bothering me."

"What letter?" I asked, and then I realized what she was talking about. "The one Ang-Li mentioned in his journal."

Ah-Ma nodded. "What happened to the letter Yili wrote to her mother? It's not with the rest of the pages she photocopied. Did Yili not want me to see it?"

"I'm sure that's not the case," I said, even though I knew no such thing.

"She's been so receptive, happy even, to know about my existence." Ah-Ma blew out a breath. "But what if there's a part of her that will never really forgive me for being taken from our family?" Ah-Ma suddenly looked so small, as if she'd shrunk into herself.

"Well, there's only one way to find out." I hated seeing my grandmother so down. "Why don't we have her over to dinner tomorrow night? Along with Clare? I'd love to get to know them better, and you could ask Yili about the letter." And I would have something to keep me distracted after Simon left for New York.

"That's a good idea." Ah-Ma gave a shaky smile. "I'll call them now."

"We'll cook together for them."

Ah-Ma reached out to squeeze me on the shoulder, and then she left to go into her room to call Yili and Clare.

I sat at the table, staring at my phone, wondering what Simon was doing. I hated feeling like this, as if I'd gotten my instincts wrong. I usually trusted my gut, and my gut had told me this thing with Simon was real. So then why weren't we together on his last night in Taiwan?

Giving a huff of irritation at myself for wallowing in self-pity, I stood, deciding to go to bed early. I didn't need a man for my happiness. I'd realized I created my own happiness, following the paths that my life led me on. If things worked out with Simon, I would be ecstatic. But if they didn't, I knew I'd be okay. I'd survived a shooting and helped Ah-Ma find her daughter. I would create my own happiness.

The next morning, I looked out the open car window, my hair whipping behind me at the hot rush of air that blew in. My heart was heavy, both at the thought of Simon leaving today and at what that meant for us.

"Wait, Mr. Thomas. I'm going to see Simon." I leaned in between the two front seats when I realized he'd missed the turn he'd normally take to get to Clare's place.

He shot me a grin over his shoulder before turning back around. "I am taking you to see him."

"You're going the wrong way." I looked behind me and then back at the driver.

"Don't worry. I know where I'm going." His eyes sparkled when they caught mine in the rearview mirror.

With my eyebrows furrowed, I sat back and pulled out my phone.

What's going on? I texted to Simon. I knew he was behind whatever was happening.

I'm not at Clare's. I asked Mr. Thomas to bring you to me.

Oh. Where are you?

You'll see.

I put my phone down, looking out the window and wondering where we could possibly be going when Simon had to leave for the airport soon. Ten minutes later, Mr. Thomas pulled up to the curb, and I saw from the map on my phone that we were at Taichung Park. My forehead crinkled. Why were we at a park?

"We're here," Mr. Thomas said. "Go into the park from there and walk to the bridge over the water. Simon's waiting for you."

I shot him a dubious look, but Mr. Thomas's face gave nothing away. I followed his directions and found the bridge that curved over the lake. As I walked up to the top, I expected to find Simon waiting there. But I didn't see him. A family of four with two small children went running by me, and a couple strolling hand in hand stopped to look out over the water. It was beautiful, but I was confused. Where was Simon?

"Livia!"

I turned my head, my eyes searching for him. I finally saw him on the water in a boat, waving at me.

"What're you doing?" I leaned over the edge of the bridge, a big smile wreathing my face. "Don't you have a plane to catch?"

"Nope." He grinned up at me and then gestured for me to come down to him. "I rented this for the hour. Let's go for a spin."

"I don't understand." I kept him in my sights as I went back down the bridge to where they were renting boats. They let me through, and I soon stood next to where Simon had brought the boat back to the dock.

He didn't say anything until I was safely on board, facing him. He started rowing away from shore. "I'm not leaving Taiwan today."

"What?" My heart started pounding, and my stomach clenched.

"That's why I had to go to Taipei yesterday." His eyes crinkled as he rowed. "I've decided to take a teaching-slash-researching job in Taipei for the next few months. At the university where I taught before."

I nodded, but my brain had not yet caught up to his words.

"You know they've been trying to get me on their team for a while." He let the oars go so that we drifted in the middle of the lake. "I never had reason to before, but now I do. I asked for a last-minute meeting last night. I wasn't sure if they would still offer me the job, so I didn't want to say anything until I was sure." He reached out and took one of my hands in his. "I'll be two hours away in Taipei, but it's better than thousands of miles away."

"What are you saying?" I barely whispered the words, still trying to process everything.

"I don't want to be in New York while you're here." His gaze was intense on mine. "This isn't a fling for me, Liv."

My breath hitched, because that was exactly what I'd been afraid he was feeling when he'd said he couldn't see me last night. "It's not for me either."

"I want to get to know you. This thing between us is too new for us to be so far apart." The look he gave me sent a little glow through my body. "I'm staying. For us."

I clamped my lips together, too overwhelmed to speak. No one had ever done anything like this for me. For us. My relationships had all been pretty casual, except for a man I'd fallen hard for right out of college. It had been my longest relationship, at almost a year, but I broke his heart when he proposed and I realized I didn't want to be with him for the rest of my life. He was fun and exciting, but he didn't have a responsible bone in his body. I was devastated when he cried after I turned down his proposal, and I'd vowed then not to give anyone else the wrong idea again unless I felt the same way.

"Liv. Livia. Say something." Simon's forehead creased, and his voice was tinged with worry.

"I . . ." I struggled for words. Words to tell him how much this meant to me, how relieved I was that he didn't think of our time together as a onetime thing. "I'm happy," I finally said, although that didn't even begin to describe how light my heart was and how much I wanted to stand up and dance with joy.

A big grin burst out over his face, and we stared at each other, both smiling so big that my cheeks hurt. "I'm so happy," I said again.

"My roommate's girlfriend is moving in, and they'll let me keep my stuff in my room for now until I get back to New York." Simon tilted his body toward me. "I'm staying. I want to be with you." He stroked a thumb over my cheek.

Instead of answering, I leaned in, and then we were kissing as everything around me melted away, and all I could think was that I didn't have to say goodbye to Simon. When we pulled away, I transferred myself carefully to sit next to him, squeezed tight against his side. He put an arm around me, and we drifted like that on the water for a few minutes, neither speaking.

"You sure about this?" I finally asked. Doubt nagged at me as I wondered why he would give up his very good life in New York to be near me. "I'm not the most emotionally stable person right now."

"Who is?" One hand stroked down my arm while he took one of my hands in his other one. "I don't want perfect. I want real. And that you are. I love the way you flew to Taiwan to help your grandmother, even despite your debilitating terror. I love that you embraced life here, searching for your aunt but also getting to know your grandmother and your history better. And I love the way you love. I can see when you give your heart, whether to your family or your friends, you give it with everything you've got."

I smiled into his shoulder, speechless at the way he was describing me. What I'd thought was weakness, he saw as a sign of loyalty.

"We can make this work if we both want it." He pulled away slightly to look into my eyes. "Time apart always makes the reunion that much better."

I nodded because he was right. This felt pretty spectacular right now, being in his arms, knowing he was staying for me. I pressed myself closer to him, inhaling his Simon smell and feeling his body against mine. "You intrigued me from the first moment I laid eyes on you."

"Same." I felt him smiling into my hair. "Life isn't perfect either. But if we have a chance at happiness, I want to grab for it. Everything else is just logistics that we'll figure out as we go along." He pulled me even closer so that my head rested on his shoulder.

I wrapped my arms around his waist, and we sat like that for a moment. "I'm so glad I met you." I looked up at him and saw the love shining in his eyes.

"I love you, Liv."

His mouth curved, and he kissed me before I could say, "I love you too."

Then he was kissing me again, and we stayed like that for many more moments as the boat bobbed gently on the water.

28
YI-PING

I looked at the time and realized Yili and Clare would be here soon. Liv had texted earlier to say Simon was staying in Taiwan, so I'd told her to invite him for dinner tonight. I'd thought Liv was going to help me cook, but she'd never appeared, and I shook my head, a smile on my face. I was glad she was with Simon. He was good for her, my Liv. My strong, strong granddaughter, who I had a feeling was finally letting in the man she was supposed to be with.

The door suddenly opened, and my granddaughter burst in, Simon in tow.

"Ah-Ma!" Liv looked so pretty, her eyes sparkling and joy lighting up her face. "Isn't it exciting that Simon's staying in Taiwan? He's going to work for the university he once taught at in Taipei." Liv looked at Simon, who gazed back at her as if she were the whole world. "He's going back to Taipei on Sunday to move into the apartment the university is providing for him, and I'm going with him to help."

"That's wonderful." I came out of the kitchen and walked toward them.

"I'm so happy." Liv beamed so wide that I was surprised she didn't take off and float up to the ceiling.

I cupped a hand over her cheek. "You deserve to be happy." I leaned closer to Simon and said quietly, "Treat her right."

He nodded at me, and I knew he would.

Liv let go of Simon and came to my side. "Are you going to ask Yili about the letter tonight?"

I nodded, giving her a small smile. I was about to say more, but the buzzer went off, and I hurried to the intercom to let Yili and Clare in. I waited by the open door, and my heart spilled over to see my daughter and stepdaughter walking up the stairs to me. They both embraced me at the same time, and we stood like that for a moment. Then Clare pulled away and walked in to greet Simon and Liv as Yili pulled me just outside the front door.

"Before we join the others, I have something for you," she said. She held out a manila envelope to me.

"What's this?" I took the envelope from her, keeping my eyes on her face.

"It's the letter my father mentioned in his journal. The one I wrote in eighth grade. I wasn't ready to see it again because it reminds me of one of the times when my father really came through for me. It's been hard losing him." Yili's eyes met mine.

"Are you sure?" I reached out and touched my daughter on her cheek, much like I'd just done with Liv. My heart thudded with a mixture of hope and sympathy.

Yili nodded. "I didn't stop to think what it would mean to you. I was thinking of myself, how I felt. But earlier today, I was reading over my father's last entry and realized you might want to see it. So here it is."

"This is the original?" I opened the envelope and took out a piece of lined paper.

"Yes." Yili gave a small smile. "I wrote it for my mother, and here you are. It's for you."

I gave her a shaky smile before looking down, my eyes scanning the words. I brought a hand up to my mouth, and when I finished reading, I looked up, tears blurring my vision.

"Oh, Yili." A lump clogged my throat, and I could only draw my daughter close to me again, marveling at how wonderful it was to hold her in my arms after all this time. My mind was finally at ease, with my daughter back where she belonged.

I pulled away and gave her a tremulous smile. "Come, let's go celebrate with the others. Each day I get to see you is a special day."

She grasped my hands in hers. "For me too."

We walked back through the door together, and my eyes settled on my granddaughter, who was laughing at something Clare was saying. I turned to Yili. "Do you mind if I share the letter with Liv?"

"Of course not. She helped bring us back together." Yili looked at Liv, who caught sight of us and waved us over. "My niece."

With one last smile at each other, my daughter and I joined the rest as Simon poured out glasses of ice-cold beer so that we could toast to the future.

We clinked glasses and Liv said, "To Ah-Ma and Yili. To Clare."

I held up my glass. "And to Simon and Liv."

We drank, and then I went to Liv's side as the others started putting out the dishes I'd prepared. Silently, I handed her the letter.

She took it from me, her eyes already skimming over the words written in English, before looking up at me. Her face was radiant, and I put an arm around her. We didn't speak, but we stayed like that for a long while, her head on my shoulder as we looked out into the dining room, where my fourth daughter, whom I'd spent most of my life searching for, talked to my stepdaughter, and Simon, the love of my granddaughter's life.

I was finally at peace.

29
SUE HUANG

1972, Georgia

Dear Mama,

I don't remember you. Either of you. For the longest time, I told people I didn't have a mother. It was easier than explaining that I had two mothers but they both left me, in different ways. Baba doesn't talk about my second mother much. I knew that she'd died tragically. And I have no real memories of my first mother. But he said that you are always deep in my heart, always with me when I need you the most.

I dream about you, a woman whose face I can't see. I can only remember the feel of you, warm and soft and comforting. When I smell a lemony scent, a memory flits through my mind, but it disappears before I can grasp it. I remember feeling safe and not worried like I often am when I'm awake. Every night, I hope you'll come to me in my dreams, that I'll finally have a mother who loves and cherishes me.

I look for you when I'm out, wondering if I'd recognize you. Would you recognize me if we ran into each other on the streets? Do I look like what you imagined when you think of me? Do you even think of me? I want to close my eyes and feel you brushing my hair and braiding it the way Clare does for me. I want to taste the food you make for me, the way my father cooks for us. I want to laugh with you the way my brothers make me laugh. And I want to open my eyes and be able to see your face and recognize you as my mama.

I imagine you're a kind woman with gentle hands. I imagine that you were sad when you lost me and have spent all this time searching for me. In my mind, you are a brave, strong woman, someone I'd be proud to call my mama. I dream of the day when we find each other again. Our eyes will meet and yours will be so happy. I can hear you say, "Daughter, I've been looking for you all these years." You'll protect me like I remembered in my dreams. All the bad things that happened to you will have gone away and we can be together again. You'll make me delicious meals because you know I love to eat. You'll read with me because we both love books. You'll be there to guide me as I grow, like you couldn't with me now. I see the tears in your eyes, and I'll say, "Don't cry, Mama. We've found each other again."

I can't wait for that day to happen. I can see it when I close my eyes, your shape appearing closer and closer, getting clearer with each step you take toward me. I know I will recognize you when I finally see you again. That is my biggest wish, to have my mother hug me when I'm sad, scold me when I do something wrong, cheer when something great happens, or cry with me when I hurt. For now, Clare and Baba do those things for me. But I know one day it will be you who will be my biggest hero and champion. And when that day comes, I will finally have peace in my heart. I love you always, Mama.

AUTHOR'S NOTE

This is not a political book; rather, it's a story about two families who lived through the martial law era of Taiwan and the hardships they endured during this unstable climate. It depicts just two of the millions of Taiwanese stories on both sides of the political divide and is not meant to represent all that the Taiwanese people experienced. As someone who was born in Taiwan and lived there until I was seven years old, I am ashamed to admit I knew nothing about what was happening in my birthplace.

It wasn't until I was asked to edit the memoir of an important political figure in Taiwan that I finally read about the 228 Massacre of 1947, the reign of the Kuomintang (KMT), the fight for Taiwan's independence, Green Island, and all the Taiwanese lives that were lost during the martial law period from 1949–1987. Around this same time, as I was doing more research, I read about how baby girls were often adopted out to other families as future brides to the families' infant sons. I had a hard time believing people really did that, but my parents confirmed it was common practice and transpired in our own family. I couldn't help thinking about how the mothers who'd lost their daughters felt because, in all my research, no one mentioned the emotional torture they must have endured in losing a child in this manner. I knew then that I wanted to write a story from a mother's point of view with the political turmoil of Taiwan as the backdrop.

During my research, I spoke to many Taiwanese people, including my parents and other relatives. I also drew inspiration from Li-pei Wu's memoir, *Two Countries: My Taiwanese American Immigrant Story*, and from the film *Untold Herstory*. Any inaccuracies are a result of my imagination. Taiwanese stories have not been widely shared until recently, and I hope I can add my voice in letting the world know more about the struggles Taiwan has been through and the resilience of the Taiwanese people as they seek to become an independent Taiwan.

ACKNOWLEDGMENTS

This book would not exist without the support of my superstar agent, Rachel Brooks. While it was out on sub, I told Rachel I was going to quit writing and become a mushroom farmer because surely watching fungi grow would be faster than anything that happens in publishing. She refused to let me quit and told me to stay away from the mushrooms. Thank you, Rachel, for believing in me and my books, and for starting the Jaded Old Hag Mushrooms Club with me.

Thank you to my fabulous editor, Chantelle Aimée Osman, who truly got how important this book is to me and to the people of Taiwan. Chantelle, you have my undying gratitude for bringing this book to life. Thank you to my phenomenal developmental editor, Andrea Hurst. This was our third time working together, and when you told me this book was exquisite, I knew it was the highest form of praise. Thank you also to Jessica Tribble Wells, my editor at Thomas & Mercer, whose high opinion of me made Chantelle offer without a phone call. To Alison Impey, the genius behind the cover. A huge thank-you to the rest of the team at Lake Union, copyeditor Bill Siever, and proofreader Nicole Thomas.

For most of my life, I knew nothing about Taiwan's politics or what was happening in my birth country for the past century. It wasn't until I was asked to edit Li-pei Wu's memoir *Two Countries* that I discovered the horrors of life in Taiwan during the martial law era. Thank you to Mr. Wu, and to Julie Lee and Gene Wu, for opening my eyes. My experience working with them was the inspiration for writing this story.

Thank you to my early readers who looked over my first chapters: Mansi Shah, Anita Kushwaha, Lisa Roe, and Samantha Verant. Thank you especially to Rhodi Hawk, who read the entire manuscript and gave the book so much heartfelt love and feedback. You all are gifted writers, and I was honored to get your early insight. Thank you to my writing friends, especially the Berkletes 2021 debut group, who continue to boost me up as we navigate this very complicated journey called Publishing.

To my mom and dad, who have always tried to protect us, even if it meant not telling us what was happening in Taiwan, thank you for allowing me to pick your brains about what life was like when you lived there. As always, my husband, Jim, and our son, Lakon, are my biggest supporters. Thank you for always making it to my writing events. Thank you to my writing companions Cash and Hanna Mai Tai, and to Pinot, Lokie, and Mochi in Heaven.

And to you, the readers. I wouldn't be able to continue writing without your support. Thank you from the bottom of my heart.

ABOUT THE AUTHOR

Photo © Dave Cross Photography

Lyn Liao Butler is a Taiwanese American author of thrillers, upmarket fiction, and rom-coms. Her thriller, *Someone Else's Life*, was an Amazon bestseller and her second book, *Red Thread of Fate*, was a finalist in the WFWA Star Awards for 2023. Before becoming an author, she was a professional ballet and modern dancer and is still a fitness and yoga instructor. She and her family, including two rescue dogs and a myriad of foster animals, divide their time between New York and Kauai. For more information, visit www.lynliaobutler.com.

Printed in Dunstable, United Kingdom